The Sexy Librarian's
Dirty 30 Vol. 3
Edited by Rose Caraway

The Sexy Librarian's Dirty 30, Vol. 1
The Sexy Librarian's Dirty 30, Vol. 2
The Sexy Librarian's Dirty 30, Vol. 3
In Medias Res
Tonight, She's Yours: Cuckold Fantasies I
Tonight, She's Yours: Cuckold Fantasies II
Libidinous Zombie: Erotic Horror
For The Men:
And The Women Who Love Them

The Sexy Librarian's Dirty 30 Vol. 3

Edited by Rose Caraway

Stupid Fish Productions

Copyright © 2019 by Rose Caraway
Published © 2019 by Stupid Fish Productions
Cover design by Dayv Caraway @BigDaddyDayv

This is a work of fiction. Names, characters, businesses, places, events, and incidents are either the products of the author's imagination or used in a fictitious manner. Any resemblance to actual persons, living or dead, or actual events is purely coincidental.

All rights reserved. No part of this publication may be reproduced, distributed, or transmitted in any form or by any means, including photocopying, recording, or other electronic or mechanical methods, without the prior written permission of the publisher, except in the case of brief quotations embodied in critical reviews and certain other noncommercial uses permitted by copyright law. For permission requests, write to the publisher, addressed "Attention: Permissions Coordinator," at the address below.

Stupid Fish Productions
P.O. Box 2962
Orangevale, CA 95662
www.stupidfishproductions.com

Table of Contents

INTRODUCTION by Rose Caraway 7
1. *Eminent Domain* by Ria Restrepo 10
2. *Sourdough* by Janine Ashbless 18
3. *The Picnic* by T.D. Rudolph 26
4. *A Floating World Song* by Kenzie Mathews 34
5. *Not Quite An Antidote* by T.C. Mill 42
6. *Benediction* by Alex Slaine 50
7. *Dyke Lightning* by Lynn Lake 58
8. *The Safe House* by Kendel Davi 66
9. *Hung Jury* by Terrance Aldon Shaw 74
10. *In The Rough* by Rachel Woe 84
11. *Tell Me* by Eddie Monotone 94
12. *Demon Lover* by Romey Petite 100
13. *Hot* by Chase Morgan 106
14. *Call Me* by Clare London 116
15. *Batteries Not Included* by Silas Bliss 122
16. *Erotic Moves* by Dr. J. 130
17. *Wet Rewards* by Sommer Marsden 140
18. *His Property* by Eliza David 146
19. *In The Practice Of Her Calling* by Alegra Verde . 154
20. *Such A Small Thing, Really* by Kiki DeLovely ... 160
21. *Confession* by Emma Chaton 168
22. *My Tantric Surprise* by M.P. Clifton 176
23. *Nights In Red Satin* by Emily L. Byrne 184

24. *Home For Good* by Saskia Walker 192
25. *Hard Art* by Jaap Boekestein 198
26. *The Mermaid's Necklace* by Maxim Jakubowski . . . 206
27. *King's Mercy* by Alexa B. Forde 218
28. *The Wicked Witch Of The Wet* by t s cummings . . . 226
29. *Boy Toy* by Jaycee Amore 232
30. *A Star Is Born* by Janie James 240

About The Editor 247
The Kiss Me Quick's Erotica Podcast 248
More Books by Rose Caraway 249

Introduction

Rose Caraway

Dear Reader,

I am so excited that you are here. Welcome!
My 'libraries of erotica' are meant to share with you stories that exemplify the breadth of what good erotic storytelling can offer. This 3rd volume in my Sexy Librarian's Dirty 30 series is ready to turn you on. This collection is wide-ranging and full of original characters driven by exciting circumstances and situations, and the talent contained within these pages deserves special mention too. Each of the 30 authors presented here contributed their unique craft and have produced tales that should immediately suck you in. They've set the stage for you, brought to you erotic elements that are sure to penetrate your dreams long after you've closed this book. We want you coming back to this library to be swept away, again and again, to experience that special breathlessness that can only happen through erotic storytelling. We want you to get turned on.

I'm always after variety—erotic energy that cuts through in the best possible way. As I'm editing an anthology, my job is to cultivate the most exciting, unforgettable stories that will give you an experience you won't quickly forget. To provide you with characters and scenarios that you won't want to deny. I want to not only offer you the flirty frills-and-petticoats of a sassy bodice-ripper, I also want you to get the back-hills country taste of

Introduction

vengeance. I want you to love a dangerous spy—experience the bitter-sweet sacrifice made for love and country. I want you to pull off a jewelry heist and not feel a single ounce of guilt while doing so. I want the heat to rise in your cheeks as you confess your deepest, darkest desires to your priest—I want you to be the priest!

Allow these characters in as you turn each page. Be the patient stuck in a hospital bed and receive the ultimate in bedside manner. Go on vacation, stare at the sea—discover that mermaids really do exist. Work, day in and day out at a café and see your long-lost love suddenly return after months and months of being gone. With every bone in my body, I want to amuse you, Dear Reader…to make you throw on your tennis shoes and go jogging in Central Park only to come upon a house made of…gingerbread? Enter a judge's chambers and witness the defense and prosecution presenting their 'evidence.' Take your chances on the western frontier and let your heart rate ramp up as you lust after two brothers. Sneak into the bedroom late at night, while your wife sleeps, and transform into her demon lover—dare to break with family tradition and get the best revenge!

It is through erotica that I want you to be encouraged on a deep and personal level so that while you are walking around in your own skin, day after day, you will feel empowered as a sexual human being.

Before each story, you will find my 'card catalog' which will assist in helping you find something to suit your mood. The stories have been 'cataloged' with each of their 'subjects' tantalizingly listed (sometimes with an air of tongue-in-cheek) and all designed to whet your appetite before you even begin reading.

I hope you enjoy these stories as much as I do. Before I go, I'd like to encourage you to leave us a review when you have a free moment. Where you found enjoyment, so many others can too. Please, tell a friend about this book. Let them know how much you enjoyed it. Word of mouth is the highest compliment. And speaking of word of mouth, please subscribe to my podcast, The Kiss Me Quick's for free audio erotica, anytime you like.

It is my pleasure to present to you, The Sexy Librarian's Dirty 30, Vol.3.

Enjoy.

Rose Caraway
California, USA

333.0
Rest

Eminent Domain
author: Ria Restrepo
category: Land Economics

subjects: 1. Gran Turismo 2. Motorcycle Club
3. Proposition 4. Sordid Situation

Rose Caraway's Library of Erotica

Eminent Domain

Ria Restrepo

Sabrina was done being a good girl. She'd followed her parents' archaic rules about how a proper young lady should behave and had never given them a moment's trouble. And where had all her obedience and loyalty gotten her? Still a virgin at the ripe age of twenty and pressured to marry a sleazy politician twice her age. It was her duty, after all, as a Ponce de León to bring honor to her family's noble name. How better to achieve that than as the wife of the future Governor of Florida, then perhaps the President of the United States?

Frankly, Sabrina thought it was pretentious that her family insisted on keeping the "Ponce," instead of shortening their surname to the more common "de León." She'd made the mistake of saying that to her father once.

He'd slapped her across the face so fast she hadn't seen it coming. "Never, ever, disrespect your ancestors! We are not and will never be common."

From that day on, she'd learned to keep her thoughts and opinions to herself.

Her anger roiling, Sabrina dropped a gear on the Maserati and eased her foot down on the accelerator. The Gran Turismo cut through the early evening traffic on the turnpike like a laser-guided missile. Sabrina could see why her father cherished the car; it handled like a dream. A wry grin curved her lips while she imagined his fury when he discovered she'd taken his baby. But that would be the least of his problems if she got her way.

Traveling south of Miami, past the more affluent communities, Sabrina retraced the route her father had taken earlier in the day. After their brunch with her would-be husband, her father hadn't been able to resist gloating about his imminent success to his arch-nemesis, the leader of the Diablos Rojos Motorcycle Club.

Sabrina's gut twisted thinking about that awful meal with Congressman Gomez. His lascivious leer had made her so nauseous that she just pushed her food around her plate and donned her patented serene smile. The good thing about her father's "women and children are seen, but not heard" mentality was that she wasn't expected to say much—or anything at all—and learned more than they realized.

While Gomez drooled over her like she was prime rib, her father talked about his plans for a multimillion-dollar waterfront complex. In truth, family honor had very little to do with her impending marriage. No, her father's greed was the real reason her virtue was being bartered away.

In a hamlet situated between two mangrove preserves, the Diablos Rojos owned a coveted piece of waterfront real estate they refused to sell. Generations before, the motorcycle club and Rojos family had settled in an area that would later be surrounded by protected wetlands. With no tall buildings in the vicinity, it was a prime location for luxury oceanfront condos. In other words, a real estate developer's wet dream. And just like their famous conquistador ancestor, her father thought it was his right to claim land that didn't belong to him.

Sabrina hadn't known what to do about the whole sordid situation—she only knew she'd rather die than let Gomez touch her. But her father made a critical error; he took her with him to tour the land that would soon be his. Of course, she was ordered to wait in their Bentley while her father and his two goons approached several of the bikers outside their clubhouse.

Safely concealed behind the dark-tinted windows, she watched the tense exchange. That's when she first saw him—Raul Rojos, president of the Diablos, and he might have been the Devil himself. In his early thirties, he was tall with a thick mane of dark hair. He wasn't classically handsome or overly muscular, but solidly built. A long scar on his left cheek marred his rugged good looks, giving him a dangerous edge. Towering over her father as he scowled down at him, Raul looked deadly. If it hadn't been for the two-armed bodyguards, he probably would have slit her father's throat.

The sight of him sparked a sensation deep in her belly she'd never experienced before. This feeling was on the opposite end of the spectrum from the revulsion Gomez inspired. Muscles low in her abdomen tightened, her breathing quickened, and the air in the car became stifling. Moisture pooled in her sex and quickly soaked through her panties. Pressing her thighs together, she tried to ease the ache between her legs, but it only made her needier. She could almost smell her own arousal over the scent of the car's rich leather upholstery.

Sabrina wanted to go to him right then, kneel at his feet, and beg him to take her. Hell, she wanted her father to watch him defile her in every way imaginable. But she didn't dare. Her father's men would've dragged her back to the car and what little freedom she had would've been stripped away. Then, there'd be no escaping her dismal fate.

By the time her father and his men came back to the car, Sabrina had formulated a scheme worthy of her father's Machiavellian machinations. She just hoped she could make a deal with the Devil and live to tell the tale.

She exited the turnpike onto the road leading to the Diablos Rojos compound. The closer she got, the harder her heart pounded in her chest, and the wetter she became. She'd changed into a flirty little sundress that was so short her father had declared it indecent and ordered her to get rid of it. Of course, she hadn't. Now, it was the only thing she wore, and the hem had ridden up enough that nothing separated her bare backside from the soft Italian leather. Shifting restlessly in her seat, Sabrina took wicked delight in smearing her wet pussy against the pristine upholstery, staining it with her desire.

Entering the Diablos compound, Sabrina took in her surroundings. On the right was the clubhouse, a windowless two-story cement-block building painted black with a large Diablos Rojos MC logo on the front. It looked like it could withstand a Category 5 hurricane or an armed invasion. The line of badass Harley's out front only made it more imposing. Straight ahead was the much more welcoming Devil's Den, their bar and grill that overlooked Biscayne Bay. To the left was Rojos Repairs, a full-service garage. There were a few men in coveralls working on a couple motorcycles and a late model Buick.

Turning left, Sabrina felt all eyes on her as she carefully pulled the Maserati into an empty bay. One of the mechanics abandoned the Buick and approached her, wiping his greasy hands on a dirty rag. His coveralls were half off, hanging down around his waist, displaying a wife-beater with black streaks. A good-looking guy around her age with his dark hair pulled back into a ponytail, he flashed her a curious smile.

Sabrina forced an answering smile as she shut down the car. Her nerves were suddenly raging, but she'd come too far to back out now. Taking a deep calming breath, she picked up her cell phone from the passenger seat and carefully got out of the car, pulling down her dress so her ass was covered.

"Are you lost, *senorita*?" He looked from her to the silver Maserati. "We don't work on cars like this."

"I'm here to see your boss, Raul Rojos."

The other two guys snickered and whispered something to each other.

"He's kinda busy right now." His forehead creasing, he shifted from foot to foot. "What is this about?"

"It's personal." That was only partially true, but she wasn't going to tell this guy more than he needed to know. "Please."

He heaved a sigh. "Okay. Wait here."

As he walked out of the garage and headed for the clubhouse, Sabrina tried to ignore the lusty looks from the other mechanics. She hoped they wouldn't bother her if they thought she had some kind of personal relationship with Raul. Pretending to read something on her phone, she avoided making eye contact.

Minutes later, there was the loud bang of a metal door slamming, and Sabrina looked up to see Raul storming toward the garage.

"This better be good, Pedro, or I'm gonna kick your ass."

Sabrina almost swallowed her tongue when she saw Raul was shirtless. He may not have been bulky, but his muscles were like chiseled stone. An intricate pattern of tattoos covered his arms, and dark hair dusted his chest before disappearing into his low-slung jeans. She couldn't help noticing that the top button of his fly was undone.

Raul stopped a few feet in front of her, taking her in with eyes so dark they were almost black. His inscrutable expression gave her no idea what he thought of her, which unnerved and frustrated Sabrina.

"Who are you?" His voice was just as deep as she'd imagined.

"I'm Sabrina Ponce de León," she said, tucking a dark-brown lock of hair behind her ear.

His eyes narrowed. "Any relation to Enrique Ponce de León?"

"Yes, he's my father."

Before she knew it, he was in her face, lording over her like an avenging angel. "You have *cojones* coming here on your own, *niñita*."

It took every ounce of willpower Sabrina had to stand her ground and not shrink away from his obvious wrath. Up close, his presence was even more powerful. But along with the fear racing through her, there was an overwhelming attraction. Her nipples were impossibly tight, and she felt her juices seeping in the gap of her closely pressed thighs.

Sabrina cleared her throat. "I have a proposition for you."

"Tell your father to shove it up his ass. He's not getting our land."

"You misunderstand. I'm here to help you keep it."

His eyebrows rose, and he backed off a bit. "This, I've got to hear."

The thrill of immediate danger subsiding, Sabrina released the breath she'd been holding. With a shaking hand, she held out her phone to Pedro who intently watched their exchange. "You'll want to record this."

Pedro looked at Raul to see what he should do.

Raul lifted a shoulder. "What the hell. Do it."

Sabrina waited until Pedro took the phone and started recording her. Turning to Raul, she asked, "Have you heard of eminent domain?"

"No," he said, crossing his arms over his chest.

Sabrina was momentarily distracted by the play of his muscles flexing. "It says the government can take your land if they need it for a public purpose."

"Bullshit!"

"That's legit, *jefe*," Pedro offered. "I heard about them taking this guy's land to build a highway through it."

Raul's eyebrows lowered. "Why would they need this land?"

"They're going to claim they need a new Coast Guard station to monitor drug smuggling."

Lowering his arms, he fisted his hands. "They can steal from me?"

"They'd pay fair market value for it, but you'd still lose all this." Sabrina waved her hand to indicate the entire Diablos compound.

"*Cuño!*" he spat, then his eyes narrowed even more. "How does that help your fuckhead father?"

"Once you're out of the picture, the state will change its mind and sell the land to my father. At a bargain, of course, as long as he builds shops, restaurants, and a marina along with his luxury condos to generate income for the county."

Raul looked like a bull ready to charge. "They can't get away with that."

"If you have enough politicians in your pocket, you can get away with anything."

She could practically see his wheels turning as he glared at her. "Why are you telling me all this?"

"Because Daddy Dearest plans to marry me off to Congressman Gomez and back his bid for governor to cement the deal."

"You don't want to marry him."

"Hell no."

"What's your proposition?"

Her pounding heart felt like it was going to burst out of her chest. "I need you to make me your slut."

Just saying the word made her inner muscles clench with longing. The idea of being his naughty plaything set her blood on fire.

Sabrina watched as his rage seemed to turn to fiery interest. An answering heat unfurled low in her abdomen, making her even needier. Not waiting for him to respond, she boosted herself onto the Maserati's hood and kicked off her sandals.

"You see, Gomez wants a sweet virgin bride from a prominent family. If I'm soiled goods, he won't want me, and my father's deal falls through. And you keep your land."

"You're a virgin." His tone was skeptical.

Slowly spreading her legs, Sabrina revealed her shaved pussy. "Father made sure of it, so I'd be a more valuable bargaining chip."

"Gomez really won't marry you if you're not a virgin?"

"He might, but not if there's a recording of me fucking the leader of a biker gang while his buddies watch." Sabrina nodded towards Pedro. "You also have me detailing their sordid plan. If any of this gets out, it would ruin them. That's leverage."

"She's fucking brilliant, *jefe*." Pedro grinned from behind her phone.

Aware of the other guys' avid interest, Sabrina kept her focus on Raul as she lowered the thin straps on her dress until her breasts were naked.

Raul stalked closer, his gaze devouring her exposed flesh. "You could just run away."

Sabrina trailed her fingers up the inside of her thigh to her drenched sex. "His men would just hunt me down and drag me back. No, I need to make him disown me. Losing my cherry to his enemy on his prized possession should do the trick."

She slid her finger between her slick slit, circling her clit while teasing her nipple with the other hand. She was so close to coming it wouldn't take much to send her soaring over the edge.

Between her legs now, Raul licked his lips. "Prized possession, huh?"

"Father loves this car more than anything. Certainly more than me."

"He's a fucking idiot."

Raul grabbed the back of her neck and pulled her against him for a demanding kiss. He took no prisoners, plundering her mouth just like she hoped he'd take the rest of her. Moaning, she stroked her tongue against his, needing him to relieve the growing ache between her legs. He smelled like smoke, and leather, and manly musk, and every forbidden thing she'd ever desired.

She was breathless by the time he pulled back and pinned her with his intense gaze. "Last chance to change your mind."

"Fuck me...please."

He yanked her hips closer to the edge, causing her to fall back onto the hood. Sabrina raised up on her elbows to see Raul rip open his fly, freeing his long, thick erection. His eyes never left hers as he dragged the head of his cock along her drenched folds.

"Sticking it to your father must really turn you on."

"Not only that," she said, nearly panting in anticipation. "I was in the car this morning. As soon as I saw you, I wanted to be yours. That you hate my father as much as I do is a bonus."

When his cock lined up with her opening, Raul thrust hard and deep, making her gasp. Unable to hold herself up, Sabrina collapsed back onto the hood, closing her eyes as she luxuriated in the bliss wracking her body. There was a sharp pinching sensation at first, then a stretching, filling, proving more pleasurable than the brief discomfort. She whimpered in disappointment as he eased out of her, but then he forcefully pushed inside her again, deeper than before.

Raul groaned. "You feel so good, *hermosa*."

His grip on her hips was brutal as he steadily pounded her cunt, thoroughly pillaging her innocence. There'd be bruises, but it only heightened her arousal knowing he'd mark her in more ways than one. That others were watching—and that her father would soon have proof of her willingly embracing her own debauchery—intensified her pleasure. It built fast and furious until she cried out her release.

Growling through his final few thrusts, Raul came inside her, flooding her with his seed.

As Sabrina caught her breath, Raul leaned forward and placed a kiss on her stomach. She looked up and basked in his warm expression. Carefully pulling out of her, he helped her sit up and gave her another surprisingly tender kiss. While he tucked himself back inside his jeans, Sabrina looked down between her legs and watched as pink-tinged cum slid out of her cunt and onto the Maserati. She gathered some of it with her fingers and wrote *FU* on the hood.

Raul chuckled, then urged her to look at him. "Do you want to return to your father, stay with me, or go off and live your own life?"

Sabrina didn't need to think about it. "Stay."

"If you stay, you'll be mine to use as I please."

"Just yours," she clarified.

He nodded, the corner of his mouth lifting. "I don't like to share."

"Then, yes, please, I'd like to stay."

Raul turned to Pedro. "You still recording?"

"Yes, *jefe*."

"Ponce de León," Raul said, looking at the camera, "I've claimed your daughter by eminent domain."

At Raul's slashing motion, Pedro stopped recording.

"Send me a copy of that video, then leave the car and her phone outside her father's mansion," Raul told Pedro. "Don't get caught."

"*Claro que sí!*"

Sabrina was biting her lip to stop herself from giggling when he turned back to her. She could see banked amusement glittering in his dark eyes. Then, he lunged for her and hoisted her over his shoulder, making her squeal.

"What are you doing?"

Raul slapped her ass and headed for the clubhouse. "Let's really tick off your father and put my baby in your belly."

Grinning, Sabrina knew she'd never regret selling her soul to the Devil.

END

RIA RESTREPO *may appear to be a mild-mannered bookworm who drinks too much coffee and spends most days tapping away at her computer. But below the surface lurks a filthy-minded sex kitten with a lurid and lascivious imagination. Writing romance, erotica, and all the shades in between, she truly enjoys entertaining readers with stories about strong women exploring and celebrating their desires.*

973.5
Ashb

Sourdough

author: Janine Ashbless
category: Frontier & Pioneer Life

subjects: 1. Floured Table   2. Brothers
3. Quiver of Cleavage

Rose Caraway's Library of Erotica

Sourdough

Janine Ashbless

Bread making demanded an early rise. Ezra had built Grace an oven at the side of the kitchen hearth, but it needed a good burn going to heat the stones. While she waited for the blaze to reduce to hot embers, she took the sourdough that had been proofing under muslin since the day before and divided and shaped it into loaves for baking. Then, she started on the next batch for tomorrow. Their nearest neighbors—the Van Burens from eight miles over, in the next valley—were planning to come visit, so they'd need the extra bread.

The cabin was snugly built, and the morning was already threatening to be warm. Their corn patch was starting to ripen, and before noon, the cattle would drift down toward the shade of the cottonwood trees near the creek. She took off her blouse, not wanting the sleeves to get sweaty or dough-stained and set to work, bare-armed, in her corset and camisole, stirring flour and sourdough starter in the big crockery bowl Ezra had bought as her wedding present. Bread making was one of the daily tasks she liked best. Much better than cleaning out the pigsty or airing the heavy layers of family bedding or—worst of the lot—pounding the laundry. But it was all better than her last job, back in Chicago, where she'd sewed leather coats day and night until her hands bled.

Maybe she'd lied, just a little, when she'd wrote Ezra and told him she had a farming background. Back home, when she was a little girl in England, yes—sure, as they said around here. But they'd moved into Lancaster, and she'd worked factory jobs from a young age in a cotton mill until she immigrated to America. She couldn't really remember her milk fever from her glanders. But it didn't matter, not now. She was his wife, and most of her work was around the house, not out in the pastures. She could shelter from the worst of the summer heat and the worst of the winter snows that this harsh land threw at them, and she wasn't on her own in filthy, muddy, violent Chicago.

And she had family again. A small one, sure. Just Ezra and his younger brother, Amos, but, with luck, there'd be children in the years to come. They were certainly working hard enough at that.

As if summoned by the thought, the cabin door opened, and Amos edged in, hanging his rifle on the wall. The pre-dawn light washed in with him, muting the cozy little glow of the fire Grace had been working by. Amos moved quietly—always cautious inside the house as if worried he'd break something. When he caught sight of her at the kitchen table, he nodded and took off his hat, respectful-like. His uncombed hair fell in a dark curtain across his eyes, and he pushed it aside.

Grace blushed, conscious that she was under-dressed for company, even family. She hadn't thought Amos would be about this early. "You been out all night?" she asked, her voice unexpectedly husky.

He turned his hat between his hands, just as awkward as her. "Sitting up for that coyote," he muttered. "Didn't see him."

She smiled encouragingly. Amos often seemed ill-at-ease in her presence. He'd wooed a bride by post via the same newspaper and at the same time as his brother had. Grace had even met the woman on the train west to the Montana Territory, but Christabel had taken ill on the journey and left the train at Minneapolis. No one had heard from her since. So, the elder brother had caught all the luck, and the younger was left waiting for his to change. Grace felt obscurely guilty, though it was not her fault; it must make things even harder for Amos to bear, having her around to remind him of his loss.

"Coffee's brewing," she told him, trying to brush a smut of flour off her cheek. "Sit down."

He filled a tin mug at the stove and sat at a kitchen chair, settling his hat in his lap, and stretching his long legs out in front of him. He wasn't as broad-built as his brother, but he was handsome in his way, with hazel eyes that looked green or brown depending on the weather. His gaze never quite met her own but slipped about the room from dresser to hearth and to the toes of his worn boots. He said nothing.

Amos was always quiet; his brother made sure he knew his place.

Maybe I married the wrong one, Grace thought, smiling to herself. But no, Ezra was the landholder and had been, in every way, the better prospect. She'd preferred the look of his handwriting too, firm and bold. And he'd worked hard, making things nicer for her around the homestead since she'd arrived. He even washed his privates and scrubbed his teeth every day just to please her.

Grace busied herself with kneading the dough, rolling it out onto the floured table-top and plunging her hands into the soft, white mass. The muscles danced in her forearms as she bore down upon it, stretching and folding and squeezing, and the familiar work made her breath come harder. The rhythm was mesmeric, almost, and it was a while before she looked up at Amos again.

He was watching her. Not her face, she realized; he hadn't even noticed her surreptitious glance toward him. He was staring at her cleavage as if entranced, his mug half-way to his lips.

Such a famished look in those eyes. Heat rose to Grace's face as she realized her culpability. Her white camisole was low-cut, the top button not even done up, and her breasts bulged softly out over the top of her corset as she leaned forward, just like rising loaves. *He's lusting after me.* The wave of heat washed down from her cheeks, through her breastbone and into her belly and down between her thighs, gathering weight and force as it went, until she thought it would wash her out down the creek and into the Missouri and out to sea a thousand miles away, all the way back to her giddy girl-days in England. The shock took the breath from her.

Without thinking—she couldn't think, not with the blood roaring in her ears like that—she flipped the dough forward a few inches on the tabletop, so she'd have to lean even deeper into the kneading. The bulge of her breasts must be more precarious now, and she felt the quiver of her cleavage with every move she made.

When she looked up at Amos this time, she made the motion obvious, though she never paused in her labors. Their eyes met, burning, and his face went stiff, like a mask.

They both knew.

It felt inevitable.

Push went her hands in the dough. She sucked her dry lips briefly to moisten them.

As if pulled by gravity, his gaze fell back to the cleft of her breasts, struggled to her face, and then fell again.

She looked at the felt hat in his lap and imagined what it must be covering. She'd seen his erection tenting his canvas pants before at odd moments— once, when she'd been hanging out laundry, and he'd been chopping wood nearby. Once, when she'd poured the hot water into his tin bath while he waited to undress and wash. She'd always pretended not to notice. Now, she wondered dizzily what his cock would feel like against her palm, her thighs, her lips.

Push. Fold. Turn. The heavy beat of life. The damp well of her sex was threatening to spill down her thighs.

Softly, almost shyly, he slid his hand beneath the hat to grasp himself. There was a plea in his eyes now.

She smiled. *Hot*, she thought. *Hard.* Full of marrow and frustration. She'd

Sourdough

like to see that.

The muscles of his forearm bunched as his hidden fingers gripped tighter.

That was the moment Ezra came thumping down the stairs from the bedroom above.

Amos managed to whip his hand out from beneath the hat before his elder brother opened the stair door, but the rest of him stayed frozen. He couldn't move from his chair, Grace knew. She straightened up sharply, pulling the great ball of dough toward her. She felt as if her whole being was about to fly apart like a keg of gunpowder.

"Morning," said Ezra, swaggering into the room behind her and surveying them both.

"Good morning, husband," said Grace, over her shoulder. Her voice would not rise above a whisper.

Amos nodded, quick and—she thought—guilty-looking.

Ezra certainly noticed something in the air. He came up behind Grace as she worked assiduously at the dough and rested his big hands on her hips. "There's a fine sight for a morning," he said, snuggling his crotch into her ass. "You enjoying it, brother? Just sitting there taking in the view?"

"I've just got in," Amos muttered. "Been out in the long pasture." He dropped his coffee mug on the table.

"There's nothing like the sight of a wife hard at work in the morning," said Ezra, ignoring his brother's words. "'Her price is beyond rubies,' as the Good Book says. 'She looketh well to the ways of her household, and eateth not the bread of idleness,' isn't that so?" His hands were working in her long skirts, squeezing her ass through the layers of cloth, gathering them up. "Bet you wish you had one, brother."

Amos glowered. He was used to being taunted, Grace knew, though it was rarely this blunt. But he couldn't move right now. If he lifted the hat and stood, his guilt would be obvious.

"Ezra," she protested, as he found his way under her dress and to the thin cotton of her long drawers. Her face was growing ever pinker.

"Hush now," he said, putting a hand between her shoulder blades and tipping her forward over the edge of the table. "You've got women's work to be getting on with."

For a moment, she thought he meant the bread until she felt him toss her bundled skirts up around her hips and reach between her thighs to the split of her bloomers. Ezra always woke with a beam you might build a bridge on, but he'd never been this bold before. Not in front of his brother.

Amos squirmed.

"Damn, this feels fine," her husband said, his fingers sliding rudely into her while his other hand worked open the buttons of his fly. "Best feeling in the world, Amos. Bet you wish you had one for yourself."

Grace grabbed the edges of the table for support and felt how terribly wet and slick she was. Simultaneously, she reeled in gratitude for the push of his thick fingers and hoped he wouldn't notice. She felt dizzy with shame. Not that Amos could actually see anything from where he was sat, of course—he was looking down the barrel of her cleavage and couldn't see anything of her ass beyond the rumpled skirts, but there was no hiding when Ezra nudged his thick cock into her, because she couldn't help gasping out loud at the girth of it.

It felt good. *So good.* She was wet and aching, and he filled her like she needed. Even the shame felt good.

"Oh," she said. "Oh."

"Damn yes," said her husband happily, shifting his grip to her hips, getting a good thrust on. He paused, nuts-deep, to inquire of his brother, "Do you think yours really took ill and died, or did she just run off with the money?"

"Go to hell," Amos groaned, fixed in his seat, staring, watching his brother start to thrust deep and slow, watching her flushed face and her open, O-shaped mouth and her jiggling breasts, glossed with gathering sweat.

Grace, panting, braced her arms against the table and tried to save her cleavage from being squashed down into the big ball of dough. She saw Amos's face, twisted with pain and desire, and it was like she could read his thoughts. He desperately wanted to stick his achingly-hard cock into her mouth, between her slick tits, and up her wet sex where her husband was rooting. His balls must have been blue with need, but he couldn't so much as touch himself for relief. He just had to watch, raging, while his brother got it on and rubbed his face in his lack. Poor, good-looking, younger brother, always at Ezra's beck and call, lusting after his wife, wanting to do a million sinful things to her.

I wish you could.

Arching her back, she let her nipples burst from behind the confines of her corset, her breasts tumbling into the damp sling of her thin camisole. Grace felt the roil of her arousal gather toward a tight, hot point, and she locked eyes with Amos. She swallowed her scream, not daring to let Ezra know how turned on she was, but it showed in her expression as she started to come. She didn't try to hide that. And when her husband spurted triumphantly inside her, she pushed back onto his big cock eagerly, swallowing it all up, keeping her gaze on Amos, on that handsome face so racked with frustration, and she let him see it all.

I'm coming. I'm coming. It's you making me come.

And it felt wonderful.

She didn't see Amos leave because when Ezra finally released her, she slid shaking down onto the table, into the flour and the dough, and covered her burning face with her hands. She just heard the younger man stomp out and slam the door.

Ezra laughed contentedly and rearranged her skirts. "Now that's better than damn rubies," he said. He went to the coffee pot and poured himself a mug. "I'll be getting on with that roof then," he remarked, as if nothing had happened.

When he'd left the cabin, Grace peeled her perspiring cleavage off the dough and walked unsteadily to the door. Ezra's seed seeped down from her sex. She felt like dough herself—pliable, well-pummeled, puffed up with her orgasm.

Into the fire, now, she thought.

She saw Ezra beyond the barn—he was working on the new house he was building for her, a home bigger and more comfortable than his old, bachelor's cabin. He seemed to have shrugged off what had just taken place entirely; he was sorting out wooden shingles for the half-finished roof. But Amos wasn't anywhere in sight. Slipping out into the yard, she scanned the outbuildings.

The stable door stood open.

Ignoring the chickens who were clustering about to demand their breakfast, she hurried across and slipped into the darkened doorway. It took a moment for her eyes to adjust, but then she saw Amos saddling up his pinto gelding.

"Where are you going?" she asked.

"Helena, I reckon," he said, not turning. "I hear they're hiring there."

"Amos, don't go," she said, laying a hand on his arm. "We can't manage this homestead without you."

"And I can't stay."

His bicep was warm and hard, and she wanted to feel his bare skin. "We'll starve!" She thought of summer hailstorms and winter blizzards and grasshoppers and floods and wolves. She and Ezra couldn't fight the whole land on their own.

He thumped the saddle down onto the horse blanket. "He should have thought of that before he took to treating me with contempt." He swung round to face her in the gloom. "I can't bear it—you moaning and panting every night on the other side of that wall! Your sweet titties and your mouth and—" He broke off, his breath harsh, his hand almost on her shoulder, not quite daring to touch. She hadn't tidied her breasts away after their escape from her stiff bodice.

"You'll find another woman, Amos."

"You think we can afford another rail ticket? That's the reason Ezra's so sore at me." He laughed bitterly. "Maybe I'll find a nice girl in Helena."

"Don't leave us," she said, sliding down to her knees in the straw, nuzzling her face up against his pants, finding the half-hard cock he was trying to master.

He groaned and grabbed at a stable partition for support as the buttons of his fly parted under her quick fingers, freeing his burgeoning erection.

Yes. Yes.

He tasted of leather and male lust, a sourdough tang that made her heart pound. But there was very little kneading necessary in this case; he was rock-hard in moments, then clutching her hair and working her throat and gasping in a few more. She had to wrap her hand around his shaft to stop him from choking her with the eagerness of his thrusts and his flood.

"Jesus," he whispered, catching his breath.

She looked up at him, licking the last of the yeasty spill from her lips.

"Don't leave me," she demanded.

He pulled her to her feet and pushed her back against a wooden wall, into a shaft of light. His fingers danced down from her face to the heave of her breasts as if unable to believe what his eyes were seeing. Then, he leaned in and kissed her.

Grace whimpered, unable to catch herself.

"Ezra's gonna kill me," he warned, as he took his lips away.

"You're his brother. He won't."

"Maybe he'll kill us both."

"Only if he finds out. And I'm not telling." But *What have I got myself into?* she asked herself. *Oh Lord, what have I done?*

END

JANINE ASHBLESS *lives with an ill-defined number of men and dogs in the North of England, The Land That Summer Forgot. She enjoys tabletop- and live-roleplaying, and travelling anywhere less wet. She writes mostly about magic, life-and-death situations, and fallen angels with big cocks and problematic attitudes.*

```
823.8
Rudo
             The Picnic
       author: T.D. Rudolph
       category: Romance/'Bodice Ripper'

   subjects:  1. Scamp  2. Unladylike
              3. Impure Thoughts


Rose Caraway's Library of Erotica
```

The Picnic

T.D. Rudolph

Mrs. Susan Chamberlain—barrister's wife, aspiring portraitist, member of the Ladies' Guild of Free Thought and Equality—rested her white-gloved hand on the sturdy wrist of her carriage driver and, using the footstool provided, swung as gracefully as she could into the polished, black coach.

"Thank you, Francois," she said, struggling breathlessly to adjust her billowy skirts. Silently, she cursed every designer of women's fashion on the continent—the majority of them men—who obviously took great pleasure in imprisoning women's bodies in painfully constricting layers of starchy, scratchy, burdensome materials. Damn them all!

"Where would madam like to take her lunch today?" Francois asked, his strikingly handsome face framed by the coach's open window.

In your room at the stables, Susan thought wickedly. Yes, she supposed that she was happily married, if by that one meant being properly provided for. But a woman had certain needs, and if they weren't being fulfilled, well, the mind did tend to wander.

"Oh, it's such a lovely day, Francois. Perhaps that place I like so much, the one down by the river, under that marvelous canopy of willows. Yes, I think I should like to go there."

"Very good, madam," Francois said. "And may I offer you my kerchief? The road is particularly dusty at this time of year."

"Why, that's very thoughtful of you, Francois. The soot, the dust—it's all so terribly harsh on a woman's complexion."

The carriage lurched, and its two white horses started out under Francois's command at a steady, unhurried pace. "Such a sweet young man," Susan mused aloud, conscious of her bottom shifting as the carriage swayed. Feeling adventurous, she dared to lean out the window while Francois, his back to her, clambered up onto the driver's bench. His tan, canvas breeches were cut quite snug across his well-defined buttocks, and for a heady moment, she was transfixed by the sight and dizzy from the unseemly ideas swirling around in her head. When she finally plopped back into the coach, she scolded herself. "No, I mustn't think that way. A man in his twenties is still practically a boy, for Heaven's sake."

At a fork in the main road, the carriage canted left, then rumbled down a meandering cart path, the taller juniper and spruce trees making way for the more water-loving cottonwood and willow. Susan knotted her bonnet securely, then placed Francois's kerchief over her mouth and poked her head out the window. Oh, yes! She could already smell the clear, sweet, mineral-rich river, the very river where she and her older sisters used to bathe *au naturel*. The faded memory still had the power to make her blush.

Soon, she spied the most perfect place for a picnic and shouted up to Francois, "Just ahead there! Pull up under that stand of willows!" She knew full well that inviting a lowly member of the laboring class to dine with someone of higher social standing was frowned upon, if not forbidden. And yet, one had to eat to keep one's strength, didn't one? Yes, of course! She should be congratulating, not admonishing herself for her egalitarian gesture. A pox on all of these antiquated social conventions!

Content, she tilted her head upward and caught sight of her driver who was bracing his fine ass against the bench, his powerful arms tugging mightily on the reins to halt the carriage. Why, she wondered, did she find this so alluring? Or was it something more primitive she was feeling? She quickly ducked back into the coach, confused by her emotions. Was Francois married? No. She remembered Henry saying he was not. In fact, it was rumored that he had something of a reputation among the domestics. *Perhaps*, Susan thought with some concern, *Francois is one of those untrustworthy men of ill repute. A scamp. A lecher. A wolf in sheep's clothing.*

Oh, dear. She would have to be mindful of how much wine she consumed, though it went so well with the cold, roasted chicken and the hearth-baked bread she'd packed. A sly smile crossed her lips. "Lead us not into temptation," she prayed silently. "Begone, any thoughts of unladylike behavior."

"We'll dine over here," Susan said, leading Francois to a soft, grassy patch of ground beneath a stately willow. Glancing back over her shoulder, she watched him struggling bravely with his burden. His arms were laden with a thick, wool blanket, a wicker picnic basket, a jug of fine, imported Bordeaux, glasses, cloth napkins, her easel, and ceramic jars of paints and brushes. Goodness, it was exhausting just watching the poor man work!

"Does madam mean that I am to take lunch with her?" Francois asked, looking puzzled by this unexpected development. "Should I not water the horses instead?"

"Nonsense," Susan replied. "Now, let's get everything sorted out. Then, we'll drink a toast to this perfect day and the blessings of beauty all around us." Not the least of which, she decided, was a strapping, robust male who positively reeked of musk and masculinity. She wondered what her libertarian sisters at the Guild would make of the flirtatious smiles she offered Francois at every opportunity. Smiles that barely concealed her...her interest? No, that wasn't the word, nor the truth. If she were honest, the gnawing, insistent hunger she felt had nothing to do with convivial feelings and everything to do with lust.

Well, then. Thank goodness that she'd recognized the symptoms before it was too late! She snickered to herself, amazed at how a few impure thoughts could make her feel so...so receptive. And yet, why should women have to hide their true feelings or otherwise behave any differently than men, who openly undressed the fairer sex with their lascivious stares, then mouthed gross indecencies as they passed by? She took several deep breaths, suddenly infuriated by the double standard. Men!

As the afternoon waned, she turned her focus to other affairs. Now, they sat, Francois half reclining, Susan with her legs tucked uncomfortably under her bottom, the coarse, heavy crinoline lining of her skirts and her waist-pinching corset making it impossible to relax her posture. And further woe, the worst had happened; she'd sampled too much from the fruit of the vine, and her cautions had slipped away as the jug of wine lost its volume. In fact, the two had scarcely touched their meal. Instead, meeting each other's uncertain glances, they'd traded sips of the Bordeaux—from the same glass—while Francois recounted his boyhood along the Mediterranean Sea, and Susan told him about her strict Christian upbringing by a domineering father.

Have mercy. Such confessions, such intimacy with a strange man—a commoner, no less—was a reckless game played, maybe even a dangerous one. But wine always did go right to her head, and as they continued to talk, she felt her niggling concerns popping like so many lavender bath bubbles. Gradually, the trappings of wealth and privilege—qualities she sometimes resented—peeled away like the sour rind of a tangerine, leaving only the sweet taste of desire. *Is it mutual desire?*

"Tell me, Francois. Have you ever sat for a portrait?"

"A portrait, madam?"

"Oh, come now, don't be coy. I should think that with such attractive features your face has been rendered to canvas many times before."

Francois lowered his thick-lashed eyes and smiled, his teeth as ivory-white and even as piano keys. Shrugging, he broke off a small piece of bread, buttered it liberally, then reached out ever so slowly and held it to Susan's strawberry lips. He looked pleased by her startled expression. "You flatter me, madam," he said, watching as she nervously ran her tongue along the ridge of her teeth before allowing him to place the morsel on its tip.

"And you take liberties, sir," she said, feeling her face turn crimson, yet not at all unsettled by his forward behavior. "Now, pour us one more glass of that delicious wine while I retrieve my paints. The sun, the cloudless sky, the trees, the splash of river against rock—I find it all so inspiring. I only hope that I can capture your likeness to your satisfaction."

Francois ignored her wishes and, instead, sprung to his knees, piercing her with his deep-set, sea-green eyes, his long, wavy hair pushed back behind his ears. He picked up his napkin and dared to brush a crumb from the corner of her lips. "Where I come from," he said softly, "it is customary to bathe after the afternoon meal. Will you join me?"

Susan, aghast, felt like she was suffocating inside her clothing, but even so, she swore she could hear her heart beating wildly underneath her clothing's many layers of material. The French! Only a French man would make such an outlandish proposal. *Is this all really happening, or am I living inside a dream?* Her head, addled with drink, swam with all sorts of images and possibilities, none of them decent. But imagine the scandal! A woman—especially a married one—caught out with a…a…

Her thoughts stopped midstream, and she gasped. "What on earth are you doing?"

Francois laughed. "Where I come from, it is also customary to remove one's clothing before bathing. It is different for you here?"

Susan watched, paralyzed and unable to speak, as Francois's rumpled, long-sleeved, cotton shirt slipped from his husky shoulders and fell to the blanket. When his hands went to the purple sash holding up his breeches, she shocked herself by seizing them, holding them for a precious second, then slapping them away.

"No," she insisted. "We cannot. If we were ever found out…it's not that I don't want to…oh, God."

Before she could stop herself, Susan's gloved hands, shaking uncontrollably, were at his waist, struggling to free the knot in his sash.

Francois gently lifted them and placed them on his thighs.

"Allow me, madam," he said. Unashamedly, he worked the knot loose, then sat back, kicked off his calf-high boots, and shimmied out of his well-worn but sturdy breeches. He was wearing nothing underneath them.

Reflexively, Susan clamped both hands over her mouth and drank him in with wide-eyed astonishment. She had seen only one other unclothed man in her thirty years, only because Henry had mistakenly thought he was alone in the house and dropped his towel after bathing. Their lovemaking, when it occurred at all, was accomplished in the depths of darkness. By contrast, Francois's stark nudity, seen in all its glory, stung her like a brace of cold water from the river's deepest pool.

"You see," Francois said, in a reassuring tone. "I am only a man, the same as any other. There is nothing to be afraid of."

Susan scooted backward to appraise him more closely. A man the same as any other? She could hardly imagine the possibility. His chest, broad across the nipples, was glistening and nearly hairless, and his stomach muscles were as taut as the rope on a ship's anchor. And his cock—dare she even imagine the word—his cock was, like the rest of him, long and lean and sinewy, and it seemed to grow and swell under her curious gaze.

Feeling her resistance crumble, she reached out tentatively as though his stiff manhood was a slender, burning candle. "May I?"

"Again, you flatter me, madam," Francois answered. "Of course, you may. But know that the pleasure will be all mine."

All yours? That was hardly the case. She peeled off her gloves, then brushed the underside of his burgeoning erection with her fingers. When it twitched, she pulled back quickly, startled. "It seems to have a mind of its own," she said, smiling impishly. "Does it always behave this way?"

"Only in the presence of great beauty, madam."

"Ah, now who flatters whom, Francois? And does it feel nice when it's caressed? Like this?"

Francois bit his lip as if to stifle a moan.

Susan laughed. "The look on your face is one of anguish, sir, not pleasure."

"I assure you that it feels wonderful," Francois whispered. He leaned back on his elbows, then raised his knees and spread them so that Susan could see his fleshy ball sac dangling suggestively. "Now, if you'd like, wrap your fingers around the shaft, and run your hand up and down its length." When she did so, he growled appreciatively, then said, through clenched teeth, "Yes. Yes, madam. Your hand knows exactly what to do. I am in heaven."

Susan smiled with triumph. She'd had no idea how easy it was to bring a man to his knees, so to speak. It wasn't the sex itself that could cause a man to do a woman's bidding, she now understood. It was the mere promise of sex—or the withholding of it—that might someday shift the balance of power from men to women. Hallelujah! Her sisters at the Guild would be so pleased to hear her revelation—minus any sordid details, of course.

"You will not speak of this to anyone," Susan scolded, meeting Francois's eyes while she vigorously jerked his cock. As it became more engorged and its mushroomy head turned scarlet, she felt an urgent need between her own legs that racked her with longing. Oh, to have the deep, moist recesses of her cunt—yes, her cunt—filled to the brim with Francois's magnificent prick. "It would be the ruin of both of us," she breathed. "You especially."

Francois, huffing like a runaway stallion, managed to gasp, "Madam, I assure you…"

"Ah, what's this, then?" Susan interrupted. Reluctantly, she pulled her hand away from his cock, then with prurient fascination bent low to study the pearly drop of pre-cum oozing from its swollen glans. She'd had little experience with the male member and its transgressions, yet she knew intuitively that Francois had nearly scaled the peak of pleasure.

This knowledge only served to ruffle her feathers. Damn the lot of men who never stopped to consider the intimate needs of the fairer sex! Not that she suspected Francois of being so deceitfully self-centered. Still, it wouldn't do to give in to his desires so readily—not without getting something in return.

"Dear, sweet Francois," she said, with an abject tone of regret. "It appears I've started a fire that cannot be put out."

"Cannot, madam?" he said. His pained expression aroused in Susan such wickedly inappropriate sensations that she had to stifle a moan.

"Heavens, no," she said. "Think of the scandal if we should ever consummate the act." She teasingly traced a slender finger from the underside of his balls to the weeping crown of his cock. "I am sorry, Francois."

"But..." Francois sputtered. "But no one need ever know." His helpless vulnerability made Susan ache for him all the more. "Please, madam. I am begging you. Finish me!"

Secretly titillated by his coarse proposal, she, nevertheless, feigned disgust. "Why you impudent lech," she said. "How dare you? Perhaps you've forgotten who you're speaking to."

"Never," Francois said, looking appropriately chastised. He rose gracefully to his knees, his stout cock beginning to lose its firmness. "I am speaking to a beautiful woman who many men desire, yet none can have. Please forgive my impertinence. I shall resign from my duties immediately upon our return."

Susan suppressed a laugh. *Dear boy, you French take everything much too seriously. And I have toyed with you long enough.* "You will do no such thing," she said. "Rather, what you will do is undress me. Quickly, before I come to my senses."

Francois, far from appearing startled, flashed a mischievous grin as though he'd known all along how the course of events would transpire. "As madam wishes," he said. "As always, I am your humble servant."

Buttons, stays, clasps, bindings, buckles—Francois laboriously removed every article of clothing from Susan's body. But when she found herself so completely exposed to his hungry gaze, the weight of imposed modesty pressed upon her, and she tried to cover herself with her hands.

"No!" Francois said, gently brushing them aside. "Let my eyes devour you. Your lips, your breasts, your ass, the downy patch of hair that hides your cunny. You see? There is nothing to be ashamed of. We are just as God made us—animals with certain appetites, no?"

Susan, despite her trepidation, lay back and opened her legs, inviting Francois to snuffle and lick at and otherwise explore with his fingers the warm, wet channel of her cunt. When he wound the tip of his tongue around and around her excitable little ruby, she cried out, never having imagined such pleasure was possible.

"I am going to fuck you now, madam," Francois said. "But not like one of your noblemen, no. I am going to fuck you like the ruffian I am."

Susan, inflamed by his crude remarks, dispensed with any ladylike pretensions. "Very well," she replied. "Then, I will be your whore, Francois. Do with me what you will."

Francois positioned himself between her legs. As he stroked his cock into full readiness, she thought, perhaps irrationally, that she would enter the events of this day in her diary and leave it where Henry would find it. Then, she would pack a bag and give up her stale, privileged life for one of unbound passion. For it was just as Francois had proclaimed—we are all, at base, simply animals. Animals with appetites.

And the most surprising revelation of all, she thought, as Francois guided the head of his cock into her wet and willing cunt, was that this included women, no less than men.

END

T.D. RUDOLPH *enjoys writing erotica, flash fiction, short stories, poetry, and the occasional angry letter to the editor. He is privileged to live and write in Santa Cruz, Ca.*

306.7
Math

A Floating World Song

author: Kenzie Mathews
category: Culture & Institutions

subjects: 1. Captivity & Submission
2. House of Pleasures 3. Lord & Samurai

Rose Caraway's Library of Erotica

A Floating World Song

Kenzie Mathews

1703
Yoshiwara Pleasure District
Edo, Japan

I have a tattoo on the back of my neck of a blue lotus opening. The Tattoo Master asked me what I wanted, and I formed my hands—wrists together, palms up, fingers bent in fragile expression. I wanted something trapped yet free. Something that found freedom in captivity and submission. The pain was exquisite. I floated, trembling with want of it, both numb and all-feeling.

With pain and breath comes clarity. In all the endlessly turning, floating world *this* is the one pure truth, this stillness of self.

Nothing is real. Nothing has true consequence except for love, and even that is fleeting.

I am Lady Asaji, an Oiran of the Tayu Order. The Ageya I belong to is the Willow House. Of all the beautiful flowers in this House, I am singular in purpose. I serve a certain need. I am loved by a specific type of client because I am the only one from Willow House who loves the whip, knives, bundled sticks, and knotted rope as much as I love the scars on my golden-silk skin. Tattoos are allowed for me as they would never be to other High

Courtesans of Yoshiwara District. In my case, tattoos add to my appeal. Pain is my pleasure.

My paint is my fair skin and crimson blood. My brush is braided whip and tiger nail. When I perform, merchants and samurai blush. When I bleed and moan in ecstasy, they moan with swollen members.

All together, we are art and beauty. All together, we are truth and life.

I have trespassed ritual and tradition. The tattoo is not my only transgression. This little bird dreams of flying into the wide skies. One day, when my debts are paid, I will open my own House of Pleasure. A House dedicated to the skills of discipline and submission and the ecstasy of pain.

This night, I perform in a private room for Lord Ezo-Matsumae and one of his noblest samurai. I peek through the rice-paper door in the corridor that connects the chambers. Yukio, my protégé and the miko of Willow House, stands behind me, her hand covering her mouth, her eyes alight with mischief.

The men are most handsome and young. Lord Ezo-Matsumae is as strong bodied as a warrior king. He must exercise with his samurai. His kimono is scarlet with golden dragons fighting beneath the sun. He seems serious, but then he smiles. He will be a fun lover, perhaps a generous patron. He reminds me of the Koi fish in our garden pond, quick and playful.

As for the samurai, he is frightful, but he makes my heart quicken. He has a wild, barely tamed look to him. He is like a black and gold lion. His blue-black topknot is thickly braided, and his face echoes his beast manner—strong, ruthless bones, a demon's blackest eyes, a cruel, beautiful mouth. The samurai who would be the wind to my willow.

I gasp, already imagining his strong fingers twisting my nipples, his teeth on my lips. I shudder with pleasure. I am wet with longing for them both.

Yukio prepared me for this night. She tied me up in knotted silk. My breasts burst away from my slender body. My arms are bound to my stomach so that I may tickle my cunny when the whip licks my back.

We enter the room proudly, smiling demurely like court ladies in our red and silver kimonos. When we reach the table at one end of the room, Yukio removes my dark-blue night-sky and silver moon kimono. I stand before the men in knotted rope, my skin goose-bumped, my nipples hard, my cunt already tingling with want.

Yukio bends me over a small table so that my bound breasts hang over the side and my captured arms are trapped beneath my stomach. I spread my legs, and Yukio ties them to the table for support. I close my eyes, waiting, hardly daring to breathe. My fingertips stroke my cunt. The whip's first strike is gentle, tentative. The next is surer, turning my moans into husky cries and broken sobs. I rise up with the whip as it bites my flesh. I surrender to the pain and hump the table when it comes down. I bite my lip and swallow blood.

Images cross my inner eye. A white heron standing in a river waits for the hunter. A fox steals the fish from a butcher's table and returns to her den and yowling kits. A court lady in a pale-yellow kimono, her long black hair like silk pouring into night takes a lover, and he is also the lover of her husband. Death, life, and love. What more is there? Then, the whipping stops.

Behind me, Yukio struggles for breath. She is a slight miko, small for her age, but she has been the house mascot and treasure from her first day here two years ago. When her apprenticeship is up, her journey will continue under my tutelage. It will be her cries that bring men to their knees. Her beauty that will rise up higher on scarred flesh and tattoos. I will pass on, a little bird that once faced storms so bravely. I will disappear into the wide, endless sky. This world, and then the next.

I open my eyes. Lord Ezo-Matsumae has risen and now stands next to Yukio. She palms my wet cunt to gather its nectar. She presses it to his mouth. Lord Ezo-Matsumae sucks her fingers and palm clean. Then, his fingers explore my opening. I thrust against him, rocking the table. His fingers tickle my clit, entwine with my own fingers, and then enter my cunt. I watch him over my shoulder. He looks lost in this moment. I cannot wait to get more of him. Grunting, Lord Ezo-Matsumae nods toward the door, motioning to Yukio that she may leave. Yukio bows and quickly darts away.

Lord Ezo-Matsumae lifts his kimono and releases his cock, thrusting it in me. We fuck wildly, the table barely able to take our movements. First, his hands rest on the table, trapping my bloody back between them, then they grip my waist when his movements hasten, his hands soon slipping in blood and upon sweaty flesh. I come quickly, and he follows, crying out. He pulls himself out of me, wiping his hands on his silk kimono as if it were mere rags. He snaps his fingers and strokes my bound legs.

The samurai rises, pulling free his wakizashi. For a moment, I freeze, terrified. It would not be so unusual for a lord to kill a displeasing concubine or courtesan. Had I displeased him? The samurai reads my face and grins before he cuts my legs free from the table binding. The blade is a whisper against my skin. The samurai catches me with one arm before I hit the ground, holding me as if I am nothing but flowers and moonlight.

I am tender. I feel regret and shame that I stain his warrior robes with my blood and comings. I attempt to pull away gently, but the samurai tightens his grip on me. I submit and let him hold my weight. Now, one hand strokes my stomach, barely touching the edge of my shaved cunny.

"Lord Ezo-Matsumae, if your samurai would be so kind to cut the bindings that trap my arms, I will have a bath prepared before Sado," I say softly, head bowed.

The lord nods. Soon, my arms are no longer tied to my stomach, but my wrists remain bound. The samurai makes a move to cut those bindings too, but I move my hands away, my head still bowed, "Please do not. It is my pleasure to serve in bondage."

The samurai nods and moves away to join his lord. I stand alone now before them, naked, my breasts still tied in knots and my wrists bound. I chime the small gong on the wall. Yukio returns, leading servants carrying a large, metal tub. We wait in silence as they bring the hot water to fill the tub.

Then, we are alone.

Lord Ezo-Matsumae starts to lift his kimono, and I rush to him. I shake my head, my eyes down, and I remove his kimono. I was right. He is beautifully muscled beneath the robes of silk. I kiss his naked chest and work my way down to lick his erect nipples. Then, I kiss his stomach until I reach his cock. I nuzzle it with my nose. As he moans, I claim it with my bound hands, willing tongue, and open mouth. He rises in my mouth and moves against me like waves crashing against rocks. Soon, he fills my mouth with his cream. I swallow and he strokes my face, cradles my cheek, and coerces me to rise. Once I stand again, he gently guides me towards his samurai.

"He is like my brother, Watari Sho-Jiro. Will you honor him as you have honored me, Lady Asaji of Willow House?"

I bow in answer. But, of course, I am a most gracious hostess. And I like a man who can handle a wakizashi so close to my skin. It promises much for the future. Watari Sho-Jiro regards me with his dark, demon eyes. I walk into his space just as Lord Ezo-Matsumae enters the metal tub. His black, bottomless eyes on me, Watari opens his obi and removes his daisho. He lays them carefully on the bamboo flooring.

Watari brings me close, his large hands cradling my upper body. Watching my reaction, he slides his hands over my bound breasts. His thumbs rake my taut nipples.

I hiss in pain. Bound as I am, my breasts and nipples are sensitive. Watari twists one nipple slightly, and I cry out, the pain sharp and sudden. A strike of lightning runs from my nipple to my cunt and he covers my mouth with his own, crushing me against his chest. One of his hands roams my back, unlocking the crusted blood and cuts before sliding over my ass. He cups my wet cunny from behind, and I rock into his hand as his tongue explores my mouth. I open my legs and mouth wider, taking him in fully.

Watari laughs in my mouth. It is a warm sound, filled with pleasure. He fumbles at his groin, and I feel the press of his cock against my stomach. The hand cupping my cunny lifts me. Watari places me firmly on his cock and carries us both down to the bamboo floor.

On his lap now, my legs wrapping behind him, I ride. His cock is bigger than Lord Ezo-Matsumae's, more painful. I am not sure which I prefer. Lord Ezo-Matsumae fits better, like silk. When the samurai slides into me, it is like joining a blade to its mark. I arch my back, taking all of him in. Watari squeezes my breasts and I scream and ride him harder. The pain of my twisted breasts and pinched nipples at war with the fire in my cunt.

When he comes, my cunny is squeezing him, juicing him for more. It suckles at him, and he laughs out loud, his demon eyes shining with amazement that I am so hungry still.

I bare my teeth and in answer, he bites my nipple before kissing me. His fingers ride my cunt, taking over for his cock. Watari bends me backward, and I lift my hips so he can fit his entire hand into my cunt. I am so wet, I drip. His hand fills me while his other plays at my clit, pulling the lips of my cunny, tickling the little button. His tongue strokes my mouth, and he nibbles on my torn lip, drinking my kisses and my blood. He hand-fucks me until I come, screaming into his mouth. Then, he removes his hands from that wet place, grabs my face, and kisses me again—a possessive, demanding kiss. I feel it long after he moves away from me.

My finger touches my mouth. Trembling, I lie back onto the bamboo, my fingers swimming in my long, black hair. It has come loose from my elaborate arrangement.

Watari rises and enters the tub as Lord Ezo-Matsumae exits it. I lie there on the bamboo, spent, exhausted, my half-closed eyes watching him. Unlike my other clients, this lord and samurai gave me as much as I gave them. It has been a good night.

Lord Ezo-Matsumae makes it even more so when he drinks from my cunny, licking it clean, sucking on my cunt's lips, his teeth nibbling like Koi fish on my clit. I am so in need again, I cannot breathe. He unties my breasts and releases my wrists from the knots. I am sore where the rope cut me. He massages the blood back into my breasts and wrists. I moan, my body pins and needles. Lord Ezo-Matsumae lifts me and puts me in the tub with Watari. I lean back against Watari, his strong body warm and protective. He rubs the soap cake on my breasts, and I close my eyes as lord and samurai bathe me. Even little birds may dream of the love of dragons and lions.

When we are clean, I dress in a new kimono, this one white with the lightest-silver embroidery of Heron in flight. Lord Ezo-Matsumae and Watari are simply dressed in white fundoshi, treating me to the beauty of their limbs and muscles. Both men carry scars from battle. I blush, thinking of running my tongue along those lines, tracing their pain, making it my own.

It is a challenge to clean the tools for tea when the body is sore and broken, but I have been practicing for years. I am graceful. Last night, I prepared my soul with prayer and calm breath. I meditated on peace and love. Tonight, we have found balance and harmony with each other's bodies. An Oiran could not ask for more.

I present a bowl of rose and jasmine water for Lord Ezo-Matsumae and his samurai to wash their hands. While they rinse and dry themselves with clean cloths, I add matcha and hot water to the tea bowl. I make the paste before adding more water. Once it is ready, I pass the bowl to Lord Ezo-Matsumae. He takes the bowl in both hands and rotates it before taking a drink. Then, he wipes the edge and passes it to Watari. The samurai rotates the bowl, takes a drink, cleans the edge, and then gives me the bowl. My eyes close while the hot tea clears my throat and fills me with warmth. When we are done, I clean the utensils and put them away.

I gather my shamisen and begin plucking its strings. I sing the song about the young lovers who commit suicide so that they can be together forever. I sing the song about the rabbit who fell in love with the hawk that captured it and devoured it to keep it close. I find it comfortable to be in the presence of these men. They make small talk, and I smile. Sometimes, they ask my opinion of so-and-so from court, or they inquire about my favorite theater. I answer honestly. I have an education like many Oiran, and I can converse on gossip, the arts, and politics. The men are entertained and amused by me.

When they have rested enough, the lord rises and bows to me in honor. The samurai echoes his lord, and I rise quickly to bow. Lord Ezo-Matsumae fingers a lock of my long black hair.

"Even this is pleasurable, lady. This nightfall of hair is strong as a katana blade but as delicate as gold filigree." He raises the lock to his mouth and nose. "It smells of cherry blossoms and peach tree flowers."

I smile.

Lord Ezo-Matsumae continues, "It is a difficulty to find women who truly love pain. I have often wondered if the butterfly loves the pin that traps her."

"I cannot answer for the butterfly, but this little bird loves the arrows that pierce her. She dies in the hunter's hand, kissing his palm."

The Lord and his samurai take their leave of me. I cannot sleep though. My cunt is hungry again, and I miss them already. I toss and turn and finally, I roll up my mat. I am deep in thought when the samurai returns to my chamber.

He opens my rice paper door without knocking. "My daimyo has bought your debts. Bring what you wish, but hurry. You are now a concubine of Lord Ezo-Matsumae."

I rise up and quickly pack my tools of trade—my whips, my knives, my ropes, my kimonos, and my lovely ukiyo-e prints—but I will miss Willow House. I turn, smiling up at him. Concubines bare sons who become lords. This is a good future to fly into. Now, I can drown in happiness as well as beauty.

END

KENZIE MATHEWS *lives in rural Alaska. She has big spoiled dogs and a ridiculous amount of books. She writes and paints when not reading or dealing with naughty dogs. She loves the fore-mentioned as well as coffee so strong it hurts to drink it, horror movies, anime, manga, and sleeping. Sleep being the real power of the gods.*

```
808.8
Mill
```

Not Quite an Antidote

author: **T.C. Mill**
category: **Science Fiction**

subjects: 1. Venom 2. Boundaries
3. Intoxicating Dazzle

Rose Caraway's Library of Erotica

Not Quite An Antidote

T.C. Mill

The *Liberty at Last* leaped into hyperdrive, and a release of tension spread across the ship like spring rain over Cyreius IX's inland meadows. The last shuttles came safely aboard after their raid on the Imperium's prison camp, rescued prisoners disembarking to a warm welcome, along with the few guards who'd joined the revolution. A handful of merchants who had provided supplies at the camp also arrived to a cooler reception, still eager to trade with rebels who hadn't had nonviolent outside contact for months.

Between the new snacks, toys, clothing, and other luxuries, and the relief and triumph of the successful attack and escape, conversation in the mess hall was louder than it had been in hundreds of hours.

Bela met Faon's eyes across a long table. Together, they stepped out. Already on short rations, neither of them had eaten anything hot since before the raid set out—he worked and waited in the hangars, she ran around the projections table in logistics—but now, in the midst of plenty, they needed other nourishment.

They found a vacant corridor and pulled each other close. She kissed him as if it could save their lives.

He wrapped his arms around her back, and she felt him pulling his gloves off. His palms and fingers seared, warm through her clothes. His hands moved around to her chest, squeezing gently but firmly with a hunger she shared.

Without breaking the kiss, Bela stepped forward, pushing Faon's body against the wall, her body against his. His touch continued to rove, his hand on the small of her back pulling her nearer. Clutching his hips, Bela shifted her pelvis, starting to rock and rub.

His moan almost sounded like a snarl of pain. It didn't alarm her, but Bela slowed her movements. Faon turned, bringing her with him. She reclined, her shoulders against a storage compartment, and lifted her legs to wrap around him. It brought her groin against him again, the friction sending heat radiating through her mound. His hands held her under the thighs, so close.

She had to keep rutting, her body singing at the contact with his, even though she knew what it was doing to him. But Faon met her with his own blunt thrusts, angling his mouth to meet hers, the kiss messy and interrupted by their panting.

"I want you," he told her. "So much it barely matters if it kills me."

Bela jerked her head away so sharply it knocked the metal door behind her.

Faon frowned, his hand rising to cradle her skull, and she searched his copper-brown eyes for a deeper, more dangerous emotion than concern for her comfort.

He had developed a squint after thousands of hours welding everything from bulkheads to weapon arrays across the ship and on the attack shuttles. She wondered what he thought about all day, if his mind had time to wander. If he was careless enough to let it. Her own tasks among the strategists kept her occupied, at least distracted. Only for a few moments, every few hundred hours, could she be like this, letting her mind go free and her body take over. Her body…

"We didn't win our freedom just to risk your life for this," she said.

"You know I won't. Not if you don't want it."

"What I want is impossible."

"That makes two of us." The wry sarcasm seemed to help him regain equilibrium. He didn't even stammer, though his lips had to be going numb from their kisses, from the poison in her saliva. It was a mild intoxicant, meant to put a target off-guard. By this point in their encounters, they'd both grown used to him slurring his words from more than the disorientation of arousal. A calculated risk, far safer than the venom that flowed elsewhere in her.

"Don't worry, Beladona. We can't. I can't. Believe me, I understand." The note of sarcasm in his voice grew less wry, less steady, and more bitter. His body trembled. "I'm reminded every time I use the heads, or the showers, or change clothes." He shifted, but they remained locked together, thigh to thigh, where she was poisoned, and he was mutilated.

Her eyes burned with her own bitterness and fury at what the Imperium had made of her and taken from him. They'd seen no need to keep a laborer like him intact. For her, they'd had different uses. Strategic ones.

She'd made her last kill five years ago—her former commander. And she hadn't known intimacy since, except what she and Faon had lately found together, what they had the time and the courage for.

A tear slipped from Bela's eye. She caught it before it could reach her lips, then licked it away. The taste was so acrid it left her mouth dry. But at least he could continue kissing her safely, which he did—this time with more gentleness, and something she feared was regret more than passion.

Her nipples rubbed in her suit, hard enough to feel through his own uniform, she was sure. Sometimes, Faon would bring his kisses along her neck, to her breasts. He would suckle them until she shouted.

She wanted more.

She and Faon deserved more.

They'd long accepted they couldn't have sex and had tried not to chafe against their boundaries or think of what they'd risk if they tried. But now, after helping to achieve this latest victory against the Imperium—after doing the impossible—Bela's back stiffened with new determination.

She stroked a lock of hair back from Faon's cheek and promised, "I'm going to find a solution."

Thirty hours later, she sent a comm inviting him to join her in a recreation chamber. Though far smaller than the *Liberty at Last's* dormitories, the reserved space was more private, low-ceilinged, but with a one-way portal that offered an amazing view of the stars.

After embracing her, Faon looked not at the stars, but at the array of items Bela had laid out on one of the floor pads. A smile tugged his mouth.

"The traders who joined us after the rescue carried some surprising things," Bela said.

"And yet, I'm not entirely surprised." He pulled her close again. "It's a brilliant idea, Bela."

She nipped his jaw. "You haven't even heard my idea yet."

"I hope I'll get to watch you…" The words trailed off in a sigh as her kisses moved lower, eventually reaching the sweet spot where his neck joined his shoulder.

"That would be nice," she whispered, over his collarbone. "But you could participate, too."

"How?"

She knelt and picked up a fluid pouch from the floor pad. "This is surgical, but it also…" Bela hadn't told the merchant exactly what she wanted it for—wouldn't bare herself like that to a mercenary stranger—but the description she'd received convinced her it could work. Desire hadn't blinded her to the risk. But the risk no longer blinded her to desire, either.

"An antidote?" Light sparked in Faon's eyes.

"Not quite. But it's a solution. Also, an emulsion."

His groan seemed to be half at her pun about the fluid's chemical makeup and half impatience. The realization of his impatience made her heart beat faster, a heaviness growing between her thighs. Finally, they'd found something to be impatient for.

"It's sterile," she explained, reaching for an Icaran beetlesilk scarf. "And watertight while also providing a measure of lubrication."

"That is brilliant."

She stood, forcing herself to grip the soft-walled pouch less tightly, so she didn't puncture it, winding the scarf between the fingers of her other hand. "It's a chance to be more than what they made of us."

"They made nothing of us."

At his words, Bela stood straighter even as the corners of her eyes prickled. Pride and hope, gratitude and anxiety and love for him, mixed and overflowed. "You're right. We've come this far ourselves."

They'd shaped their own fates, escaping the Imperium, resisting it—even now, even here.

Faon knelt on the other floor pad. Bela dropped the gel pouch and scarf to join him. His fingers danced over the buttons of her suit while she unzipped and folded back his off-duty uniform. She moved slowly, caught in the wonder of seeing his body. Then feeling it. His skin was tawny, a few shades lighter than hers, smooth and taut over the muscles in his shoulders and chest with just a touch of softness at the waist that she found delicious to her fingers.

He cupped her breasts, then bent to suck on their hardening nipples and nip the flesh around them. He was too tender to leave marks, yet so thorough that Bela began dissolving, held up only by his hands on her hips, her hands braced on his chest and side. His heart beat against her fingertips. Her pulse sang beneath his teeth and tongue and down in her cunt, below the billows of her suit bunched around her waist. Unsteadily, she pushed off her clothing the rest of the way and fumbled for the scarf and gel.

She coated both sides of the fabric, then lay back on the floor pad. The gel felt cool as she positioned the silk over her sex and slowly spread her legs wide. Not uncertain that she wanted this. No. But she'd never invited anyone's mouth to her cunt before. It would have been a quick way to finish her targets, but they usually weren't interested.

She'd chosen the waterproof scarf as an extra barrier, one she could feel, because she needed to feel one. To be that much more certain.

Faon touched her thighs as if her body was fragile, sharp, or precious. He lowered himself, breathing hard, his eyes as bright as the stars. Through the thin silk and slick, faint warmth of the gel, she felt the deeper heat and hunger of his mouth.

He licked with short, exploratory strokes at first, pressing the silk between her folds as he followed each curve. He mapped her—she discovered herself under his tongue—moving inward until he circled her clit. It grew harder, hotter, throbbing with the coiling sweep of his attention. Every so often Faon pulled back, and although Bela wanted to cry out at the loss, breath stopped in her throat when she saw his expression.

"You're so beautiful," he said.

When he added his fingers, massaging all along her sex, pulses of smooth sensation transmitted through the gel. Not only was she being touched at last, but some property of the fluid seemed to magnify that touch so that she barely felt the silk and forgot to miss the feeling. Pleasure flowed all along her body, dancing under her skin, deep into her muscles and nerves.

"Perfect." She tried to say more, to tell him how good he was, but each new movement swept her away.

The next time he pulled back, she grasped his shoulders and bent to kiss him. It was the sweetest thing to ever touch her lips. Not so much for the taste. The gel had a sharp tang, richer than vinegar, more astringent than citrus juice, but she was familiar with poisons as was Faon, to an extent, after all their kisses. Unbothered, they pursued each other's warmth and thrilling softness. The kiss transformed into wine and spices, an intoxicating dazzle.

He swept a finger across her lips and smeared it over her breasts—not that there was any danger to neutralize on her flesh there, except for a shimmer of sweat. But the enhanced sensations soon had her crying out, bucking her hips.

"Is it time for…?" He didn't finish the question. But the words he'd spoken weren't slurred, just broken off—from excitement or, perhaps, uncertainty.

She looked with him at the items remaining on the pad beside them. Their gazes rested on the dildo.

"If you want to watch me use it, I can do that," Bela said. "Or both of us can. Together."

He kissed her once more, briefly but deeply, and nodded. "Together."

"Okay." She'd hoped he'd agree, but it still made her shake. "Turn around."

She had a second length of silk waiting. She applied a dab of the gel, then pressed it along the cleft of his offered buttocks. Bela kissed him there, pressing her tongue to the center of the fabric until she could feel out the muscular ring, tracing it. His hips jerked under her hands. He rocked, pressing back against her.

"It feels…good," he said.

It had been too long since anything had felt good to him. Bela did her best to make up for it. Slow strokes, then playful laps mixed with the edges of her teeth, teasing through the silken barrier, knowing the gel enhanced each sensation for him as it had for her. She rolled the tip of her tongue along the whorl, then pressed at its center, steadily, until he opened for her.

Until he said, "Now. Now."

She took both silk straps, wiped off the gel, and looped them together. Then, she positioned the dildo in the resulting harness the way the merchant—a thorough salesperson, Bela had to admit—had shown her. "Don't move," she murmured, when Faon almost rose to help her. "You're so breathtaking that way."

She caught a glimpse of his face, the heat spreading across it, as he ducked his head.

For too long they had thought themselves too broken to be beautiful. But they were, and it was such a pleasure to see and be seen. If he'd wanted to watch her, Bela would have been glad to give him a show, though for five years she hadn't missed penetration, not the sensation or the memories it sometimes brought and hadn't thought to seek it on her own with a toy. Not that such luxuries, even crude handmade ones, were often available aboard the *Liberty at Last,* anyway. So, when she'd seen one, she'd taken it, wanting every option.

She positioned the dildo's base, slicked with a dot of gel, over her mound and tightened her makeshift harness until the now-familiar slippery warmth embraced her clit. More gel went generously over the tapered length.

She came into him slowly, a single long, smooth glide. He gasped as it entered, a jolt she felt running through his legs before he spread them wider. There came another gasp when, after a few seeking rolls of her hips, she found the angle that reached his prostate.

Bela pulled back for another stroke, but he pressed himself against her, onto the toy. The movement rolled its slickened base over her clit, and it was all she could do not to thrust in wildly.

With an arm around his waist, she drew him to her until the firm flesh of his ass met her mound, brushes of skin around the dildo's base and silk straps. Not enough to be risky—arousal dripped along her thighs, but there was the gel between them, and she could trust it—still, enough to leave them both shaking at an intimacy they had never anticipated. That they would never take for granted. She held him there, filled to the root, cradled by her pelvis. She kissed his shoulders and ran her hands up through his long hair. Rocking into him, she heard his gasped response, knowing she'd sparked more pleasure deep inside.

His head angled back, and a harsh, hungry sound escaped his mouth. Bela began to withdraw more with each stroke and return a little harder. Though her movements were outwardly gentle, the gel enhanced them, and his newfound openness magnified them. Their vulnerability made every sensation grow until she drowned in the ecstatic rush of her blood. Heart and hips pounded in a rhythm made smooth and slick.

Muscles in his waist and back rippled as he met her thrusts with his own. Eventually, Faon pushed against her with such force that Bela found herself back on her heels. After a moment, grinning, she shifted into a stable kneeling position and leaned, bracing on her hands, her hips thrust forward and up. "Go ahead, my gorgeous love."

She watched him work himself against her offering—down to the base, and up, the ruby-colored toy disappearing between his round cheeks. The flex of his spine and the swivel of his hips mesmerized her. Vision merged with feeling as he sent rapture spiraling from her clit throughout her entire body.

Bela shifted the position of the dildo with a firm grip, guiding it until his gasps became higher and rougher. *So, this is how he sounds in orgasm.* A flush of joy filled her, her face aching from the unfamiliar pull of a wide, amazed smile.

His buttocks brushed her knuckles. She placed her free hand on the small of his back, feeling more muscles work. When his rhythm began to flag, when his heart beat so hard she could feel it through his spine, she gently nudged him up and rose to her knees. She pushed the dildo deep into him and lay her body across his back, kissing the ends of his hair, his vertebrae, his shoulder blades, and all she could reach.

One arm settled around his waist. With the other, she reached for the gel pouch one last time, messily slicking her fingers. She slipped one in alongside the dildo to feel him, flesh within flesh.

He was hot, and tight, and raw without injury, tender without pain. Despite the risk—for all the cautious steps she'd taken, it had been a risk, one she couldn't quite confront the scale of even now that it had paid off. The sweat rising on his skin tasted clear. His heartbeat was rapid with excitement but didn't have the dangerous thread she'd learned to wait for in her targets. She remembered the symptoms just to rule them out and let the past be lost in the present. He was strong, and well, and whole. They both were. As she made the finishing thrusts, Bela unraveled into her own spasming release. It was almost frightening in its unfamiliarity, but nothing about it was painful.

"Bela!" He shouted her name as his limbs gave out beneath them.

They sank to the floor pad, trembling. She withdrew from him and rolled to lay on her side. He turned his face to her. His eyes danced across her features as she studied his, framed against the stars.

Faon lifted a hand to his cheek and brought it away, shining with a captured tear. He held it out—an intimacy that felt instantly right—and Bela gathered it on her tongue.

"You taste wonderful," she said.

"Like what?"

"Simple salt." It was difficult to explain why that was wonderful, but she wanted him to understand, to believe how delicious he was. For not being poison, not something she needed an antidote for. For being evidence she no longer required an antidote at all.

But he smiled, not seeming to doubt her. He said, "It's the taste of joy."

END

T.C. MILL *is a writer and freelance editor living in the Midwest, which is one answer to the question "What do you do with a philosophy degree?" She's interested in writing about sex, vulnerability, and power, especially when it can be made queer or feminist.*

203.0
Slai

Benediction

author: Alex Slaine
category: Public Worship & Other Practices

subject: 1. Gravest of Sins 2. Confessional
3. Pleasures of the Flesh

Rose Caraway's Library of Erotica

Benediction

Alex Slaine

"Forgive me, Father, for I have sinned..."

The smell of lemon polish and incense permeates the small confessional box. It sticks in my nose and throat, adding a smothered feeling to the claustrophobia that's threatening to send me running. I don't care for churches. The dim light filtering through the screen illuminates dust motes in the air. They softly dance and dip. For a moment, I am distracted watching the way they move. The soft sound of breathing from the other side of the rattan partition pulls me back to the present.

"It has been three weeks and four days since my last confession, and I'm afraid I've lost count of the many crimes against our Lord I have committed," I say.

"Would you perhaps like to start with the gravest of your sins?"

His voice is like cool silk sliding across my mind. The sound puts me at ease even as his question causes my gut to clench. How do I determine the gravest of my sins when in reality I do not regret even a single one? Habit makes me come here, makes me confess, but deep inside, in the place I hope no person or spirit can see into, I don't truly believe I have done wrong.

"I have tempted and indulged in pleasures of the flesh, Father," I whisper, fighting to keep the edge of a smirk out of my voice. I have tempted and indulged, true, but that seems like an understatement.

"Would you care to elaborate?"

"I have fraternized with women and men, sometimes together. I have acted out scenes of depravity in public for the pleasure of others. I have been gluttonous for sex, alcohol, and food. I have coveted the material and emotional possessions of others..." My voice trails off, and I wait, listening to the soft breathing of the priest. I don't realize I am holding my breath until he speaks again.

"Go on, my child."

"The worst of my sins is that I have tempted a devoted man, Father."

"Is this man married?"

"No, but he has commitments that make him unavailable, and I have had relations with him despite knowing that."

"Have your liaisons caused him harm? Have they caused you or anyone else any harm?"

I sit and think for a long moment. Harm is objective, in a space between good and bad. I haven't broken any laws of consent, and he comes to me eagerly and often.

"Perhaps you can tell me, Father," I whisper.

"If you are here to confess, my dear, then you must do so with an open and honest heart. God already knows all. Share with me your trespasses so that he may forgive you."

Taking a deep breath, I wonder where to start. "This man, he comes to me of his own free will. He submits to his pleasure and, in turn, it gives me pleasure."

I think back to our most recent session. I remember it so vividly that I am suddenly no longer in the church but in a modest rented room with simple furnishings and anemic lighting.

I see him standing there before me in the shadows, waiting for my orders. He's tall and broad in the shoulders. His clothing during the day hides his impressively muscled body. When we meet, he knows to be both naked and silent. I like him in a very particular setting, and until the scene starts, he is only a part of the room. Nothing more.

The soft, brown carpet cradles my heels and dampens my footsteps. The hotel is close to the freeway and the sounds of early evening traffic filter through the thin walls and shake the windows.

Removing my jacket, I drape it lazily over the back of the small chair that is part of the writing desk set against one wall. Aside from the bed and two nightstands, there is no other furniture in the room. I know the bathroom will be clean but spartan as well; this isn't about indulging in luxury. We meet here because it is a necessity for both of us, and we do not distract with bells and whistles.

I know the exact moment he's registered my appearance because his cock jerks and a bright pearl of pre-cum weeps from its head. I don't blame him.

I look amazing. I don't put any special effort into my appearance for these meetings with him; I always look spectacular. He is mostly in the shadows, but I can see the muscle ticking in his jaw when he grinds his teeth. The tension riding him is palpable, and I like it.

"Turn around and face the wall. I don't want you looking at me," I say.

I might as well be commenting on the weather. He turns and does exactly as told, exposing his naked back and ass to me. He is as still as a statue with his nose a hair's width from the plaster. I watch him take several deep breaths as if to reign in his anticipation. I know he's been here for most of the day. Check-in was at ten, and it is half past six now. I never tell him when I will arrive, which requires him to always be waiting and ready at any moment.

Setting my bag on the desk, I begin unpacking the supplies I have brought with me. Adjustable bar restraints for his ankles attach to a second bar—an ingenious contraption. It connects to a set of steel rings he will meet for the first time tonight. I retrieve several pairs of surgical gloves, bottles of lubricants in varying viscosities and stimulants, and leather cuffs for his wrists. Lastly, I remove a gag and two of my favorite floggers from my kit. I have a dinner date later in the evening, so this is all I have brought for our session.

"Lie on the bed and turn your face toward the window," I tell him. "If I catch you looking at me, I'll tie you up and fucking leave."

He hastily obeys, and I go into the next room where I proceed to make several calls. None of them are particularly important, but the extra time he spends waiting for me only builds the suspense and makes him more eager to comply with my every wish and command.

After a lengthy conversation with the owner of my nail salon about the error her receptionist made booking me with anyone other than my regular manicurist, I hang up and step out of my heels. I am silent as I make my way back to the bedroom where I see he is vigilantly looking at the window even as his cock remains hard and at attention. His eyes are staring blankly at the drapes, but I know I have his full attention.

"I have something very special for you today, Edward—not that you deserve it. Would you like to know what it is?" My tone is light, but my question is a test. Everything I allow him to experience is special.

"I need only know that it pleases you, Regina."

"Look at me, Edward."

His face turns slowly like he's anticipating a trick or punishment. He stares through clear-blue eyes at my face for long moments while I mirror his expression of calm. It's a wordless exchange as we both slip into our predetermined roles. We know that once we begin, only his pre-negotiated safe word will stop what is about to happen.

"Confirm your signal to stop," I say, quietly.

"Grace, Regina."

With that confirmed, I begin my work. His wrists are bound together and positioned so that his arms stretch high above his head. I do not tether them to anything. It will be up to Edward to control himself. Next, I strap his ankles into the supple leather cuffs connected to the spreader bar which holds his legs wide open. The whole time his body is still but plaint, and his gaze never leaves my face. I know he will stare at me, unblinking, until I order him to look away again.

I won't.

Next, I put on a pair of the surgical gloves and take his shaft in my hand. It jerks involuntarily at being touched after so long without stimulation. His skin is flushed and fever-hot, searing my hand through the black neoprene. With a few drops of lubricant, I massage him slowly, making sure his penis and testicles are meticulously coated in enough of the silicone so that when I fit the two adjustable steel rings around them, there is no discomfort. I do not intend to hurt Edward in any way with this game.

The second bar attaches to the rings, effectively binding him in such a way that if he tries to move his legs, he will be forced to pull on the rings encircling his most sensitive flesh. It's an attractive and titillating way to keep him prone. His breathing is labored, and while I can tell he is trying to keep from making noise, it is a struggle.

We stare at each other in silence for a long moment, while I rub the thumb of my right hand against my index and middle fingers. The feeling of the lubricant sliding between them and over the surgical gloves is wicked. Edward's eyes dart quickly between mine and my hand, and I grin as a fine sheen of sweat mists his body, making his pale skin glow in the dim light of the hotel room.

"These should keep you from coming," I say, gesturing to the contraption I have forced his erect cock into. "But in case they don't, you may not. Do you understand?"

He nods eagerly, and I wonder if he realizes he's also moved his hips or if it was involuntary.

"I want the fucking words, Edward," I say, darkly.

"I will not come, Regina."

With that, I begin my work, applying a generous amount of warming lubricant to his inner thighs. I take my time kneading the thick muscles beneath his skin. His body is hard, and he works tirelessly to keep himself in excellent shape, even though I know it is not required for his job. Another active form of restraint and submission, I suspect. His skin is slick, and as the lube warms him, I watch another round drop of pre-cum seep from the head of his needy cock.

I work my way up and apply more lubricant to the base of his shaft, tracing the upward-jutting appendage with my fingers. I encircle him, but I do not stroke him. The blood trapped by the rings makes him swell impressively, and his taut skin is angry in shades of amethyst and concord. The warming sensation will push him closer to orgasm. To deny himself will be a challenge.

Now, I begin to stroke him, taking his cock in a bruising grip and sliding my hands up and down his length. Every so often, I reach down to palm his testicles, rolling them this way and that. I do all of this while looking him in the eyes.

As sweat beads and glides down the sides of his face, Edward stares at me worshipfully.

Just when his balls begin to tighten, pulling as close to his body as the rings will allow, I stop. I let him catch his breath and slow his pulse, and then I begin again. We do this many times. The duration of what he can take shortens with each glide of my fingers over his hard length until he begins to writhe in the restraints. I watch him try to pump his hips up and down, seeking to grind harder against my palms. I let him chase his climax for a moment before releasing him completely.

Removing my gloves, I pick up my preferred flogger. It has four thin falls constructed of braided leather with glass beads woven into them every four inches. It is the color of fresh cream, complimenting the burnished caramel of my skin pleasingly. Turning back to the bed, I see Edward is tracking my movements again. His lips press into a thin line, tension masking his features when he sees the impact tool in my hands.

I trail the fringed ends lightly over his body, tracing the lines of his form. With a quick flick of my wrist, the first strike lands on his abdomen. This is my favorite place to use the flogger. Despite his toned and chiseled body, the flesh of his stomach remains soft and vulnerable. Like a predator, I enjoy access to the most vulnerable flesh of my prey.

The falls kiss the deep v of muscles, again and again, mere inches from where his erect cock stands straight and proud, confined in the metal rings. With each stinging collision, an angry red welt marks him. In moments, his body is decorated in ribbons, and Edward's arms are shaking with the effort of holding his bound wrists above his head.

I lose myself to the rhythmic slapping of leather against skin. My motions are fluid and in sync with his breathing. In what feels like seconds, more than thirty strikes have endeared him. Each one leaves a faint mark to remind us both of what we have done here today and what he can withstand. I stop then, despite his failure to use his safe word. Edward pushes his boundaries with every session, but he cannot push mine. He's had enough.

Sliding my hands into another pair of gloves, I carefully remove the rings around his shaft and testicles and begin to massage him again. This time, with a cooling lubricant that will cause his skin to buzz and tingle when it meets the warming glide that has continued to assault his sensitive skin throughout his flogging.

His cock twitches and jerks in my tight grip, and I watch as a quiet sense of panic enters his eyes. He cannot possibly fight the urge to come any longer, not without the rings. The anticipation and his training have kept him on the edge for too long, and I can see the strain on his control.

We stare at each other for a second that lasts an eternity. I nod my permission.

"Thank you, Regina." Edward sighs as hot semen begins to leak from the *swollen head of his cock.*

His cum leaves him slowly at first, sliding down his length and pooling around my fingers where they grip him brutally. Soon, the lazy rush of his climax turns into spurts that arc and jet to land on his stomach and chest.

I stroke him to completion, allowing his orgasm to rise and crest in waves, drawing it out and milking every last ounce of pleasure from him.

He continues to thank me as it flows. I do not think he realizes he whispers my name like a benediction. "Regina...Regina...Regina..."

Eventually, he is wrung dry, and his soft moans and harsh breaths are the only sounds in the room. His muscles have gone lax, exhausted from our session.

I massage him gently as I remove his remaining restraints.

And then what did you do?"

The priest's voice shocks me out of my recollection. I have been talking for a long time, recounting my most recent acts, within the solace of the confessional. He has been mostly silent, aside from the occasional rustle of fabric and shifting of weight that can be heard from the other side of the screen. If I didn't know better, I would wonder if he was enjoying my story, taking pleasure in my exact retelling of that afternoon.

I don't have to wonder—I already know.

"I think confession is over, Father," I say, softly. The church is quiet, and I know we are the only ones here. "What penance would your God have me pay for my sins?"

"What sins, my child?"

"Tempting a man." I seem to lose my voice before confessing the one detail I have omitted from my story. "The man is a priest. I have aided him in breaking his vow of chastity. Is that not a crime against God?"

I hear the priest turn in his seat, and when he speaks again, his voice seems to whisper directly into my ear. I can feel his breath through the screen, gusting against my face with each word. "No my dear, it is he who has committed the crime, both against God and unto you for making you complicit in his sin. Only he can repent."

"I don't think a few Hail Marys are going to cover this one, Father."

"Perhaps not, but it is a start."

"So, there is hope for him after all."

He makes a sound of agreement, and then we are quiet for some time. Separated by the screen and many intangible things, the intimacy of the moment is surprising, and when I hear his door creak as it opens, I lean back with a sigh and close my eyes.

A knock echoes softly in the small space, and seconds later, the door to my own side is opened.

"Have you come to repent, Father?"

"If I may, Regina."

I keep my eyes closed and uncross my legs, sliding my skirt up inch by inch until my pussy is exposed to him. He falls to his knees and crawls between my legs. I can feel his breath, hot against my thigh, and I let him wait for my permission to begin until his breathing has turned to panting, and his eagerness is like an electrical current in the air of the small booth.

"Let's start with a dozen Hail Marys, Edward."

END

ALEX SLAINE *is a fiction writer based in Seattle Washington. Specializing in erotic tales featuring strong female protagonists with adventurous tastes in a variety of consensual kinks and feminist undertones, Slaine's time not spent writing is usually dedicated to three cats and brewing another pot of coffee.*

```
349.1
Lake
```
Dyke Lightning

author: **Lynn Lake**
category: **Rural Jurisdictions**

subjects: 1. Southern Night 2. Illegal Liquor
3. Vengeance

RC READERS CAUTIONED
CONTAINS VIOLENCE

Rose Caraway's Library of Erotica

Dyke Lightning

Lynn Lake

The Merc thundered down the backwoods road, through the hot, steamy, moonlit night. The car was a '52, specially modified, lights doused.

A woman stepped out of the dense brush on the side of the road and flashed a light, twice. The Merc's back-end slewed across the narrow road, the big car shuddering to a stop.

"You Zora?" the woman with the flashlight drawled, shooting a brief beam into the open driver-side window of the rumbling vehicle.

"Yeah. Where's the stuff at, Beulah?"

Beulah snorted, swiped at a string of black hair licking her face. She was tall, thin, slatternly, her hair done up sloppily, many strands dangling down. She wore a dirty checked shirt and a greasy pair of blue jeans. She'd been handsome once, still was to a certain extent. Her dark eyes were glazed.

"You ain't a Fed, are you? Been plenty of them boys sniffin' around lately."

"Would I know which road to take if I wasn't working for Sweet Mama? Whippoorwill's the password, ain't it?"

Beulah burped, giggled. "Follow me, sweetheart."

Zora killed the Merc's engine. With the motor off, the sounds of the rural southern night filled the thick, sticky air—buzzing insects, the haunting call of a peacock, the snarl of a big cat somewhere deep in the moss-laden forest.

The trail was twisted and tangled but short. It led to a clearing. A small, wooden shack stood in the clearing, next to a large still. A fire burned low and orange under the giant copper tank, a pipe running off from the tank dripping clear liquid into a steel vat. Moonshine, white lightning, illegal untaxed liquor.

Beulah stopped in front of the shack, turned the torch full-on Zora. "My, my," she commented, moving the yellow beam slowly up and down. "Sweet Mama sure does know how to pick 'em, don't she?"

Zora's red hair flamed in the light, fanning down to her shoulders. Her young, pretty face was tanned golden-brown. Like her bare arms and legs, it was just as smooth. Her slitted green eyes were watchful, intense, her full lips wet like the night air. She was dressed in a tight, white t-shirt and a cut-off pair of blue jeans. Her breasts bulged from the shirt, her hips and butt filling out the shorts.

"You ain't no bobbysoxer, are you, sweetheart?" Beulah slurred. Her voice was thick with more than just liquor.

"How do we get the stuff from here to the car? Carry it?"

The torch beam burned on the twin indentations sharply poking Zora's top. "Where did Mama ever find you?"

"Sweet Mama didn't find me. I found Sweet Mama."

Beulah snapped the flashlight off. The full moon lit the scene in silver. "We run a hose. Down the trail to that big 'ol tanker car of yours. The ground slopes from here to the road. Smart, huh?"

It took them only five minutes to run the hose from the vat, down the trail, to the fifty-gallon tank hidden in the trunk of the Merc. Beulah slotted the nozzle into the mouth of the tank, unpinched the hose, and the white lightning flowed.

"It'll take about fifteen minutes to fill," she said. "However will we pass the time?" She ran a finger along one of Zora's bare arms, then roughly grasped Zora's shoulders, and mashed her mouth against hers. Beulah shoved Zora up against the side of the Merc with the force of her passion, her lips moving, tongue alive.

Zora hooked her arms around the woman's skinny body, let Beulah's tongue flood her mouth. Their breasts squeezed together, Zora's large and firm and pliant, Beulah's small and hard, nipples pressing. Their bodies throbbed, hot.

Beulah jerked her head back. She stared into Zora's narrowed eyes, breathing hard. Her long, veined hands slithered under Zora's t-shirt, snaked up onto the redhead's breasts. "Oh, my!" she gulped, as she felt the bare, mounded flesh.

Beulah clutched and squeezed Zora's breasts with her damp hands, shot trembling fingers up to the pointed tips, and clasped and rolled Zora's nipples. Diving her ragged head down and mouthing one of Zora's blossomed buds through the thin cotton, sucking on one then the other, she hungrily fed on the young woman's ample breasts, her gasping breath reeking of shine.

Beulah dropped down to her knees on the grass, on fire with desire. She tore Zora's shorts open with fumbling fingers and yanked them down the woman's legs. "My God!" she breathed, staring at Zora's lush, ginger-furred pussy.

"It...it gets so lonely..." she started to explain.

Zora grabbed her by her straggly black hair and pulled the woman's face into her cunt, cutting off the words. Beulah plunged her tongue into Zora's slit.

Zora shivered, wettened breasts jumping, fingernails digging into Beulah's scalp. Beulah grasped Zora's plush buttocks with her grimy hands and squirmed her tongue into the woman's pussy, intoxicated by the tangy scent and sweet taste. She brushed her teeth against Zora's clit. Then, she flattened her tongue out and licked Zora's slit from deep in between the woman's legs to the tip of her clit. Again and again.

Zora shuddered, and Beulah lapped faster and faster, hard-stroking the woman's puffy, pink lips, licking and swallowing.

An owl screeched in the sultry night, capturing its prey. Zora bucked against the car and cried out. Her orgasm shined on Beulah's face.

The older woman shakily got to her feet, pushing aside matted strands of hair. She licked her thin lips and said, "My turn, sweetheart."

Beulah unbuttoned her shirt and shrugged it off her bony shoulders, unfastened her jeans and shoved them down, baring her skinny legs. Her wiry body glowed pale in the moonlight, her pussy a jungle mass of dark fur.

Zora smiled, slipped up behind the woman and pushed Beulah against the Merc. Then, she reached in, plucked a sap out of the trunk of the car, and thudded it against the back of Beulah's skull. She caught her unconscious body, and then dragged it off to the side of the road.

Zora walked back down the trail to the still. She pulled the hose off the vat, letting the moonshine gush out onto the ground. Then, she took a cigarette out from behind her ear, lit it, sucked it, its tip burning red.

Then, she flicked the cigarette into the spreading pool of liquor.

Zora strolled back along the twisted trail to the road, the leaping white flames of the fire lighting her way.

A car swerved out in front of the Merc on Highway 5. A woman jumped out of the vehicle, ran around to the driver-side window. "You Zora? Hauling a load for Sweet Mama?"

"Just come from Beulah's still. She's lit on the stuff, that one."

The woman grinned, kissed Zora on the mouth, long and hard and wet. She pulled her head back and smacked her lips. "Yup, that's Beulah, all right—100 proof. Best proof there is if you ain't no Fed." She stuck her hand into the open window. "I'm Clemmie. Be your blocker tonight. Road's been crawling with Feds lately."

Zora squeezed her hand, turned it over, and kissed the soft, smooth, shapely back of it. She licked, staring into Clemmie's big brown eyes. "I look forward to you being on my tail."

Clemmie ran back to her vehicle, a '51 Rambler, and pulled in behind Zora. The Merc leaped forward, shot down the black stretch of country highway, the Rambler in hot pursuit.

Both cars were a mile or so short of the river, and moving fast, when two other vehicles suddenly sheered out of the brush on either side of the highway and gave chase. Zora stomped on the accelerator. Clemmie kept pace, the howl of racing motors filling the night.

The Merc's headlights swept up onto the sign just before the bridge over the Dixie River. The car roared up the incline and catapulted onto the high-spanning bridge. The Rambler followed, the two black cars close behind.

The metal grates of the bridge hummed beneath the speeding Merc. Zora glanced at the rearview mirror, saw the lights of the Rambler suddenly sweep off in an arc. She twisted her head around and watched Clemmie swing the Rambler to a skittering stop right across the mouth of the bridge, sideways, blocking the path of the pursuing cars.

Neither vehicle could stop in time, without smashing into the Rambler. The lead car sheared off to the right, down the steep earthen embankment. The trailing car jumped to the left, plunging down the embankment and plowing into the mud at the edge of the river. Men boiled out of the stuck cars, raced back up the embankments.

Zora slammed on the brakes. The Merc screeched to a stop in a cloud of blue smoke. She shifted into reverse, trod the accelerator. Tires spun and whined, and then the car rocketed backward. The Merc's rear end crashed into the Rambler broadside before Clemmie had a chance to get the car straightened out again.

The woman scrambled out of the passenger side of the vehicle, into the waiting arms of the Feds.

Zora shifted back into drive and drove hard and fast into the night.

The Merc skidded to a stop at the top of a dirt road that sloped off the small town's Main Street and down to a warehouse by the river. Behind the plywood walls of the nondescript building, Zora knew, were stacked crates of moonshine. The warehouse was the main storage and distribution center for the surrounding three counties.

Zora parked at the top of the steep grade, got out and walked around to the rear of the vehicle. She had to pry the damaged trunk open. Then, she picked up a rag and unscrewed the cap on the moonshine tank and stuffed one end of the rag into the rounded opening.

She pulled a cigarette from behind her ear, propped it between her lips, then lit it. Then, she lit the rag, walked back around to the open window and shifted the car into neutral.

One push was all it took. The big Merc rolled down the hill, rapidly gaining speed, aimed straight at the front door of the warehouse.

Zora took a long drag on her cigarette and blew smoke just as the Merc smashed into the building below. Wood splintered, and glass crashed. An explosion rocked the steamy night.

Zora ran down the deserted street to the docks, where a speedboat was tied up. Behind her, a massive fireball mushroomed up from the warehouse, fueled by white lightning, flaming high into the starry sky.

Dropped off your first load, huh?" Sweet Mama said, eyeing Zora from the southern comfort of her massive four-poster, canopied bed. She was lying back against a stack of pillows, body wrapped in a red silk robe, her long, bare legs crossed at the ankles. Sweet Mama was soft and sensuous of form, hard and shrewd of mind.

Zora nodded, her large, taut breasts shivering beneath her tight, white top. Slender, tanned legs swished together as she approached the bed. Most of Sweet Mama's minions were never granted access to the woman's boudoir. But Mama had asked Zora to check in with her special after she made her first run.

Zora had made good time downriver to the antebellum mansion. None of the night's destruction and disruption had reached the woman's shell-like ears yet. "That's right, Sweet Mama," she said, stopping alongside the bed.

"You can call me Savannah, darlin'. All my most intimate acquaintances do." She slowly unfastened the sash on her robe, pulled the silken wrap open.

Her naked body shone rich and creamy-white under the muted lights, breasts big and blue-veined, capped by cherry-red nipples. Her waist was narrow, hips wide, pussy furred honey-blonde. "I'm not even old enough to be your mama, truth be told."

Savannah uncrossed her legs, showing off the glistening damp of her cunt. She slid her hands under her breasts and cupped them, thick, soft flesh. She lifted a tit and lowered her head, suckled the fat nipple into her mouth and nursed on it, bright blue eyes watching Zora from behind long, dark lashes. Sweet Mama was a woman of appetites.

Zora smiled, her green eyes slitted. She pulled her t-shirt out of her shorts, up over her head. Shook out her fiery tresses, then turned her back on the woman and unbuttoned her shorts. She bent forward, sticking out her bum, then slid the fringed jean shorts over the glowing bronze orbs of her buttocks. The skimpy garment sighed down her lithe legs. She kicked it up onto the foot of the bed, to join her discarded, shrunken top.

Zora climbed onto the bed, on top of Savannah, needing to get close to Sweet Mama. She pulled the slick, shining nipple out of Savannah's mouth and fastened her own mouth onto it.

"Oh, darlin'," Savannah murmured. "You've gone and done proved two things—you ain't no Fed, and you've got mighty fine taste."

Savannah reached over to the mahogany nightstand and picked up a wine bottle, tilted some of the clear contents down her throat. "This is the good stuff, darlin'," she breathed, watching Zora tug on her engorged nipple.

Zora lifted her head from Savannah's breast, and the woman put the mouth of the bottle to her lips, feeding Zora the special stock. Then, Savannah poured the liquor onto her own breasts, bathing the plush mounds in alcohol.

Zora scooped Savannah's tits up in her hands and squeezed the damp, heated pair, licked their supple surfaces, tasting smooth white lightning.

"Mmm," Savannah moaned, pouring out more of the contents of the bottle. Liquor streamed between her tits and down between her legs, drenching her pussy.

"Follow the lightnin' trail, darlin'."

"That's exactly what I did," Zora responded, dragging her tongue down the woman's cleavage and stomach and into the blonde fur of her pussy.

"Oh!" Savannah cried, jerking, Zora's probing tongue finding Sweet Mama's sweet spot.

Savannah dove her fingers into Zora's flaming hair and hung onto the woman's bobbing head. Zora swabbed Savannah's puffed-up clit with her tongue, then swiped up and down the woman's swelled-up pussy lips. She licked hard and long, lapping with a vengeance.

"Here, darlin', here—I've got something for you." Savannah emptied the rest of the liquor over her shimmering body. Then, she pulled Zora up, inserted the mouth of the bottle into the woman's ginger-furred pussy, and pushed the long, slender neck inside.

Savannah pumped Zora with the glass bottle, fucking her. "Stick your fingers in me, darlin'!" she hissed. "Fuck me!"

Zora covered Savannah's sopping mound with her hand, sunk three fingers inside, and pressed her thumb against the woman's bloated clit. She held her breath, riding the thrusting neck of the bottle, finger-fucking Savannah.

They came together with fiery intensity, screaming. Zora quivered out of control, the bottle buried to the curved hilt. Savannah vibrated, her juices squirting out from around Zora's plugged-in fingers.

They lay together afterward, Sweet Mama gently stroking Zora's cuddling body, her legs spread wide and breasts splayed, body and eyes languid. She groaned when the antique phone on the nightstand rang. And when she reluctantly reached for it, Zora reached down for her shorts at the foot of the bed.

"Hello. What? Where?"

Sweet Mama took a wild swing at Zora's head with the phone receiver. Too slow and too late. The young woman had already pulled Savannah's other arm up and shackled her wrist to the frame of the bed with the handcuffs she'd taken out of the back of her shorts.

"You blew up one of my stills, my warehouse?" Sweet Mama rasped. She rattled her cuffed wrist. "You are a Fed, aren't you, you little cunt?"

Zora stepped away from the bed, taking her shorts and t-shirt with her. She pulled a cigarette out from behind her ear and propped it in between her glossy lips. "No, I'm not a Fed, Sweet Mama. But my daddy was. He's went missing a year ago while investigating your operations. Those are his spare set of handcuffs he kept at home."

Savannah's blue eyes blazed with cold fury. "So, you're goin' to turn me in, in honor of your daddy, huh?"

Zora lit her cigarette and took a good hard pull. The tip flared red-hot. "Wrong again, Sweet Mama. I'm going to see you burn for what you did."

She flicked the cigarette onto the bed, between the horrified woman's legs. It struck like lightning, setting the liquor-soaked sheet ablaze.

END

LYNN LAKE *lives in the Great White North which she tries to keep red hot – partially – through her erotic writing. Cat-lover, game-player, connoisseur of old movies and new eating places, she used to balance numbers on a full-time basis but now juggles words part-time.*

355.1
Davi

RC READERS CAUTIONED
CONTAINS VIOLENCE

The Safe House

author: Kendel Davi

category: Military Life & Customs

subjects: 1. Surveillance/Interrogation
2. Rogue Agent 3. Deadly Curves 4. Strip-Search

Rose Caraway's Library of Erotica

The Safe House

Kendel Davi

Storm clouds created an all-consuming darkness that swallowed the winding dirt road in front of our vehicle. My training prepared me for nights like this. Instinctively, I knew where I was, but my specific purpose wouldn't be revealed until we reached our destination. When the Bureau sends an unmarked vehicle to your residence with no warning, you know it's a matter of national security. The young agent that sat across from me in the back of the black Suburban sneered as a fellow agent gave him an injection to kill the pain.

"Sorry about your arm," I stated. "I was young once. Haste without thought always gets you hurt." I gripped my cane and glanced out the window. The agent was lucky I'd only broke his arm. If I'd gotten to my nightstand, there'd be one less person in the back of this vehicle heading toward Rho Manor.

Most major cities contain satellite hubs maintained by the Bureau, designed to keep the country running in case of an emergency. Rho Manor is just such a place. It was once a flourishing dairy farm until the water supply mysteriously became contaminated. Even from the sky, it looked like a wasteland, but 150 feet underground rests a fortress that would put the Pentagon to shame.

The Suburban skidded to a stop in front of the dilapidated farmhouse. I adjusted the straps of the suspension sleeve on my prosthetic leg. This was a souvenir from my last assignment in the field. The gravel here was difficult to navigate on two healthy limbs, so I knew I had to be extra careful on just one.

"Shit, Trenton. You almost killed one of my best trainees. Glad to see you haven't changed," Garrett said. He smiled.

The years hadn't been kind to him. His once mountainous frame now slouched. Stress wrinkles accented his ice-blue eyes, and a thin line of stubble was the only trace left of his thick mane of red hair.

"Good to see you, Chief. So, what do you need from me?"

"Zareen. We got her, and she requested you."

The name chilled my blood. Zareen was the reason I'd lost my leg and had almost lost my life. It was a name I hadn't heard in years. The memories of our time together both haunted and aroused me. As the elevator made its descent through walls of reinforced concrete, my mind swirled. *How did she get captured? When did she arrive in the United States, and why in the hell would she want to talk to me?*

Garrett whisked me to the monitored interrogation room.

For the first time since the explosion that had claimed my leg, I saw her. Zareen was chained to a grey aluminum table by her wrists and ankles. Her raven hair was splayed out, covering her face. Even in this constricted position, she was still volatile. I knew that better than anybody in this compound

"She surrendered without a fight," Garrett stated. "In fact, she assaulted a TSA agent in customs to draw our attention to her. If he'd just arrested her, he'd be fine, but he tried to play hero and ended up with a broken rib that punctured his lung."

I had witnessed her doing that to a bodyguard when we were working in Dubai. That was before her government collapsed during the Arab Spring, and she was forced to go rogue.

"She made it very clear the only person she'll talk to is you."

I glanced at the monitors and swallowed my fear before heading to the interrogation room. The hinges of the thick metal door echoed through the hallway. My quivering hand squeezed my cane as I followed two heavily-armed guards into the cell. The buzz of the fluorescent lights was the only sound in the room. The succulent aroma of Zareen's sweating body in the closed space peaked all of my senses.

"Zareen?" I softly called out.

"Trenton?" she replied. Her voice was dry and husky. Zareen's hair cascaded across her face as she lifted her head, and her hazel, almond-shaped eyes pierced into me. "I've really missed you, Cowboy. Why don't you give me a kiss for old times' sake?"

As much as I wanted to get close to her, I didn't know which Zareen sat across from me. Was this the former collaborator, the rogue agent, or the ex-lover who'd almost killed me?

"Just a kiss?" I joked.

"Who knows? Right now, I just need someone who can sit alone in a room with me when I'm not chained to this table like a fucking animal!"

I wasn't sure if that was a good idea. If she tried anything, she'd be taken out in a matter of seconds.

"You heard the lady. Uncuff her."

The larger of the two guards clutched his weapon. The other one knelt down and unlocked the shackles on Zareen's ankles. She kicked her leg free, and both guards jumped back and drew their weapons.

"Give me the damn keys," I huffed.

I snatched the keys from the guards.

"She's shackled and unarmed and you act like this? I don't want her to blink and you accidentally shoot her." I led the guards to the door. "No matter what you see or hear, I don't need to be bothered." I opened the door and signaled them to leave. "That goes for you too, Garrett," I yelled.

"Understood," he replied from the squawk box in the ceiling.

The guards shut the door behind them, perhaps sealing my fate as well. I unlocked the cuffs and sat on the far end of the table.

Zareen grabbed her wrists and massaged the circulation back into them before placing her hand gently on my thigh.

Her touch brought back a deluge of memories. Her toned, naked body flashed in my mind with all the dark tattoos of her kills artistically displayed on her sandy flesh. There was an empty spot above her heart she'd reserved for a very special target. My recollections were encapsulated in fear. A simple scratch from a poisoned fingernail would end me quicker than I would feel the pain. Yet, the visions allowed my normally dormant cock to swell with excitement. I placed my hand on top of hers, gave it a squeeze, and cautiously waited for her response.

Zareen smiled, and I let my guard down as far as my training would allow. She was still beautiful, but behind her bloodshot eyes was a restlessness that seemed to need solace. Her gaze drifted to my erection, and her smile grew into a smirk.

I was just as surprised as she looked. Shrapnel from the explosion had damaged some of the arteries to my groin. Erections were elusive and sometimes painful. Zareen was the last person I'd been intimate with, so I thought my erection could be the result of sense memory.

Zareen released my thigh and stood up. "When I found out you were alive…you don't know how long I've wanted…"

Her voice trailed off. I sensed her focus was cloudy, and I slid closer to her.

Zareen quickly regained her composure. "The Syrians, North Koreans, the Russians…five years of trading information with all three, and they've been working together the entire time. I know what they're planning, and I can't allow it to happen again." She took a step toward me.

I tensed up but held my ground.

"I have all the intel on me," she said, taking a few steps backward. "But you have to find out where it's hidden on my body to get it. They strip-searched me twice and found nothing."

I glanced up at the cameras, knowing every action was being scrutinized in great detail. I thought she was joking until she unzipped her pants and yanked them down to her ankles. My eyes locked on her light-colored underwear. The outline of her pussy displayed itself through the damp cloth. It took everything I had not to toss her on the table and bury my face between her legs. A part of me felt this could be a trick, so I stepped behind her and kept a safe distance.

"Turn around and spread your cheeks," I coldly stated.

"I was hoping you'd to that for me, Cowboy," she responded.

Her playful attitude angered me. I reached forward and snatched her panties off her body, raised her soaked undergarment to my nose, and inhaled deeply. Fuck, she smelled delicious. I wanted nothing more than to close my eyes and live in her scent but hesitated, afraid to take my eyes off her.

"I don't have any gloves," I whispered.

"I really don't give a fuck," she responded. She placed her head on the table, reached back with both hands, and spread her labia, giving me a full view of her cunt.

I fought to contain my lust but lost that battle within seconds. I tossed Zareen's panties onto the table in front of her, placed a hand on the small of her back, ran my fingers tenderly between her cheeks, and gently entered her warm opening. Her wetness clung to my fingers. The squelch from her cunt drowned out the buzzing of the fluorescent lights and devoured my lucidity until the scraping sound of her fingernails along the chipped paint of the table crept up my spine. I bent my fingers inside of her.

She groaned and flexed her cunt around my fingers before glaring at me over her shoulder. "I wish that was your cock inside of me," she gasped.

You're not alone, I thought. I surveyed the room for an area the security cameras couldn't cover. I was willing to risk it all for the sensation of being engulfed by her one more time. I fluttered my fingers inside her before yanking them away, leaving her body shivering on the table. My fingers glistened. I placed them in my mouth, savoring every creamy drop, praying that a little hair of the dog would help maintain my focus. Instead, her taste left me wanting more. I quickly spotted the one space I knew the cameras couldn't reach.

"Come on, Zareen. We both know how this is going to end."

"Do we?" she responded, turning around.

I scratched my chin and gave a slow nod to signal my intentions. We'd used this signal in the past to alert each other to our urgent needs on assignment. I stepped back slowly, guiding her to the camera's blind spot on the other side of the room. As soon as I reached the safe zone, Zareen clutched my belt. I leaned against the wall for balance as her eager hands pulled down my pants and underwear, freeing my cock. I gripped my cane, waiting for her to take me into her mouth, but an eerie silence fell over the room. I looked down as

Zareen trailed her fingers along the raised scars on the stub that remained of my left leg.

My leg had been amputated just above my knee. In my haste to leave tonight, I hadn't pulled the suspension sleeve all the way up. The keloids had no nerve endings, but for some reason, I swore I felt her touch. She gently traced the raised wounds with her fingertips as if she were reading about my trauma in Braille. Then, she looked up at me with woeful eyes before giving the longest and deepest of the scars a kiss. The active nerves around the scars fired at the touch of her sensual lips. Her kisses moved up my leg, and her tongue traced along the surgical crevasses. With each kiss, my cock ached with anticipation. My breath became shallow as her mouth moved to the head of my cock. Her tongue caught a gleaming drop of precum, smearing it around my glans before she took in my full length.

"Oh, fuck!"

I shut my eyes and allowed myself to submit to the power of her mouth. If this was a diversion to catch me off guard, I'd be happy to die just like this. It had been years since I had any release and was determined not to waste this moment, but Zareen seemed to have other ideas. She pulled her head away from my oversensitive, damp cock.

I opened my eyes as she yanked her shirt over her head. Her naked body looked even more exquisite than I remembered. Her erect, russet nipples begged for my tongue to flick them. The tattoos of her victims, coiled around her soft but deadly curves, were works of art. I noticed the place she'd left vacant over her heart was now filled with a name—my name. It was bigger than the rest and done with a deep-red ink.

My training overcame my desires. I grabbed my cane and tapped the tip on the concrete floor. The cane was also a .22 caliber rifle. At close range, a simple twist from my wrist would send a bullet into the victim's brain, pureeing gray matter as the projectile ricocheted inside their skull. I tapped the cane once more to load the weapon and then aimed it at her.

"You weren't supposed to be there," she said, her eyes watery. "I told you to stay put, but you didn't listen." She stroked her fingers across my name on her breast. "I got this when I thought you were dead but now…"

There was something in her voice that radiated honesty, and I lowered my cane.

Zareen pushed me against the wall. Her tongue slipped into my mouth as she hooked her arms around my neck, lifted herself up with the power of her arms alone, and delicately lowered her wet pussy onto my cock. "Fuck me, Trenton," she whispered.

Zareen clenched her pussy around my shaft, and I was lost. I tossed my cane aside and drove into her. Each thrust I delivered brought back painful memories of the last time we'd seen each other. The stench of my burning flesh. Zareen running away, looking back at me through the flames and screaming my name.

I grabbed Zareen by the neck and squeezed. She grabbed my wrist but made no attempt to pull my hand away, sinking herself onto my cock and pushing her orgasm to the edge.

A violent vibration ran through her body. As she came, she tenderly whispered, "I'm sorry."

I didn't know what she was apologizing for, but something in my soul allowed me to just accept it. I placed my hand over her heart and traced the outline of the tattoo of my name. I didn't think about my damaged leg. All I wanted was to be with her. I threw my cock into her with all the power I could muster, fucking her hard, trying to forget the pain. Each filthy word of encouragement she whispered in my ear lifted me to the point of freedom. I felt my orgasm rise and buried my face in her hair to muffle the groans of pleasure that spewed from my soul. With a valiant thrust, I flooded her cunt.

I held her, my cock still pulsing inside her. This reunion of our bodies had made me feel whole again. For the first time in years, I felt virile. The explosion had done damage to more than just my leg, and this had been better than any government-approved therapy session. For a moment, it felt like everything was as it used to be between us. Then, Zareen pulled me in for a kiss, and a sharp, searing pain ripped through my lip.

"Goddammit!" I threw her across the table and cupped my lip. Blood poured from my mouth as I felt around to gauge how much damage she'd done. She'd bitten me hard enough to split my lower lip wide open. Fresh pain refueled my anger. I rushed toward her, determined to take her down until I spotted my cane in her hand.

"I always loved you, Trenton," she calmly said. Then, she placed the tip of the cane under her chin and gave it a twist.

Bang! Her body slumped to the floor. I stood there in shock before scurrying toward her, but she was already gone. The clank of the metal door opening broke my daze. I held her tight as several agents rushed into the room. Garrett pulled me away from her corpse.

I squeezed my lip, attempting to stop the flow of blood, and felt something hard and sharp embedded in my wound. I pulled out the object. It was a small microchip, covered with my blood.

"I'm pretty sure everything you need is on this," I mumbled, handing it to Garret.

He looked at me, his expression stunned.

I did my best to collect my thoughts as I looked at the tattoo of my name on Zareen's dead, naked body. A lifetime in prison or in the witness protection program would've destroyed her spirit. She'd ended this on her terms. I had to respect that in some way, no matter how much it hurt.

"Let's get that stitched up. We can deal with how we're going to explain this to the higher-ups later," Garret said.

I nodded as the pain from my lip rushed through me and leaned on Garret for balance as he led me past the stretcher where Zareen's body had been placed. I gazed upon her one last time. In a job where emotional connections are elusive, even dangerous, I'd risked everything to love Zareen.

"Until we meet again, Zareen," I slurred. As the medical team took her body away, I felt a part of me leave with her, but I only had a brief moment to grieve. I was still an agent with a job to complete and was whisked away to receive medical treatment before giving my official statement about the events that had occurred in the cold belly of Rho Manor.

END

KENDEL DAVI *spends way too much time on a computer either writing, doing graphic design, or video editing. When the sun calls his name, he can be seen listening to classic jazz as he walks around Los Angeles looking for inspiration in used bookstores or local coffee shops in Koreatown.*

347.0
Shaw

Hung Jury

author: Terrance Aldon Shaw
category: Civil Procedure

subjects: 1. Judge's Chambers 2. Jury Tampering
3. In Flagrante Delicto

Rose Caraway's Library of Erotica

Hung Jury

Terrance Aldon Shaw

ady lawyers!" District Judge W. Hardin Longfellow shrugged off his robes with a weary sigh. "I assume you both know why you're here?"
"Your Honor!" The defense attorney raised her hand. "If I may? I'd like to—"

"Purely a rhetorical question, counselor." The judge draped his robes over an antique hall tree that dominated one corner of the room like a set of trophy antlers. The chambers in the small county courthouse were on the shabby side, with cheap veneer paneling where fine oak wainscoting would have graced grander surroundings. "Let's get down to it, shall we?"

"But, Your Honor!" The young woman persisted. "My client—"

"Your client is a single-celled organism with serious boundary issues, Miss Bubachevski. A fact which, your most valiant efforts notwithstanding, everybody on that jury is unquestionably aware." The judge grimaced as he sat down behind the desk.

"But—"

"Ah!" He raised a finger for silence. "The Constitution of these United States guarantees even a scraping of unregenerate pond scum like Mr. Enos 'rhymes-with-you-know-what' Reeks is entitled to the due process of law as much as we'd love to ignore that pesky little fact."

"Speaking of pesky little facts," the prosecutor interrupted, "I must ask if

Your Honor deems such language appropriate?"

"I was wondering when we'd be hearing from you, Miss Apple. Were you always the quiet one in class?"

The prosecutor was clearly not amused. "Your comments are clearly biased, sir. Need I remind you that it's our duty as officers of the court to avoid even the appearance of—"

"Give a bimbo a law degree!" The judge rolled his eyes.

"—and that such remarks could be interpreted as sexual harassment?"

"Are you quite finished, Miss Apple?"

"I—"

"What is it that leads either of you to believe I was, somehow, born yesterday?" Hizzoner spoke evenly. "Hell! I was practicing law before your daddies discovered their peckers were good for more than just taking a whizz."

"Objection!" The defense attorney shot out of her chair. "Oh...sorry."

"Dumbass." The prosecutor stifled a cough.

"That, however, is not the question before us this afternoon," Judge Longfellow said. "The question is why in blazes, given you two young ladies' behavior, should I not immediately declare a mistrial?"

Silence.

"Thought so," he said. "In fact, I am well aware of these issues, Miss Apple. But, seeing how the two of you have both been caught with your tits in the proverbial ringer—*in flagrante delicto* no less—I am inclined to call it even and move on. What the bar association doesn't know won't hurt it."

"Huh?" The defense attorney seemed confused. "What are you—"

"Oh, give it a rest, Bambi," the prosecutor sneered. "Can't you see he's figured it out?"

"Screw you, Candi," the defense shot back. "I don't know what you're talking about."

"Enough, you two!" Judge Longfellow pounded the desk with his fist. "It's already been a sow's anus of a day, and the last thing I want to do is referee a cat fight. Got it?"

"Yes, Your Honor."

"Good." The judge continued, "This simple, open-and-shut case is rapidly turning into amateur night at a demolition derby. And why should it be thus, aside, that is, from you two D-cupcakes constantly trying to one-up each other in front of that jury? You, Miss Bubachevski, batting those big brown eyes as you finger the top button on that blouse, virtually inviting the men to undress you. And you, Miss Apple, not to be outdone, pouting like a porn star just before the cumshot, all the while tossing those platinum locks back across your shoulder. Hell's bells! You'd make a mockery of a mock trial. I haven't seen shenanigans like this since law school. Speaking of which, the two of you graduated in the same class at State, am I correct?"

"Yes, Your Honor," they said together.

"Neither particularly distinguished?"

"No, Your Honor."

"Dead heat for smack-dab in the middle, as I understand, which might explain these competitive antics of yours."

"Uh-huh," the defense said.

"I suppose," the prosecution agreed.

"So tell me, how did you young geniuses finance your less-than-distinguished essay through the halls of Academe?"

"That's hardly relevant!" the defense protested.

"And yet, I ask, Miss Bubachevski. So?"

"I worked as an exotic dancer."

"And did you have a stage name?"

"There's no shame in honest work," Bambi insisted.

"True, my dear, but jury tampering is another matter. So, how did they introduce you when you strutted out on that stage?"

"Foxxy Boob-a-licious." She blushed.

The other woman snickered.

"And what of you, Miss Apple?" Judge Longfellow swiveled in his seat, fixing the prosecutor with a rheumy stare.

"*I* worked my way through as a paralegal," Candi said, haughtily.

"Bull*shit!*" the former Foxxy Boob-a-licious muttered.

"All right!" Candi admitted. "I worked for an escort service on the side. Didn't even have to change my first name."

"Candi Apple…Bambi Bubachevski." The judge smirked. "Hard to be taken seriously with names like that."

"Mmm."

"Yuh."

"And I suspect both of you view this trial as a chance to break out of this podunk purgatory finally and do something other than standard contracts and wills for little old ladies the rest of your lives. Get your pretty little behinds to the big city and real careers while the getting's good. Or would I be mistaken in these rather clichéd assumptions?"

"No, Your Honor," Candi said.

Bambi nodded.

"So, the question is what are we going to do about all this?"

Silence again.

The judge tented his fingers. "Only one thing interests me here, ladies, and that's speedily disposing of this case, preferably with as few loose ends as possible. However, since you both apparently missed that day in law school when they talked about plea bargains, we'll need to find a more creative way to skin this particular feline."

"What did you have in mind?" Candi winked.

"We're listening," Bambi said.

"That's better." The judge put his feet up on the desk. "For starters, the two of you are going to confess—and I mean every detail down to the last soiled garter. I shall consider what happens afterward. So, who'll be the first to come clean?"

"Me." Bambi sighed. "It started during jury selection. I knew the odds were against me going in, and I needed an edge. Enos might as well be wearing a sign that says 'Look at me! I did it!', and there isn't much I can do about his appearance. The man does not clean up well."

"Indeed," Hizzoner said. "Continue."

"All I needed was one person on that panel to go my way, just one reasonably sympathetic individual, and I'd have a hung jury. Not a great strategy, I know, but better than nothing."

"So?"

"So, how to make an impression? It could be as simple as brushing up against one of the male jurors on the stairs during the lunch recess—innocently enough as far as anyone could tell. Let him feel my hip against his for a second, give him a quick hair tickle as I pass, maybe stop and bend over, let him rear-end me. If I do it right—subtle enough to seem like an accident, obvious enough to be unforgettable—he gets the message, yet we haven't exchanged a word about the case."

"Geez!" Candi wrinkled her nose.

"You're just jealous because you didn't think of it first." Bambi sniffed.

"Very clever, Miss Bubachevski." The judge nodded. "And the lucky fellows in question?"

"I identified three potentially-susceptible jurors," Bambi said. "Number four, the retired mechanic, a widower, clearly lonely. Number nine, the old deacon, pillar of his church who can't take his eyes off my tits. Then there's number seven, the kid fresh out of school. I assumed he was a virgin based on how he'd never make eye contact when I questioned him during *voir dire*. I saw lots of guys like him when I was a dancer—too shy for their own good, totally nervous around women. All they really need is a little encouragement. Give their egos a few good strokes, and they're practically eating out of your hand. Figured all I had to do was plant an idea in his head."

"Such as?"

"Defense Exhibit A." Bambi stood and lifted the hem of her skirt to reveal the lacy black garter belts beneath.

"Lovely," the judge murmured. "Anything else?"

"Exhibits B and C." Bambi undid the top buttons on her blouse before bending forward, offering a panoramic view of her cleavage.

"Holy—" The judge sat up, clearly taking notice. "So—"

"You stalked him!" Candi said.

"Did not!" Bambi snapped. "I very discreetly followed him into the men's room downstairs. Court was adjourned for the day, and the building was practically abandoned."

"What happened then, Miss Bubachevski?"

"He was draining the dragon when I walked in. Didn't see me until he turned around, still halfway unzipped. I didn't say anything, just offered Exhibits A through C, backed his cute butt into a stall, and gave him a lap dance."

"Details, counselor. Remember?"

"Of course." Bambi came around the side of the desk with a vampy, hip-swinging swagger. "If Your Honor will permit me to approach?" Moving to music only she could hear, the defense attorney danced, swaying and spinning as she shoved her ass at the judge's chest, sliding it slowly down to his crotch, then back again before turning around. A few more buttons undone, she straddled his lap, drew his head to her bosom, and buried his face between her magnificent bra-straining boobs. "Like this, only…"

"Mmmph?"

Bambi hiked up her skirt and ground her silk-pantied pussy into Judge Longfellow's lap, narrating as she teased. "That poor kid was so hot and bothered by the time we were through, I thought he was going to have a seizure."

The judge came up for air. "And you're sure no one else witnessed this?"

"Didn't think so at the time." Bambi stood up. "But, as it turned out—"

"I did," Candi said. "Knew exactly what Jane Airhead was up to when I saw her sneaking out of the gents'."

"Yet," Judge Longfellow chided, "instead of reporting your suspicions like a goody-two-shoed officer of the court?"

"My competitive hackles were up," Candi confessed. "Figured if some skanky brunette had what it took to sway this guy, I sure as hell had what it took to sway him back—not to mention the other jurors she'd made contact with."

"Do tell." The judge took a bottle of bourbon along with a tumbler from one of the desk drawers.

"I found juror number seven in the restroom where my distinguished colleague had left him. He was sitting there with a dazed look on his face, jacking off in the stall."

"Is that all, Miss Apple?"

"Not quite." Candi strode heel-to-toe like a runway model around the other side of the desk. "If I may offer People's Exhibit A?" She tore off her blouse. Her glossy camisole spilled over a pair of pertly-luscious jugs like high tide in fuchsia. Kneeling at the judge's feet, the prosecutor let the garment drop away. "The guy was scared out of his wits," she whispered seductively, stroking Judge Longfellow's hand. "Scared and totally turned on at the same time. Not sure he could've talked even if he remembered how. In any case, I didn't say a word."

"Not the way I remember it, counselor." The judge took a sip of his drink. "I believe your exact words were, 'Need any help with that?'"

"Wha—?" Candi started.

"Oh, God!" Bambi covered her mouth.

"How do you suppose you were found out in the first place?" Judge Longfellow asked. "Who do you think was occupying the stall at the far end? Didn't bother to check, did you?"

"So you—"

"It was that damned tenderloin I had for lunch yesterday. Made me a captive audience, as it were. Heard the whole thing through the door. Care to amend your statement, Miss Apple?"

"Okay. I asked number seven if he required assistance. He indicated in the affirmative. That's when I took matters into my own hands. If I may demonstrate?" Candi reached for the judge's zipper.

His cock sprang out like a jack-in-the-box.

"Nice gavel, Your Honor!" She worked the shaft, hand over hand, coaxing it to greater heights before laying it flat against her breastbone. "Mmm!" She squeezed her knockers around it as she glided subtly up and down. "The people will stipulate for the record that juror number seven was hung like a horse's handbrake and that, further, I did knowingly, of my own free will, and, basically, for the sheer hell of it, titty-fuck him to within an inch of his life. Just. Like. This."

"Ahh!" The judge tossed back his drink with a single swallow.

"May I approach?" Bambi was naked from the waist down now; only her garters and stockings remained as she moved in to press her sable-soft cunt against the judge's face. "If it pleases the court, I'd like to offer additional testimony at this time."

"Uhh!" The judge nodded, turning to flick his tongue at the defense attorney's clit.

"May I interpret that as an okeydokey?" Bambi bore down and, for a while, the only sound in the chambers was the steady rhythmic slip and slide of the judge's cock between the prosecutor's hooters, along with the sharp, slurp-sloppy, egg-beating noise of his tongue working in and out of the defense attorney's sopping folds.

Candi slipped a hand into her panties, getting herself off, her scrumptious natural knockers yo-yo-ing buoyantly around the judge's overheating rod.

Bambi moaned as she cupped her own melons, fingering her nipples until they etched the front of her D-cups. Leaning forward, she let her long hair fall along the side of Judge Longfellow's face, tumbling into a silken pool across his heaving chest.

"May I cross?" Bambi inquired.

"Your witness," Candi said.

Together, they lowered the back of Judge Longfellow's chair until his head rested on the low credenza behind the desk. Then, the women switched. Shucking off the rest of her clothes, Bambi genuflected between the judge's thighs, dragging her bare knockers and her sharp-pointed nipples over his knees as she rose up to swallow his dong.

Candi had already stripped off her skirt and panties. Now, she took a wide sideways step to stand astride the judge's face. "I suppose somebody ought to object, given that we're calling for speculation on the part of the witness," she cooed, triumphantly.

"Overruled!" the judge shrieked a second before Candi lowered her pussy to his mouth.

She rocked slowly forward, teasing with her sloppy sideways pussy-kiss.

Meanwhile, Bambi made her argument below, her lips forming a tight seal around the judge's prang, nodding and bowing her head, drawing it down and back as she swirled and swizzled her tongue about the shaft.

"Ahh!" An ominous groan rumbled up from the back of Judge Longfellow's throat, though he could form no words with his mouth full of Candi. His nose was pressed tightly against her clit, his tongue jammed deep into her snatch. Below, his dick trembled and spasmed as if anticipating release.

"Oh!" Bambi disengaged. "I think he's about to make his ruling!"

"Uhhhhh!" The judge shot his wad across Bambi's ba-zooms just as Candi's cooch exploded like a geyser, squirting all over his face. "All right! All right!" he panted out the words at last. "I've made my decision."

Bambi rubbed her tits over the judge's shuddering shaft, then swallowed his balls with a greedy slurp.

Candi continued to hover tantalizingly out of reach, her svelte pussy glistening, mere inches from Judge Longfellow's lips.

"Jurors four and nine are clearly tainted. Both are excused forthwith."

"But, Your Honor!" Bambi whined. She gave his balls a pleading lick. "I worked so hard!"

"Would you prefer a contempt citation, Miss Bubachevski? Disbarment? A criminal indictment? We can't impanel another impartial jury. Not now. Change of venue is impractical, expensive, and utterly pointless given the almost-certain outcome of a second trial. So, this is what's going to happen. Two alternate jurors will be seated, and this trial will proceed without further incident as if none of this ever happened," said the judge. "That acceptable to all parties?"

"But—" Bambi ran her tongue hopefully up to the tip of his cock.

"What about juror number seven?" Candi said.

"All things being equal, after carefully weighing the evidence presented here, I'd say we can count on his being scrupulously unbiased from here on in. Only question's whether the lad prefers blondes or brunettes." Judge Longfellow smiled crookedly. "Guess you'll have to win him over with the eloquence of your summation after all."

"So, that's it?" Candi stepped clear and bent over to retrieve her clothes.

"Not quite." The judge wiped his face with a handkerchief and poured himself another drink. "Under the circumstances, I think the two of you should reconcile your differences."

"What?"

"Kiss and make up." Judge Longfellow cleared the top of the desk with a swipe of his hand, sending a flurry of papers to the floor.

"Your Honor?" The women stared at him incredulously.

"On the lips, if you please. Right. Now."

"Well, if you insist." Bambi rose and stepped toward her colleague as Candi puckered up sourly.

Hung Jury

"Not those lips." The judge nodded his head to indicate precisely which lips he meant. "So?"

Candi rolled her eyes, then surrendered. She lay on her back atop the desk, and Bambi joined her, their faces in each other's pussies, grazing, bussing, licking, and sucking. They writhed and wrestled together, blond over brunette, and again, jet over platinum, panting, whimpering, hyperventilating, trembling, and coming. Their rivalry seemed to melt into languid sighs of climaxes without end.

"Oh, Gaaaaaaaawd!" Bambi cried out.

"Mmm!" Judge Longfellow took a leisurely sip of his drink as he sat back and watched. "*Lady lawyers!*"

END

TERRANCE ALDON SHAW *once thought about becoming a lawyer. Subsequently, he decided to go into a more respectable line of work and write erotica. The idea for Hung Jury came to TAS while he was serving on a jury in a vehicular homicide case many years ago. Now, with three novels and nearly 80 short stories to his credit, TAS has no regrets about his choice of careers. He lives and writes in rural southeast Iowa.*

364.1
Woe

In the Rough

author: Rachel Woe
category: Criminal Offenses

subjects: 1. Cat Burglar 2. Cable Ties
3. Gloved Finger

Rose Caraway's Library of Erotica

In The Rough

RACHEL WOE

Vashti strummed her magenta fingernails against the glass countertop as she contemplated the array of gemstones glinting in the showcase below. If time were more precious than money, she could've considered herself rich. As it was, she spent most of her time these days making money for someone else.

"You're slouching, Vashti." Edmund Gorski, the proprietor of Gorski Jewelers, appraised her from the office doorway.

She straightened and manufactured a smile. "Only for a moment, sir."

"See that these are added to the collection." He handed her a velvet-lined case dotted with engagement rings. "Try and keep yourself upright until the end of your shift." Gorski slinked away as silently as he'd emerged.

Vashti dropped her shoulders along with her smile and surveyed the empty storefront. Why Gorski insisted on staying open late on weeknights was beyond her.

She unlocked the showcase and arranged the new rings beside the old. The bell on the entrance door jingled. Vashti swallowed a yawn.

"Welcome to Gorski's. How may I—" She jutted her hip; no need to fake a smile for this fine customer. "—help you?"

The well-dressed man cast an eye around the shop. "I'm looking for an engagement ring."

A disappointing request. "We have some new arrivals if you'd care to have a look."

He approached the counter, his gait smooth and unhurried. Vashti pegged him to be a few years older than herself, perhaps in his late-thirties. He scanned the assortment.

"See anything you like?" She stroked her collarbone. He may have been shopping for a ring, but as far as she was concerned, the man was still on the market.

He pressed his hands to the glass. His wide palms and long fingers were perfect for pulling hair. "I'm having trouble deciding on a cut."

"Does your girlfriend wear much jewelry?"

"She seems to favor quality over quantity."

"In that case, perhaps she'd like a classic round diamond. Unless you think she'd prefer the sentimentality of a heart-shaped stone." Vashti pointed to each cut as she named it.

He tapped the glass. "Which would you pick?"

"Me?" She loved this part. "Oh, I couldn't—"

"Don't pretend you haven't thought about it. How long have you worked here?"

"Eight years," she said.

"That's a long time to stay in one place. You must love your job."

"It has its moments."

"What could be more riveting than hawking overpriced jewelry?"

Vashti laughed, keeping an eye on the office door. "I suppose I've always wanted to travel."

"A woman with a sense of adventure." His eyes glinted. "Where would you go?"

"Paris maybe. Berlin." Vashti stared longingly into the case, recalling a time when she'd relished her proximity to such extravagance. In all her years of employment, she had only managed to obtain a single piece of jewelry. "Anyway, enough about me. What do you do?"

"I specialize in acquisitions." He blinked, slow and feline. "You still haven't answered my question."

Vashti barely had to scan the display before pointing out her favorite. "This one. A full carat, platinum band. The radiant cut maximizes the surface area, making it appear larger."

"Would you mind trying it on?"

She smiled. "If you insist."

Vashti slid the dazzling piece onto her finger.

"It looks good on you," he said.

She heartily agreed.

"How much?"

"Nine thousand."

He rubbed his chin, his expression thoughtful. "I'll think about it. Thank you for your time, Miss?"

"Turani." She offered her hand. "Vashti Turani."

Rather than shake it, he kissed the knuckle just above her ring finger. "Your assistance has been invaluable, Miss Turani."

She watched him go, wishing more than anything that she could follow.

The clock chimed ten. Vashti performed the requisite nightly duties, switched off the lights, then went to collect her purse from the office.

"Aren't you forgetting something?" Gorski called from the storeroom.

"Sorry?" she asked through gritted teeth.

"Tonight's inventory."

Vashti's lower back seized at the thought of standing for one more minute, let alone another hour, in three-inch heels. "I assumed you were doing it."

"I'm afraid I have a prior engagement."

"But I just pulled a double."

Gorski frowned.

Vashti challenged his stare but ultimately conceded. She needed this job more than she hated Gorski.

"Don't forget to set the alarm before you go home," he said.

As soon as Gorski left, Vashti sank into the chair behind his desk. She kicked off her heels and fanned her toes. If she was going to spend the next hour stooping and straining, she resolved to make herself as comfortable as possible.

In the bathroom, Vashti shrugged out of her silk blouse and unclasped her bra. She relished its absence, tracing the pink groove left by the underwire, then let her gaze drift to the glint of metal and precious stone dangling from her left nipple.

Acquisition of the quarter-carat diamond had not been premeditated. Alone in the storage room one evening, she'd come across an ugly pendant harboring treasure and had secreted it into the crotch of her panties. The cool metal pressed against her skin had sent a rousing shiver up her spine. Once home, Vashti broke out her pliers and replaced the stone with a cheap crystal, then attached the diamond, in its white gold setting, to the hoop dangling from her nipple. The next morning, she'd returned the pendant to its box where it remained.

Vashti re-buttoned her top, noting a hint of sparkle through the delicate fabric. She pinched the tips of her breasts and hummed at the twinge of pain-laced pleasure. It'd been too long since she'd been touched by rough hands. She closed her eyes and reached beneath her skirt to rub herself through her panties. Just thinking about how the diamond had felt between her legs was enough to make her moan.

A loud clang from the storefront woke Vashti. She composed herself, then tiptoed out to the showroom and switched on the overhead light.

A figure loomed over the register.

Vashti gasped.

The intruder spun around, his face hidden behind a black ski mask. He must've noticed the security light wasn't flashing and picked the lock on the front door. Vashti had refrained from enabling the alarm because it was motion sensitive, and she needed to be able to move freely around the store.

Of course, she hadn't counted on falling asleep and leaving the entrance vulnerable.

Vashti backtracked through the office door.

The man moved toward her, pausing to switch off the lights.

Her blood pounded in her ears. She ran for the phone, but he caught up to her, pinning her arms to her sides.

"You're not supposed to be here," he growled, anchoring her to the desk with his weight.

Pens, loupes, and diamond scopes dug into her abdomen. Then she spotted Gorski's coffee mug. Flailing her legs, she managed to loosen one arm as he moved, evading her feet. Seizing the mug, she pivoted and pitched it at his temple.

"Fuck!" He ripped the mug from her grasp.

Shifting onto her back, Vashti tore the mask from the man's head and slapped him hard across the face—his familiar face.

The well-dressed patron from earlier that evening scowled. "You shouldn't have done that." He withdrew a handful of cable ties from his pocket and hauled her over to Gorski's chair. In a matter of seconds, he'd secured her wrists and ankles, though she'd managed to knock him back twice in the process.

The man raked a gloved hand through his hair. "What the hell are you still doing here?"

"Inventory."

"At eleven-thirty?"

"My boss is kind of a dick." Under different circumstances, Vashti might've found this scenario arousing. Now, it was all she could do to keep from dry heaving. "Are you going to hurt me?"

The man avoided eye contact like a window shopper who'd only stopped in to try on something extravagant.

"You've seen my face," he said. "That makes you a liability."

Fear sank like a stone in Vashti's stomach. "You're going to kill me?"

"I don't know." He paced around like a caged animal.

Vashti had a hunch the man was in over his head.

"Well," she said, "how would you do it? Stabbing would be messy. Maybe strangulation? A gunshot to the head?"

"Do you see a gun anywhere?"

"No." She swallowed hard. "And I don't see a killer either."

He stopped pacing and came to stand between her knees. "Want to bet your life on that?" He studied her mouth. "I should've gagged you."

"Why? It's not like I'm screaming. You want to clean the place out? Fine by me. I couldn't care less about Gorski's bottom line. You want assurance that I'm not going to rat you out? Untie me, and I'll help you ransack the place. We can split everything fifty-fifty."

He cocked an eyebrow. "You're kidding."

"Look, the security cameras run on an analog system. Once we're finished, I'll give you the tape. Consider it leverage. Turning you in would mean incriminating myself."

Time held its breath.

He reached into his jacket pocket and withdrew a large folding knife.

Vashti's throat closed like a fist.

"Eighty-twenty," he said.

She squinted. "Seventy-thirty."

He slid the knife beneath her wrist and severed the tie.

Vashti switched on the display lights and unlocked the showcases.

The thief unzipped a black duffel bag and began plundering.

Using a gift bag, Vashti began to collect her own bounty, arbitrarily at first, then as her heart rate slowed, with discernment. She had the advantage of knowing the wholesale price of every item and wasn't about to bother with rose gold just because it was shiny.

She cleared her throat. "So, acquisitions, huh? That's cute. How long have you been burgling?"

"A while."

"How long's a while?"

He didn't respond.

The thief moved swiftly between the displays. Vashti liked that he was lithe like a cat, yet muscular enough that he could still toss her around. Too bad she'd been too distraught to appreciate his strength when he jumped her in the office.

She tried again. "What should I call you?"

He turned, his expression dubious. "Nothing. You shouldn't call me anything."

"You know my name." She crossed her arms.

"No, I don't."

"Sure you do," she said, "you're a thief. Attention to detail is your bread and butter."

The man said nothing.

Vashti sighed. "I guess I stand corrected."

"About what?"

"Thinking you were good at this."

Finally, he met her gaze. "Vashti."

She smiled. "I want a name. It doesn't have to be yours."

The thief nabbed a sapphire necklace with a platinum chain, a piece she'd been coveting for months. "Call me Jasper."

They pilfered from opposite ends of the counter, working their way toward the center. Vashti caught Jasper staring as she hooked an entire row of bracelets onto one finger, and then bagged them.

"You're remarkably good at this for someone who's never stolen before," he said.

"Who says I haven't?"

He studied her and smiled.

Vashti liked the way his eyes thinned when he smiled. She bent at the hip, offering a view of her curves as she reached for a gold brooch.

"Maybe you should consider a new line of work," he said.

"From shop girl to cat burglar?"

"At least you'd get to wear the jewels."

A case of earrings found a new home in Vashti's bag.

Jasper didn't bother removing the plastic cylinder from a set of designer watches before shoving them into his duffle bag.

"What do you do with all of this stuff?" she asked.

"I have a fence," he said. "Someone who pays cash for stolen goods. Not around here, though. Only an idiot would sell jewelry close to where he stole it."

They approached the engagement ring showcase. Jasper ran a gloved hand over the glittering assembly and teased one from its slot. Vashti recognized it as the ring she'd selected earlier at his behest.

"May I?" he said.

Vashti shrugged, and Jasper slid the ring onto her finger.

She smiled. "Is this a proposal?"

Jasper's gaze bore into her, as though he were seeking something familiar—perhaps a kindred spirit. Her nipples hardened and judging from the intensity of his stare, she was willing to bet he'd noticed.

"There's more in the back," she whispered.

The claustrophobic storeroom felt even more cramped with Jasper beside her. They ransacked entire shipments of bracelets, emeralds, cufflinks, and canary diamonds.

He raised a yellow gem to the light. "Exquisite."

Vashti's pulse fluttered. It was now or never. She touched his arm.

His brow arched along with his bruise.

Vashti stood on her toes and offered her mouth.

Jasper took the bait, his hand smoothing over her backside.

She hummed at the heat of his lips against hers, thinking of the cable ties in his pocket and the way he'd tossed her around the office.

"Put your hands in my hair," she said.

He weaved his fingers through her locks.

"Now pull," she said.

He tugged, and she moaned.

"That's how you want it?" He forced her head back and kissed her throat.

"Oh, yes."

He pinned her to the metal shelves and slid his tongue into her mouth as he reached for the top button on her blouse.

"Rip it," she growled.

He tore through the buttons, his eyes widening. "So, that's what you stole."

Vashti's heart pounded. She pulled him close.

Jasper pressed his thigh between her legs and pinched her nipples.

The soft leather felt wonderful against Vashti's bare skin as did the way he pawed at her, possessively, like she was something to be coveted.

Jasper thrust a hand beneath her skirt and cupped her mound.

She was already throbbing. She needed more—more skin, more sin, more Jasper. She tugged his jacket off, and he did her one better by removing his shirt.

He kept the gloves on.

Reaching under her skirt again, he drew her panties to her knees.

Vashti gasped as he slid a gloved finger inside her, then glided the moisture over her clitoris. She practically purred with need.

Jasper licked his fingers, tasting her, then dropped to his knees. He fitted his tongue between her folds, then licked and sucked with fervor as if he wanted to get drunk on her.

Vashti pulled his hair and bucked her hips. She humped his face as his tongue rolled over her clitoris. Normally, she had to fight for her orgasms, but this one hit her like a train. Lights flickered behind her eyes as she came, pinned between Jasper's mouth and the shelves at her back.

He kissed her clitoris one last time, making her shiver.

"Come with me, Vashti. I'll make you my assistant. We'll fly to Paris, Berlin, anywhere you want."

Her heart swelled like a balloon. She felt like she could float away. Jasper's world of danger and intrigue was the sort of life she'd always wanted, and here he was, offering it to her with a side of mind-shattering orgasms.

She slid her panties off and pushed him onto his back. Jasper may have had her beat when it came to brute strength, but he was still a man with a needy cock and a sensitive underbelly. She straddled him, unfastened his jeans, and eased them down his legs. His erection jutted toward her, thick and gorgeous.

This man was going to take her places. She was sure of it.

Vashti stroked his cock.

His gaze narrowed as she licked a bead of pre-cum from the tip. "You're a rare gem, Vashti," he said.

"I know." She bunched her skirt around her waist and took him deep inside her.

Jasper's open mouth closed over her piercing, and Vashti stole the opportunity to fish around in his pockets. She scraped her nails down his chest, leaving red streaks. Grasping his jaw, she turned his head to expose his neck to the whims of her mouth. Her inner muscles hugged him on all sides.

Jasper gasped as Vashti ground downward, taking him deeper. She'd never felt so exhilarated, so close to being free. She fucked him hard, then soft, fast, and then slow, until the pressure inside built so high that it burst.

And when it did, she knew what she had to do.

"Tell me, Jasper." Vashti leaned forward, lacing her fingers with his and stretching his arms overhead. "You were planning on claiming all that loot for yourself, weren't you?"

"At first, yeah," he said. "Before I realized what you are."

"And what's that?" She fucked him slowly.

He closed his eyes. "A natural," he said. "Like me."

"Yes." Vashti grinned. "Just like you."

She squeezed his wrists as she bucked and fucked and gave and took. She rode him until his whole body shuddered, clenching her muscles, taking everything he had to give and more than he could know.

Vashti ran her hands over his chest, then rose to her feet, letting his cum drip down her legs. "Thank you, Jasper."

"My pleasure. Now, let's get the hell out of here." He tried to sit up, but his arms caught, secured via cable ties attached to the storage unit. "What the?"

"Yeah, about that trip." Vashti used Jasper's shirt to clean herself off. "I think it would be better if I made this one solo."

Realization dawned across his face. "You cannot be serious."

"I assure you, I am." She knotted the front of her blouse.

Jasper's leg shot out, his heel hooking his jacket.

Vashti snatched it up, withdrawing the switchblade from the front pocket. "Looking for this?" She zipped it, along with her gift bag, inside Jasper's duffle bag.

"But why?" he asked.

Vashti heaved the bag onto her shoulder. "Because I want it all. No offense, Jasper, but after slaving away as Gorski's employee, becoming your assistant hardly sounds like a promotion. I want my freedom, and I can't thank you enough for granting it to me."

"Seems more like you're stealing it from me."

She shrugged. "Semantics."

"Aren't you forgetting something?"

"The cameras? Lucky for us, Gorski's a cheap bastard. They've been down for weeks. Also, that steel shelving unit is bolted into the floor."

Jasper sighed. "Doesn't matter. I'll find a way out of here, and when I do, I'm coming for you."

"You already have, Jasper." She smiled. He looked even more gorgeous with his wrists tied, his pants down, and her claw marks decorating his chest. "Perhaps we'll come together again someday."

With that, Vashti collected her heels from the office, blew Jasper a kiss, and slipped out the door.

END

RACHEL WOE *is a forbidden love junkie who probably watched too many* *inappropriate movies as a teen. A longtime lover of risqué fiction, she used to smuggle* Story of O *and* The Sleeping Beauty *trilogy to school, folded inside brown-bag book covers. On the rare occasion when she's neither reading nor writing, you can find her camped out at the back of the cinema or on the hunt for a perfect Irish eggs Benny.*

135.0
Mono

Tell Me

author: Eddie Monotone
category: Dreams & Mysteries

subjects: 1. Sex Dream   2. Freud
3. Everyone is Staring

Rose Caraway's Library of Erotica

Tell Me

Eddie Monotone

When we both worked at the bookshop during university, we'd take our afternoon breaks together. Now that we have degrees and proper jobs, the habit has stuck, so this Saturday afternoon we meet up for coffee as usual. It's a spring day, warm and sunny, and we manage to find a quiet café near her house. We make conversation, but I find myself doing all the work; she seems distracted and uncomfortable.

Eventually, it's too much for me to ignore. "Okay. Don't take this the wrong way," I say, "but you're staring at me like a weirdo."

"Oh, God. Sorry. Yeah, I'm all…" She trails off and waves her hands in front of her face.

I raise my eyebrows.

"You're going to laugh," she says.

"Possibly. What's up?"

She looks away, plays with the cup in front of her, and chews her lip. "So, I had a dream about you last night," she says.

"Oh yeah?"

She smiles. Her cheeks look hot. "It was kind of, um, you know…"

"What?"

"Well, it was…I'm not sure if I should say…"

"What? Just say it."

"All right. I kind of had a sex dream about you, okay?"

My first reaction is to laugh, but she looks so embarrassed that I stifle it. "Oh?" I say.

"Yeah. It was quite, um, explicit. So, I feel super awkward around you now."

I smile, and she hides her face in her hands.

"I thought telling you would take away the awkwardness, but apparently, I was wrong. Argh. Pretend I never said anything."

"Well, it's too late for that."

"No?"

"I can't just forget the fact that your head is full of inappropriate images of me."

She grins. "Neither can I, apparently."

We drink our coffees in silence for a moment.

"So, was I good?" I ask, eventually.

"Oh my God. You can't ask for details! It was very personal."

"So, pretty good then?"

Her cheeks get redder. "Yes, okay? It was good. You were good."

I grin, and even through her discomfort, she smiles back.

"Well, I'm pleased I could be of help," I say.

"I wish," she mutters.

"Eh?"

"Yeah, well, I may have…carried it on when I woke up," she says, with a little smile.

"Huh?"

"Well, you know, you wake up all hot and bothered, so you…take care of things. You know what I mean."

"I see. Did you think about me then, too?"

She takes a sip of coffee and flicks me a smile over the rim of her cup.

"So, just to be clear," I say, trying to keep my face straight. "Last night, you had a sex dream about me, the details of which you refuse to divulge, and when you woke up this morning, you had a wank thinking about me."

"Jesus, why not tell the world! You're acting like you want it printed on a t-shirt or something."

"Yes. That would be pretty cool, actually."

She laughs. "You say that, but you still don't know what kind of sex we were having."

"And I won't until you tell me."

"It was just…it was just a bit weird, that's all. Not stuff I usually think about."

"I'm intrigued."

"So am I. Freud would be too, I'm sure."

"Okay, you pretty much have to tell me now. Otherwise, I'll just assume the worst."

She gasps in mock outrage. "What's the worst?"

"I dunno," I say. "Cattle prods and teddy bear outfits. Various girls…"

"Well, it wasn't quite like that. No." She pauses for a moment and stares at her coffee. "You can't tell anyone," she says. "And no judging."

"Promise."

"Okay." She takes a breath. "We were in class, only there were heaps of people there, like lots of people we didn't know. And I was…I was naked, and everyone was looking at me. And I was going to leave, but then you were there, and you took your clothes off as well." She smiles but doesn't make eye contact.

"And then you tied me up."

"Huh?"

"And you fucked me on the desk while everyone watched. Bent me over and fucked me from behind in front of a room full of people. Left me tied up on the desk with your cum running down my legs." She pauses, looking down at the table. "And when I woke up, I was soaked and so horny that I finished myself off. I haven't come that hard in ages."

"Wow." I don't know what else to say. I feel myself getting hard.

"I keep thinking about it. It's weird." She fiddles with her empty cup, turning it on the table. "I'm kind of turned on now from telling you, actually." She says it quietly, her voice uneven.

"Yeah?"

"Yeah."

"This is making you wet?"

She takes a deep breath. "Yeah, it really is."

I look around the café. It's practically empty, and the two girls behind the counter have their backs to us as they do something technical to the espresso machine.

"Show me," I say.

"What?" She looks up, surprise in her eyes.

I lean back in my chair and flick my gaze under the table at her bare, crossed legs.

She scrunches her mouth, then shuffles forward in her seat, hikes her skirt up a little, and spreads her legs. The pink triangle of cotton between her thighs has a darker patch in the middle, the moisture soaking through from between her lips.

"I've been like this all day," she says, quietly. Her fingers run lightly over the wet cotton.

I can't stop looking. My cock presses tightly against my jeans. I tear my eyes away to find her looking straight at me. We lock eyes for what seems like a very long time.

"How loud are you when you come?" I ask.

"It depends. I can be quiet."

I smile at her, my heart beating fast in my chest. "Go on then."

"But—"

"Dare you."

She looks at me, wide-eyed. "I can't."

"Don't pretend like the idea doesn't appeal."

"No, it does. It really, really does." She rubs herself a little harder through her underwear. Her cheeks and neck are flushed. "Tell me if anyone's looking," she says.

"Will do." I glance around the café again. Nobody's paying us any attention.

She slips her hand into her knickers, runs her fingers slowly over her pussy, and pushes one finger inside herself. Her back arches, and her breath catches. Her finger slides in and out of her pussy.

"Tell me more about your dream," I say, trying not to let the excitement ruin my voice.

"It's the middle of the morning," she says, quietly. Her eyes are closed. "Sun coming in the windows. My arms are tied up behind my back with rope, and I'm bent over on the desk, my face resting against the wood." Her fingers twitch inside her pussy, the knuckles outlined through the wet cotton. "It's warm in the room, and your skin is cool against mine. Your hand is on the back of my neck, holding me down on the desk. Everyone is staring, nobody's saying anything."

Behind the counter, one of the café girls looks over at us. I freeze, but she turns away again.

"There's no foreplay. You just start fucking me really hard, but I'm so wet you slide straight in. You smell like clean washing. Your cock is warm inside me. Everyone keeps watching." Her voice shakes a little, her chest heaving. She's got both hands between her legs now, one fingering her pussy, the other rubbing her clit. She's soaked. The tops of her thighs glisten, and the chair between her legs is wet.

I want to lean back, see more, but I'm scared my staring and erection will be too obvious.

"You come inside me, and I feel it filling me and spilling out of me. And then, you're gone. You leave me there, still tied up and bent over the desk. Your cum is running out of my pussy, and everyone is still staring at me."

Her hands are frantic, her mouth open, and her eyes screwed shut. Her body jerks. Spasms contort her on the seat. Her legs shake. She bites her lip and cuts off a cry, her voice catching in her throat as she tries to keep herself silent when she comes.

I watch, in awe, as the waves tear through her.

Slowly, her eyes open. She takes her hands out of her underpants and puts them on the table, closing her legs. Her fingers are wet.

I grip the edge of the table to stop my hands from shaking.

She looks at me, her lips trembling, and her eyes wide and bright. Her face looks as hot as mine feels.

"So, coffee again next week? Maybe it can be your turn to play with yourself in a café," she says, with a shaky grin.

"Forget that," I say. "Next week, we're finding some rope and a desk and some people to watch me fuck you. Unless you have a better dream in the meantime."

"I'll be sure to tell you," she says.

END

EDDIE MONOTONE *is a writer, illustrator, cartoonist and parent from New Zealand. While his main efforts at smut are in comic form, he enjoys writing prose as well–because there are some stories that "show, don't tell" just doesn't apply to.*

175.0
Peti

Demon Lover

author: Romey Petite

category: Ethics of Recreation

subjects: 1. Sleeping Wife 2. Night-Thing
3. Nocturnal Emission

Rose Caraway's Library of Erotica

Demon Lover

Romey Petite

Sometimes, I help my wife pretend she has a lover. He comes to visit her only in the dark. He doesn't really have a name; I call him the night-thing.

This is how I do it.

I don a full-bodied, midnight morph-suit, and an adjustable belt with a ring-like holster. A strap-on appendage easily eclipses my genitalia. Cloaked in a veil of tight spandex and other flexible polymers, I creep like a shadow into the master bedroom to peel away the top-sheet and unwrap her from the blankets. I night-crawl along to squat over her slumbering form like a limber, spidery masseuse as she lies there unsuspecting in naked, still quietude on her stomach.

Crouched there, I am a beast prepared to spring; atop a sleeping beauty.

I hear her murmur sweet nothings then—sleep-talking as she floats just beneath the surface of the waking world; remaining briefly suspended in that uncertain place between consciousness and what lies beneath.

I sit down. My wife wakes with a start, seemingly ready for a fight.

She immediately starts to struggle. I can feel her reaching for the switch on the bedside lamp. I catch her by the wrist before she can.

The light must stay off.

One of the rules is that she isn't allowed to look at me. At best, I permit her to catch an occasional peripheral outline of the morph-suit's vague contour. I, on the other hand, can see her shape quite well, having grown accustomed to the dark. I peer down at my wife's pale body beneath me as it laps up the moon's rays, and I watch her through the thin, dark, veil of the night-thing's featureless, vapid void of a face in an otherwise black amorphousness.

I seize my wife's other wrist and—with gravity as an advantage—pin it down to the soft mattress; that's when she really starts to struggle.

Twisting beneath me, she pretends I am a stranger to her, an intruder; rest-assured, that is all part of our ritual. For my part, I hold on tight—like a gargoyle to a cathedral—refusing to be thrown from her back. With her consent, I continue to uphold my part of our prearranged mutual contract—one which could be revoked at any time—if, for example, my wife decided she is no longer in the mood.

I know it's you, hubby, she'd say and just as when Psyche frightened away the shy Cupid by candlelight, that would be that for the night-thing.

Tonight; however, my wife doesn't decide to break our magic spell. Instead, she deviates from the script, temporarily ceasing in her thrashing around just long enough to reach around and gently spread her buttocks. On cue, I slip the heavy appendage into her and squeeze it deep inside her belly. As soon as I do, she slides one hand down beneath her stomach to her delta of Venus where she proceeds to play with herself, coaxing the fleshy swollen folds between her legs.

This is allowed.

Pushing into her negative space, I can feel a suction within her. I thrust practiced and piston-like, with the surrogate priapus attached firmly to my body. Simultaneously, as the night-thing withdraws from her, she struggles, plunging back toward me, gaping around it.

Occupying a position of raw libidinal power and thwarted, tumescent pleasure, I cannot feel her, but I pretend the night-thing can; it fills me with a ticklish, throbbing jealousy.

In minutes, my wife moans loudly, tracing around her sex, throwing her body back against her invisible lover. When she tenses, then exhales at last, the artificial appendage attached to me emerges to glisten in the dim, silvery moonlight, slipping out from between the haunches of her glowing flesh. In frustrating mockery of my own quivering helpless hardness, the grooves and artificial veins of the night-thing's cock are covered with her milky jelly.

This is a nocturnal emission—not mine, of course, but hers; evidence of my wife's wet dream.

Pacified, she forgets me and drifts off to sleep while I continue to remain there—sitting astride her lower back. When her breathing grows rhythmically slow and steady, and I can be truly, completely certain she is asleep once again, I climb down from my wife's back and tip-toe across the floorboards. With utmost care, I turn the doorknob with my insect-like fingers, then I creep away down the hall, closing the bedroom door behind me, to signify the night-thing's departure from this realm.

It's taken a few tries, but now it can all be performed in near-complete silence.

At last, alone, before the master bathroom mirror, I take hold of the zipper at the rounded base of my skull and pull. Emerging from the night-thing's guise I see I'm a sweaty, disheveled mess. Looking down, I feel how hard I still am—the real me—under the spandex. Unclasping the useless artificial appendage's holster, I drop its clumsiness into the sink-bowl.

I can stand it no longer; turning the valve, I step into a hot shower.

That is where I finish myself off. I free my fantasy by washing it down to the intermingled body hair that has gradually collected in a kind of nest around the shower filter. When satisfied, I towel off, proceed back to the sink, and begin to rinse off the night-thing's unwieldy member with soap and water.

I'm careful about germs—even going so far as to wash the manufacturer's crude attempt at sculpting an approximation of testicles.

When I'm done, for a moment, I hang it on the adjacent cart-like shower-caddy to dry. It looks absurdly utilitarian there—especially next to the shampoo bottles, body washes, and my wife's porous pink loofah. It even has a built-in suction cup—perhaps in the event one should take into mind to mount it in a convenient position, location, or height with the intent of repeated use.

The idea would amuse me and perhaps surprise our maid as well but, no, my wife can't even bear to look at it for shame; she only wishes to feel it caressing her depths—in the dark.

There is just one more thing to do.

I bend down and pick up the morph-suit lying in a heap on the tile floor. I toss it into the laundry with ample detergent; washing it, too, with warm water. The night-thing's visits are regular enough that the suit must always be clean.

This is the most important rule:

Before morning, all traces of the night-thing must be scoured, tumble-dried, and returned back to their hiding place in the old shoebox on the closet shelf, or I'll run the risk of ruining the illusion. Once this is done, usually by the wee hours of morning, a faithful husband will cuddle between the sheets to join his wife's warm body as the little spoon. If he knows anything, he does not say a word.

In order for the arrangement to work, it must never be directly spoken of.

At breakfast the following morning, the married couple will discuss the headlines, their separate work schedules to see when they'll overlap, and trivialities involving co-workers and colleagues. Only, now, the pair will talk of all these seemingly perfunctory aforementioned things with a renewed tenderness, vigor, and novelty toward each other wherefore such subjects had otherwise felt rehearsed. Still, in time, there will certainly accumulate feelings left unspoken; things that go unexpressed in our passive, pleasant exchanges.

For that reason, I have no doubt he'll pay another visit to sort us out again soon, her demon lover, the incubus.

END

ROMEY PETITE *wears pinstripes, wire-rimmed spectacles, and suspenders. He loves reading and writing fairy tales, myths, and short stories that blend the sacred and mundane. Because of his habit of daydreaming in shop-windows, he has often mistaken for a mannequin by passersby. Take care and be absolutely certain it is really him, before going up and whispering secrets in his ear.*

355.1
Morg

Hot

author: Chase Morgan
category: Military Life & Customs

subjects: 1. Counter Surveillance
2. Undercover 3. Drunken Confession

Rose Caraway's Library of Erotica

Hot

Chase Morgan

HOT I'd been staring at the three letters on my screen for at least thirty minutes. One simple word texted to Matt, my friend and partner, would force him to enter this room and fuck me. He wouldn't just fuck me, he would fuck me so that anyone watching would believe we'd been involved in a ravenous affair for months.

My text would deprive him of the right to decide. To Matt, the word "HOT" would indicate the Gianelli crime family had wired the hotel room for sound and video and that our lives would depend on a believable performance.

"Heather, did you send it?" Matt's wife and my dear friend, Julie, was on speaker phone as I stared at the unsent text.

"Are you sure we should go through with this, Jules?"

"Sweetie, we've been giggling over this for months. Yes, I'm absolutely positive."

I sighed and wondered for the hundredth time if this was some kind of weird friendship test. "If I press send, your husband is going to come into this room and fuck me. In a dress I borrowed from you no less."

"Not just any dress, it's the fantasy dress," Julie said.

I dropped my head back and looked at the ceiling. I could hear Julie's breathing on the other end of the line. "Maybe we should talk about it over coffee one more time, just to make sure."

"Heather, please."

"I just don't want to mess things up between you guys. I think the world of you both."

"And we love you which is what makes this perfect."

"He's going to feel so guilty, and what if he's not that into me? That's a double whammy for him."

"Okay, hon, now you're reaching."

Julie was right, I was reaching. I knew Matt found me attractive. I caught a few lingering glances throughout the years which wasn't proof in itself, but Julie told me he'd said work was the only thing keeping me from finding a good man. His exact words had been, "She's beautiful, an amazing mother, and very fun to be around. I think she just splits her efforts fifty-fifty between her son and work, and there's nothing left for her in the end."

That conversation left me conflicted. I was happy that a man as good as Matt would say those things about me, but I was sad he'd so accurately captured the truth. I'd brought a few dates home in recent years, but it was just to scratch the itch.

Julie wasn't shy about the fact that Matt was a man of many talents, and there had been an extreme lack of talent between my sheets for far too long. I'd crushed on Matt for years, in the innocent way single women crush on their friends' husbands. It wasn't a creepy sexual crush. It was mostly a "he's one of the good ones" crush. I'd never really considered what it would be like to sleep with him until Julie brought it up. Now, I couldn't get it out of my mind. But I also felt like he would struggle with guilt until he got home, and Julie put the second half of our plan in motion.

I was worried about Julie too. What if Matt went home and didn't tell his wife? I knew Matt had as many things safely tucked away in his brain as I did. Things you don't share outside of work and especially not with your family. What if Matt locked this away too?

Julie assured me that regardless of how much training he'd undergone, and how loyal he was to the Bureau, her husband wouldn't keep this from her.

"Jules—"

"Besides, you started this," she cut me off. "Your tipsy tongue at my birthday party is what put this thing in motion."

I had told her that I thought she and Matt were the sexiest couple I knew. The statement was true, but what compelled me to verbalize it that night, I'll never know.

She hadn't mentioned my drunken confession for almost two months. I'd desperately hoped she'd been equally tipsy and didn't remember or just didn't hear me. But over coffee one morning, she'd finally asked, "What did you mean when you said we were the sexiest couple you know?" Her question hadn't been the catalyst for our current situation, but it was definitely the foundation.

I'd been undercover with the notoriously violent Gianelli family for almost a year, leaking information that aided their money laundering scheme while building our case. My cover was easy enough to believe because the majority of it was correct. I was a government employee who didn't get paid enough. My ex was the epitome of a deadbeat, and I had no idea how I was going to put my son through college next year.

Organized crime had been determined to find a way into the government subsidized, Oliver Corporation, for years. Over the last several months the crime bosses believed I'd started an affair with Matt who was undercover as Paul Fisk, a senior manager working with me at OC but in an area I couldn't access. The information Paul could provide was exactly what they needed and would be instrumental in making the mob family hundreds of millions; it would also make our case solid enough to put the dirty family away for the rest of their lives. This was one of the biggest cases in the FBI's recent past and if we could close it, we would go down in the history books.

Through our counter-surveillance, we knew the Gianellis followed Matt to the hotel for all of our meets, but there was no indication they'd ever tried to wire the room. Matt and I usually spent about an hour hanging out in the room before he mussed up his hair and left with a satisfied look. I was as close to Matt as I was to Heather. We spent an hour alone together in a hotel room twice a week. We talked about our sons, what he was going to buy Heather for their anniversary, all of my failed dates, and the myriad of other things true friends talk about. The intimacy in these hotel sessions was in no way sexual, but I was always left with a sense of guilt. If Matt and I had these exact conversations in a coffee shop, I wouldn't have given them a second thought, but something about the hotel room made it feel seedy. My unease continued to build, and after a few hotel rendezvous, I broke.

Over coffee with Julie one morning I laid out the basics of our ruse. Without divulging any of the operation's specifics, I told her that Matt and I had been meeting in a hotel room, pretending to have an affair.

Julie reached across the table and placed her hand on mine. She looked me in the eye, smiled, and told me about a drunken fantasy she and Matt had discussed.

Before I knew it, we'd formed a plan, and I was sitting on the hotel bed wearing Julie's beautiful black dress and matching heels—the same outfit that had been a part of their fantasy. I touched the fabric of Jule's dress and wondered what her husband's hands would feel like when they roamed my body.

My phone chirped, breaking my reverie. It was a text from Tom. *We're clear.*

I replied with a thumbs-up emoji and buried my head in my hands. Tom and Stan were the other agents on our team. Tom was positioned in the lobby, and Stan was outside watching the streets. We'd been safely using this hotel in our operation for months, but to fulfill Julie's fantasy, and mine too, I was about to make Matt believe the Gianellis had wired the room.

"Jules, I have to go."

"Please, Heather, promise me you'll go through with it. We're ready for this!"

"I will."

"Promise?"

"Yes."

"Thank you. Good luck. And please have fun!" Her excitement was contagious. But I still hadn't pushed send.

I stared at myself in the mirror, then down at the phone. I wanted to fuck Matt, and Julie wanted me to fuck him; my only real concern was that Matt was an unsuspecting player in this plan.

In their fantasy, a friend spilled something on Julie's dress, and in the process of dabbing the stain, a stereotypical threesome occurred. The twist was Julie's hidden desire for Matt to be a little guilty. I'm still a little perplexed by that part.

Above the unsent word was Matt's last text, sent twenty minutes ago. *On my way.* He would be here very soon.

My phone chirped with a text from Stan. *He's pulling in. Usual tail sitting about 5 cars back.*

I sent another thumbs up emoji. Maybe I would just tell Matt what Julie wanted. He could go home, pretend like we'd slept together, fake a little guilt, and she could play out her fantasy none-the-wiser.

My phone chirped again. It was Julie. *Please, fuck my husband.* Her text was straight to the point and the final nudge I needed.

The *Delivered* notification sat accusingly under my text to Matt. I felt pangs of uncertainty mixed with desire as I reconsidered how he might feel about our duplicitous scheme. What if Julie didn't tell him that we'd planned this? Surely she would; I was 99% sure the ultimate goal of our scheme was the ménage they'd fantasized about, but what if he was pissed?

The lock on the door beeped. My mental debate was over.

"I've been thinking about you all day." Matt entered the room, already in character.

"Shut up and kiss me."

Matt closed the distance between us. He wasn't Matt, my best friend's faithful husband anymore. He wasn't Agent Dixon, the partner I'd worked with for years. Now, he was Paul Fisk, the disgruntled government employee and insatiable adulterer, raking his fingers through my hair and taking my head in his hands.

If pressing send had been like a shot of adrenaline, Paul Fisk slipping his tongue past my lips was like getting shocked with a defibrillator. Electricity coursed through my body when I surrendered to my carnal desires and let my tongue meet his.

Transformed into his lover, I grabbed Paul's scruffy jaw with both hands and lost myself in the embrace. The way his tongue snaked to meet mine caused my mind to race back to Julie's comments regarding her husband's other talents.

The muscles in his shoulders flexed beneath my hands as his fingers traced their way down my back. I nuzzled under his jaw while I slid his jacket over his shoulders. I knew he was carrying and would be conscious of the cameras seeing a supposed-government stiff with a gun.

I carefully removed the .380 backup pistol holstered at the small of his back. Feigning awareness of the cameras, I tucked the gun inside his folded jacket as I placed it on the table.

Paul Fisk spun me around at the waist. He kissed me and ran his thumbs over my breasts to the straps of his wife's dress. Julie and I shared clothes often, and there's no doubt he knew the dress was hers. I wondered if he would remember that it was part of their drunken fantasy and if it would tip him off to our plan or just add to his guilt.

Matt didn't seem capable of meeting my eyes. He stared at my shoulders as he hooked his thumbs under the straps of the dress and slid them back and forth playfully.

"Shoes please," I purred.

Matt kissed my shoulders and worked his hands down the dress. He caressed my thighs and trailed his fingers down my torso. He was seductively checking to make sure my backup pistol was not strapped to the inside of my thigh.

I caught our reflection—a momentary image forever burned in my mind. There I stood in the dress they'd fantasized about. It complimented my curves, and the lacy lingerie I wore underneath made me feel sexy beyond words. The role of mistress was exhilarating.

Though it was the alter-ego Paul kneeling at my feet and slowly helping me out of my shoes, I knew Matt was going slow to steady his resolve. I pulled him up for another kiss and searched his eyes for any flicker of recognition the dress might have brought, but he still couldn't hold my gaze.

I dropped to my knees and ran my hands over the front of his pants. His cock was already stressing the zipper. I looked up and began to unzip him. My smile increased with every bump of the descending metal pull. I freed his cock and took it into my mouth, thinking that if I made the first big move, it might help ease his apprehension. The salty pre-cum that touched my tongue betrayed whatever Matt might be feeling inside.

The affair became a reality with every pass my lips made over his thick shaft.

Paul moaned with pleasure as I worked him with my hands and mouth, but Matt kept his eyes closed.

Wanting to be lost in this moment, I reassured myself that he might feel guilty now, but he would be off the hook soon after he got home and Julie fucked his brains out.

Within minutes, his balls began to rise, and he gently pulled on my head.

"Stop, or I'll come."

I stood, trailing my tits up his body.

In the past, when I'd caught Matt's stolen glances, he was almost always looking at my breasts, now he was transfixed. He cupped them and ran his lips over the apex of my exposed cleavage. His stiff cock stood between us like a crooked bridge, but Matt seemed hesitant to expose me.

I slipped my thumbs under the straps of the dress and pulled them away from my shoulders, acknowledging that it was okay.

Matt nuzzled my neck as he took the straps from me and peeled the dress down to my waist. "God, I love your tits." Paul the Philanderer seemed to speak for Matt, the guilty husband. He ran his thumbs over the lace covering my hard nipples.

The seductress in me wanted to tease Matt as long as I could, but the slut in me wanted to find out exactly what Julie had been bragging about. "Eat my pussy, Ma-ahh." I almost called him Matt. I turned the error into a moan as he lay me back on the bed.

Paul undressed. He appeared to be even harder than when his cock had been in my mouth.

I stared at his erection and teased him. "You have to earn the bra with the panties."

Paul's look acknowledged his understanding, and he knelt between my legs. He pushed the dress up to meet the top half at my waist and slid my panties off. The most graphic thing Julie ever told me was that Matt had the most skilled tongue she'd ever experienced. I closed my eyes with her words echoing in my head as her husband's warm tongue bathed my pussy. "Oh, fuck, that feels good!" I moaned.

He explored every inch of my pussy before finally looking up at me with lust in his eyes. *Is that real lust?* Regardless, his skill was unquestionable, and he made me come in record time. My thighs pressed the sides of his head like a vice. "Oh, my, God!"

As my world drifted back into focus, I let my thighs relax, and Paul kissed his way up my body. He took his time with my breasts while my clit recovered.

"I guess you've earned it." I arched my back so he could remove my bra.

There was no faking the look on Matt's face when he saw my bare tits for the first time. Paul licked, sucked, and fondled them with the fervor of a man who loves breasts.

I was ready to fuck but didn't want to deny him this moment; there would only be one first time Matt got to play with my tits. When he moved up to kiss me, his cock passed between my legs, and my pussy ached. I needed to feel him inside me. I rolled Paul onto his back and ran my hands over his shoulders and down between his legs. Holding the base of his cock with one hand, I bunched the dress so he could watch. I hovered over the tip. "Are you ready to fuck this pussy?"

Based on our coffee talks, I assumed Julie and Matt were no strangers to dirty talk, and I hoped it might perpetuate the confidence he was starting to show.

"Please," was all he mustered, but he maintained eye contact.

I lowered myself down. His rigid thickness spread my swollen lips and filled me. I only slid down the full length of him twice before the base of his cock was drenched with my wetness. I stared at him, grinding harder and faster, but he was fixated on my bouncing tits.

"God, your cock feels amazing." I was already racing toward another orgasm.

He took my breasts in his mouth and fondled them, and then watched his shaft being swallowed by my hungry cunt.

"I'm not sure how much longer I'm going to last," Paul growled, finally locking eyes with me in that way lovers do.

I leaned back on one arm to support myself and rubbed my clit with the other hand. Without support, the dress fell forward. I ground harder, forcing him deeper inside me.

Paul lifted the dress, his eyes darting between my sex and my swaying tits.

My nipples grew tighter as I approached another orgasm. "I'm going to come again," I said, looking up at the ceiling. I rubbed my clit furiously.

Paul froze when I squeezed my inner walls, begging for his release. He gasped, and his hot seed fed my pussy.

The second burst from his cock sent me over the edge. My orgasmic slit milked his pulsating shaft and for a moment, we were locked in a breathless tangle of climaxes.

I exhaled and collapsed on his chest. For several minutes, we remained in a sweaty, panting, pile of flesh. Paul's cock lost strength and slipped from me, followed by a river of our mixed passion.

I rolled to his side, so I wasn't crushing him but kept my legs intertwined with his. We kissed lazily, and his hands continued to explore my body. But, as we talked, his eyes drifted away.

"God, I needed that. It was a fucking crazy day in the office." Matt was back in control, playing for the cameras he thought were watching.

Truth be told, the cameras really did exist, but they had been installed by me, not the notorious crime family. I hadn't even told Julie about them. I figured if things went well it would be a fun surprise later. If not, I would have a little something for my late-night musings.

"What are those assholes making you do now?"

I continued the facade, burning to tell Matt he was safe and was going home to an extremely horny wife and that maybe soon all three of us would fuck. But I didn't.

Matt spent a few minutes discussing the work information I would pass onto the Gianellis, but his gaze never left my chest. I'm not sure if he was staring at my sweaty breasts or retreating back into the faithful, guilty husband role.

"I'm going to grab a quick shower," he said.

"Okay, babe." I waited until I heard the water running and texted Julie.

Hot

He'll be headed home soon. I think he feels terrible.
He's going to be okay, trust me.
I feel bad that he feels bad.
No, no, no. It's going to be okay. How was it?

My fingers danced across the keys and erased several responses. The only appropriate answer was *HOT*.

END

CHASE MORGAN *began writing erotica for his wife while away on business trips. As his muse and biggest supporter, she encouraged him to take a stab at sharing his filthy mind with the world.*

384.12
Lond

Call Me

author: Clare London
category: Telecommunications

subjects: 1. Financier Extraordinaire
2. Secret Webcam 3. Onanism

Rose Caraway's Library of Erotica

Call Me

Clare London

"Section 3b." Vic's voice is low and steady on the other end of the line. "The cross-reference is to Appendix II, not I."

"Right. Got it." I strike it out on my copy, laid out on the desk in front of me. A bold, red stroke of the pen. We're only a third of the way through the document, and he's found plenty of errors.

"I probably should have done this face to face with Jon during the meeting, right?" His words are apologetic, and yet his tone is provocative.

"It's okay." My ear is buzzing slightly from holding the phone so close for the last half hour. "He's pretty busy with Board business, and this is what I'm employed for, anyway." That came out rather churlishly, and I bite my lip. I don't begrudge the time at all. It's part of a senior paralegal's responsibility, after all, besides the fact it's given me the opportunity to share more time with Vic.

Vic Chambers, financier extraordinaire, number one client, tall, dark, striking, built like a Greek god, but with sinful, mocking eyes more like the god's wicked, unruly, black-sheep brother.

They talk about him around the office in hushed whispers. Some with amazement, some with spite, and some with plain, naked desire. I've never spent time with him without my boss around.

Until now.

I glance up, but no one passes my cubicle unless they need to see the big man himself. Being at that end of the corridor has both disadvantages and advantages. "I meant, it's my job."

Vic laughs gently. "And you get all the tough ones, right? Looks like you have plenty to do, from what I see."

"Me?" I'd spent the whole meeting passing documents to and from my boss, shuffling papers and trying not to catch Vic's eye. That way, I could keep some semblance of concentration.

"You think I didn't notice you?"

There's a sudden, warning edge to his tone, and I feel inexplicably hot. "If you'd like to move on to Section 4, there are several issues around the quarterly audit headroom requirements."

"I'd like to move on, but not to Section 4." His voice has dropped to a murmur. "I saw you looking at me."

"I'm sorry?" I squirm in my seat.

"I saw you, your hot dark eyes, the flicker of your lashes, the lick of your lips every time you drank your water, running your fingers along the edge of the table. That red nail polish, so sharp and bright against the cool, pale, wood. Feeling it. Caressing it. Glancing at me when you thought no one was looking."

"No." I daren't look at my shaking hands.

"The pulse at your throat quickening. Your blouse tightening across your breasts as if the nipples swelled beneath."

Dear God.

"You were squirming. I bet you're doing that right now."

I can barely speak. My throat is tight, and my skin tingles. Paralegals are either so predictable, or he has a webcam in here.

"I bet you're hot, too," he murmurs. "You looked hot in the meeting."

"The air-conditioner's misbehaving."

"You were misbehaving," he says. I can hear the laughter bubbling under his words, honey-rich, lapping them. "Weren't you?"

"If you have some kind of complaint, you should let Jon know."

"No way." He laughs aloud, but it's still a murmur.

Goosebumps spring up and down my spine. The heat pools between my legs, high up my thighs, deep into my lap.

"No complaint. Far from it, in fact. I like you hot. I like it a lot. You had me squirming, too. Did you realize that?"

"No." This is more like a whisper.

"I didn't hear that."

"No, I didn't know."

"Good. I like to surprise." There's the rustle of paper from his end of the line. "Don't be afraid to speak frankly to me. I insist on it. I want to hear what you think about things. What you feel."

"Me?" I'm repeating myself, but my tongue feels thick in my mouth, and my thoughts are even thicker. "Jon doesn't like—"

"I don't want to fuck Jon," Vic says, shockingly matter-of-fact. "He wasn't the one making me squirm. Making my mouth dry, my belly tighten. Making my cock swell in my pants. Making my hands itch to touch it. To rub, to grasp it. To imagine it's somewhere more caressing than my palm, feeling far hotter and sweeter than my fingers can make it, coaxing it deeper than a mere fist can do."

Fuck. I look around again, but the corridor is still quiet. "Maybe we can meet. Outside of work." Am I stuttering?

"Of course." He laughs. "That'll happen. But I can't wait for that now."

"You can't?"

"I've been listening to your voice all this time, talking about sub-sections and tabs and strike-throughs. You have a sexy voice, you know? All the times you say, 'Got it, that's it.' The sound of your pen tapping on your teeth. Well, I'm ready. Go ahead. I'm hard already."

"I...I didn't..."

"You're wet too, aren't you?"

I nearly drop the phone. Where the fuck is that secret webcam?

"You're aching. Your pussy clenches as if my cock were already there, inching thickly inside you. Your clit is swollen, your throat aches to moan. Are you thinking of me, right now? Are you thinking of what you want me to do?"

Oh God, yes.

He continues as if he doesn't really expect an answer. "You're wet, thinking of me. Wishing I was there and not here, on the other end of a line. Sitting opposite you again but not with the rest of the legal team. Just me, looking at you. And you, looking back with those bedroom eyes you have. Maybe not bedroom. Maybe just fuck-me eyes, right over the Board table. Now eyes. Hard, fast, deep eyes. Quick eyes."

The noise that comes from me is a whimper. I think Vic likes the sound of it.

"Touch yourself. Drop those panties—they're white, aren't they? There will be lace involved—and touch your clit. Rub gently, then harder. Press a fingertip into your pussy and imagine me there."

Dizziness hits me. "Of course, I can't—"

"Do it." His tone is sharp. "My cock is out already. My pants are open, I've pushed them down my thighs. My dick is so thick it's painful, it's curving out from my balls. I'm holding it in my fist. It's hot and heavy. Fills my palm. I've got to relieve it, you see, so I'm moving my hand up and down. Pumping. Slick skin against skin. Can you hear it? I keep lube in my desk, did you know?"

Of course, I fucking didn't. Under my own desk, I lift the hem of my skirt and slide down my panties. He's right of course—they are white. My skin is so sensitive, the lace scrapes it, sending tiny vibrations back up to my crotch. My fingertip hovers over the ache at my pussy, the bud that craves touch.

"Say something."

I swallow, hard. "What should I say?" I press on my clit, afraid to caress, afraid even to touch with any gentleness. The heat trickles out from my core, tendrils of it bathing me in damp need. My ass clenches, my thighs grip to the seat cushion. I start to circle the nub. I creep a finger backward to my entrance, a slim finger that's determined, yet nothing like his cock. I know that without any hard evidence.

Hard. Unintentional pun. My desperation speaks for me. I thrust quickly, sharply, fucking myself with a terrible mixture of relief, agony, and fear of discovery.

"Not good enough," Vic murmurs.

His voice is a stroke to my nerves, yet I snap back. "Not keeping lube in my office drawer? It's not on the stationery re-order sheet." I lick swiftly, messily, around my fingers, wetting the valleys between them, then thrust two back into me. "I can manage without."

"No," he chides me, then chuckles. "I mean, your conversation isn't good enough. You must tell me more. How do I make you feel?"

What the hell does he think? "Good." I gasp. The wet, slick channel around my fingers is sticky with saliva. A coil of suspense sits in my crotch. It's all a hit, straight to my groin. My hips stutter up from the chair.

He makes a tutting noise of complaint. "Tell me. Every word you say makes me harder. Every gasp makes my cock jump in my hand. I'm sliding down in my chair, spreading my legs. My balls are tight, so hard. I want you to make me come. In fact, I want you…to fuck me."

I'm puzzled. "How can I…?"

"You're in charge." He's panting, his voice ragged. "My cock is plunging in, pushing into you, swelling inside. But you're calling the shots. You want me to follow orders. You're fucking me, you hear?"

The rumors about him had never even hinted at this.

"Oh, God." I can't hold back the moan. My nerves shiver from my cunt to my scalp. I'm splayed on the chair, open to view, yet praying he's the only one to see.

He whispers something I don't catch, and I laugh shakily. I wonder what size his cock is. If he's cut or uncut. I imagine I can hear the slick, sucking noises as his hand moves, sliding the sheath back, exposing his slit, the purple-red head. Jerking off.

"You." I can't make coherent sentences. *Who could?* "At that meeting." *Purple-red head.* A bead of pre-cum, imagined, craved. "So fucking hot. Smart, clean suit. Dirty fucking eyes. Playing with me. Can't." My legs hurt, the muscles tensing. "Need." I push my panties right off my ankle, tug my skirt up to my waist. I'm pumping myself too hard, he's right about needing the lube. *Too desperate.* I start panting. I'm gripping the phone between my ear and my shoulder, the edge of it hurting my neck.

Vic's voice slips in and out of volume. He's groaning.

"So hot." There are tears in my eyes. The edge of my seat is digging into the back of my legs. My shoes are lost somewhere under my desk. Sweat trickles down between my thighs. "I want to fuck you. I want to make you come. I want to make you sob with it. Do you hear me?"

"I hear you. You're clear. Don't stop. Don't fucking stop. I'm..." His voice trails off in a growl. I think that may even be the sob I'm looking for.

I laugh, my own cry not far away. It's clenching in my belly, the pain, the ecstasy, the raw desire. My whole groin feels swollen, my lips, my clit, the flesh between my legs. My fingers flick in and out of me, spreading the dampness. Skin is hot, slippery. Even my asshole flexes in anticipation of climax. "I'll do what I fucking well please." I can barely grunt the obscene words. "You hear that?"

He gasps loudly. "Yes. I. Please."

"I'm fucking you. You thrust when I say. You grip where I want it. You wait for me. For my call." I slow my strokes, just for a moment, biting back the need to speed over the cliff. "You come when I say and not before."

Vic gives a strangled moan. "I want..."

"Yeah." *So do we all.* I can imagine him now, the designer suit pants creased with sweat, the silk necktie loose, his other palm flat on the desk, holding himself in check. Handsome, unruly, black-sheep man. Throat tight, eyes rolling.

Waiting for my order.

I grin. It's more of a grimace. To hell with any secret webcam, I don't care what I look like. I'm in Vic's mind. He's in my head. I see his eyes, hear his frustration keening, feel his dick throbbing as it thrusts in and out of his hand, in and out of me. I can't stop myself.

"Now!" I groan and squeeze my clit. The flesh shudders and throbs. My back arches. Juice bathes my fingers. Mind swimming, I grab the edge of the desk. My papers slide everywhere.

His voice is too loud. I'm assuming his PA is at lunch, but that's his problem. He's shouting, cursing. It's a stream of nonsense, it's hoarse. It's hot. It's for me.

"Tonight," he's gasping. "You and me. Yes?"

I smile as the lassitude creeps over me, heartbeat slowing, blood easing, muscles relaxing. Sticky thighs. Warm crotch. Satisfied for now.

"Did you hear me? Yes?"

I don't answer.

I let the phone drop back onto its base.

END

CLARE LONDON *took her pen name from the city she loves, and where she juggles writing with her other day job as an accountant. She's written in many genres and across many settings, with award-winning novels and short stories published both online and in print. Her work features romance and drama with a healthy serving of physical passion, as she enjoys both reading and writing about strong, sympathetic, and sexy characters.*

418.0
Blis

Batteries Not Included

author: Silas Bliss
category: Applied Linguistics

subjects: 1. Anniversary 2. Instructions
3. Fellatio

Rose Caraway's Library of Erotica

Batteries Not Included

Silas Bliss

Pulling into his parking slot, Ryan saw an envelope secured to the aluminum rectangle with his engraved apartment number by a pink ribbon. That would be Sarah. She had been doing that lately, leaving little gifts or notes where he would find them.

He had texted when he left the office, telling her that he was on his way. Pulling his phone out, still on silent from a meeting, he saw the banner showed a message from her. "Watching porn."

Confused, he looked back at his previous message. He had asked her what she was doing. *What the fuck*? He wondered if someone else had her phone or if maybe a friend had dropped by to see her and was messing with him. "Sarah?", he typed.

The response came immediately. "Took U long enough. Would have thought U would be more intrigued by my message."

Ryan's fingers skimmed the keyboard. "Phone was on silent from a meeting. Just saw your reply."

Dots danced to let him know she was typing. "Text me when you park."

Ryan shot back, "I'm here now."

More dancing dots. "Did you open it?"

Ryan looked at the envelope. He typed "No", and Sarah asked him if he knew what day it was. Ryan sent back the date, and she replied with a smiley face along with a request that he follow the instructions. Ryan sent a question mark. After a moment of radio silence, he opened the envelope. Inside, a simple piece of stationary wished him a happy anniversary and instructed him to see the attendant at the apartment's front desk.

Walking in, he thought about it. It had been about three and a half months since the night they'd met. He had noticed the slim blonde when he'd entered the diner. He'd assumed she was an actress because she was wearing a dress that would not have been out of place on the set of a Laura Ingalls Wilder movie. The strange clothing, lack of makeup, and antiquated braids did little to mask a stunningly attractive woman. Because L.A. is a town full of impossibly beautiful women, he'd thought he had her pegged until he heard her ask the server for the cheapest meal on the menu.

It had taken him a few minutes to get her name, Sarah, and convince her to allow him to sit with her. He told her his story—moving to California as a boy with his mother, seeing her struggle to become an actress, what it had cost her. Sarah must have sensed his sincerity because she opened up to him.

Ryan had assumed he would be offering some career advice to a starstruck young girl from the deepest crevice of some flyover state, but the truth was darker. Sarah had run away from a fundamentalist cult in Kentucky and the husband to whom she had been given as a teenager. After years of abuse and fear, she'd come to Los Angeles. She was looking for her cousin, the only other person she'd known to have left the group. She had been unable to find her and was close to being out of the money she had taken to finance her escape.

They'd sat and talked until the diner closed. At 1:00 a.m., the owner had shooed them out, so he could lock up and go home. Ryan told Sarah he was taking care of a neighbor's cat and houseplants while they were away for an extended shoot overseas. He assured her that the neighbor was a close friend who would be thrilled to have her spend a few days in the apartment if she promised to pet and play with the cat. Ryan said that the poor thing was starved for attention by the time he got to it every evening. Sarah resisted but finally accepted the offer. Close to sleeping on the street, she told him she saw few other choices.

Over the next few weeks, Ryan fell deeply in love with Sarah. She had grown up without television and had never been to a theater. They spent hours watching everything from *Star Wars* to the Marvel movies. She loved all forms of fantastic fiction, and Ryan got to watch movies so familiar to him that he'd memorized every line of dialog through fresh eyes.

Sarah was smart but undereducated, having been removed from school after the 10th grade. Ryan got her a part-time job doing odd tasks at the talent agency where he worked. She had quickly become everyone's first choice if they needed something important done the first time perfectly. She had taken and passed the G.E.D. and was beginning to talk about college. In less than four months, he had watched her change from a frightened woman-child into a vibrant, curious adult.

On an evening two months ago to the day, she had entered his apartment and gotten into his bed. That was the anniversary to which she had referred. Tomorrow would be the anniversary of the day he had asked her to marry him.

At the front desk, he was given a small package wrapped in the pink ribbon that had become Sarah's signature. He opened it in the elevator. It held a pink, satin choker. A small box built from a child's building block set had been attached to it. Beneath the odd contraption, a printed piece of paper proclaimed "Congratulations! You are now the proud owner of the new Love-Bot 3000. When this control unit is attached, your new high-tech companion will become operational. The initial mode is fellatio. Please complete this activity to open further options." Below that, bold copy read "Batteries Not Included".

"What the fuck?" This time, he said it out loud.

There was a note on the floor just inside the apartment door. "Ryan, I can't ever thank you enough for what you have done for me and given to me. No words could even come close to expressing my love for you. I should not ask you for anything more than you have already done, but I will. Give me this one more thing and play along. I know you have been patient with me sexually. I have had to get past a lot of things. I know how much you love oral sex, and I know I'm not good at it. The truth is that I'm just never sure what to do. I've been watching videos and reading things on the web. I think I must know more now than almost anyone about blow jobs, but I'm still not sure what you like or what you want exactly. It's hard for me to ask, and I know you would never tell me even if I were doing a terrible job. So, please, just play along."

Ryan walked into the living room and found Sarah standing naked, rigid like a doll in a package. Another pink ribbon hung around her neck. A second printed card read "Please attach the control unit. Precise instructions are required for optimal results. Please tell the Love-Bot 3000 exactly what you want her to do to you."

Ryan tried to talk to Sarah, to tell her she didn't need to do this. He told her he loved her and that he could wait as long as she needed until she was comfortable.

She didn't respond.

After a few more attempts, he sighed and buckled the choker around her neck.

Sarah fluttered her eyes and moved her neck and arms in a funny, robotic way. Ryan laughed, he could see Sarah struggling not to laugh herself. She bit her lower lip, took on an exaggeratedly stiff posture. For the first time, it hit him that his insecure fiancée, who disliked making love above the covers, or even with the lights on, was standing before him completely naked.

Ryan walked around her, examining her beauty in a way he'd never been able to do before. He ran a hand down her shimmering blond hair to where it ended at the small of her back. He stood behind her and grasped her firm ass cheek while sliding his other hand up and down her tight waist and flat stomach. Moving up to her breasts, he found hard nipples. Growing hard himself, he grabbed a breast in each hand as he pressed himself against the immaculate curve of her bare ass and kissed her neck.

"Okay," he said, "Let's do this."

Sarah turned to face him. Unclipping the card from her neck, she handed it to him.

Ryan wasn't sure what to do, then he remembered the instructions and said, "Initiate fellatio?"

Sarah sank to her knees. She unfastened his pants and took him into her mouth.

It felt so good he did not realize at first that she wasn't moving. He looked down at her and at the card in his hand, seeing the line about exact instructions and said, "Um, move your head back and forth."

Sarah moved her head in a smooth, robotic motion.

Ryan laughed, and so did she. "Stop," Ryan whispered. He took her hand, helped her to her feet and led her to the couch. He sat down and guided her to her knees between his legs. "Okay," he said. "This is weird." Her gaze dropped, and Ryan quickly added, "But hot. I mean, it's really hot! I just need to get my head around it. So, okay. Um, kiss it."

Sarah's lips parted, and she pressed them against the head of his penis.

Ryan let out a quiet moan. "All over. Kiss it all over."

She moved back and forth, kissing every inch of the shaft and head. She nibbled the tender area under the head.

He gasped. "There, right there." Ryan lifted her silk curtain of golden hair and moved it to afford himself the best view. "Kiss it hard," he said. "And give me your hand."

She lifted a hand to him. He pressed it around the top of his cock. "Kiss it, harder."

She squeezed him between her mouth and hand.

"Yes, like that," he moaned. "Harder."

Her lips parted, and the smooth surface of her teeth slid and ground into his flesh. The sensation of soft lips framing the hard pressure points of her teeth drove him insane. "Bite it," he said. It was a request, almost a plea.

She hesitated.

"Bite," he said. This time, it was a command.

She took him fully between her teeth, slowly increasing the pressure until she sensed his threshold. Sarah held him with the bite, alternating between relaxing her jaw, then increasing the tension to take him over the line. She worked her way around the head of his cock, up and down the shaft.

The action elicited gasps and cries of pain and delight from Ryan. "Oh yes. Just like that."

Sarah made a slurping noise.

"Wait." Ryan's voice was husky, barely a whisper. "Don't swallow it, hold it in your mouth."

Sarah did as he requested, and Ryan positioned her head, so her mouth was just above the head of his cock. Her eyes were closed. As he stared at her, the intensity of the love and desire he felt made him want to weep with joy.

"Now," he said. "Open your mouth. Let your spit run down me. Let me see it."

Sarah seemed to hesitate, opening her mouth a tiny bit. A little of the liquid ran down her chin onto him.

"All of it. Open wide and cover me."

Saliva coated her chin and ran over the head of Ryan's penis. He stared in fascination as the shimmering strands connected his cock to her tongue.

"Play with it," he instructed.

Sarah didn't move.

Sensing she was unsure, Ryan said, "Give me both your hands." She did, and Ryan placed his hand over hers and moved the tips of their fingers up and down his shaft and head. He drew saliva between her lips and his body, creating temporary connections. "It unites us," he said. "Makes us one."

She moved her lips around the head. Her tongue worked the glistening strands as she held her mouth open wide, allowing every drop to fall. Sarah's hands, now shining with moisture, worked him, creating an overwhelming symphony of ecstasy as she played Ryan like a musical instrument, her eyes closed.

Seeing the look of rapture on her face, Ryan fought the beginning tugs of pleasure that would signal the onslaught of orgasm. "Wait," he said. "Open your eyes, Sarah."

She stared at the muscles of his stomach.

"Look at me," he said. "What this is really about is the connection. I mean, I'm so turned on right now it's all I can do not to come, but it isn't just about that. It's about you too, wanting to do this for me. I want to look into your eyes. I want you to see me and know how you are making me feel."

Ryan could see that it was difficult for Sarah at first. She seemed embarrassed by the intensity of the moment. Finally, she lifted her gaze to meet his, holding it for a few seconds before looking away.

He saw her struggle. "Look at me. If this isn't about us and what we have, then it is just sex. We make it special, make it mean something when we share it. Look at me."

"I'm not doing this just for you. I thought so in the beginning, but this is for me too. Every bit of it," Sarah said, tension seeming to leave her. "I love this, not only the activity but the idea of it."

She took him deep into her throat. Her gaze didn't waver as she pumped and sucked. She kissed her way down to his balls where she took one, and then the other into her mouth. She nibbled his inner thighs and worked her tongue back up to the sensitive part on the head of his cock.

Ryan no longer gave her instructions. She didn't seem to need them now.

This was all he had ever wanted, for her to relax and enjoy herself. No one activity and no specific action mattered. He only cared that her old bonds and restrictions were stripped away so that she could be exactly what she wanted to be.

He put a hand on the side of her head, and she leaned into it without stopping the task at hand…and mouth. Sarah brought her hand to his and squeezed as she stared, without blinking, into his eyes.

Ryan swam in pleasure until he was shocked back to awareness by the realization that he was about to come. The very idea of oral sex had frightened Sarah at first. She had been raised to believe it was a disgusting perversion, forbidden, even after marriage. When they'd initially talked about it, she had expressed doubts that she would ever be able to do it. Ryan had accepted that and moved on. Two weeks ago, she had attempted it, but she'd warned him that she would never be able to stand cum in her mouth. She just couldn't imagine it, she'd told him. He had accepted this and was grateful when she used her mouth to arouse him before finishing him with her hand or intercourse.

Unable to delay release much longer, he began gently pressing back against her forehead.

She pushed forward harder.

He put both hands on her head and tried to push her back, but she shook her head. Both of Sarah's hands were now firmly wrapped around Ryan's wrists, pulling his hands away, forcing them up to his chest where she pinned them as her gaze left no doubt in his mind that she no longer accepted his commands. The Love-Bot 3000 had become a fully autonomous being.

"Stop Sarah." He gasped. "I'm going to come!"

She released his wrists, wrapped her arms around his waist, and sucked so ferociously that his orgasm originated from a combination of pleasure and pain so intense that it made him cry out. His legs and stomach shook as he began to feel the rolling explosion of warmth through his body. His cock pumped against her tongue, and he cried out as his entire awareness became a system of delights orbiting the gravitational pull of Sarah's mouth.

When Ryan's shaking subsided, Sarah slowly released him. She pressed her tongue tightly against the underside of his dick. "Do you know what that spot is called?" she asked.

Ryan shook his head as another shiver of ecstasy worked its way along his spine.

"That is your frenulum," she said. "It is very sensitive." Sarah nibbled her way down his cock, then pressed her tongue against the base before sliding it back up. "This extends your climax and squeezes out the last drops."

Ryan made a quiet sound of pleasure before collapsing completely. Sarah followed him down, pulling him back into her mouth to gently probe and roll his softening cock with her tongue. He lay there jerking and shaking with tiny post-orgasmic jolts of pleasure, unlike anything he had ever experienced.

When full awareness returned to Ryan, Sarah lay with her head on his stomach. His dick, now completely lifeless and soft, was still in her mouth.

He pulled her up and kissed her, gently at first, and then deeper, tasting himself on her tongue.

"I love you," he said.

"I know, or I wouldn't have done that."

"Why did you?" He stroked her hair again.

"I just told you," she said.

"No. I mean, why did you take it all? Why did you swallow? You didn't have to do that."

"Because I want to be everything to you. If you want something, I want to give it to you."

Ryan kissed her again, touched her choker, and then the little box attached to it. "Did you make this?"

Sarah nodded.

"It didn't work, you know."

"Oh, I think it did." Sarah twirled his soft dick with a finger.

"No," Ryan said. "I mean, the card said you would follow my instructions. I tried to push you away and told you to stop, but you didn't."

Sarah unclipped the choker, and then slid the little box off the ribbon. She held it up and opened it, showing that it was empty. "The instructions clearly stated that batteries were not included." She dropped the choker onto the floor, then crawled on top of Ryan. She kissed him on the nose. "In order for it to work, you have to put batteries in."

Ryan laughed, and Sarah pressed a finger to his lips. She reached for his cock with one hand and turned his head to the side with the other. In his ear, she whispered, "Now that you've broken it in, can you imagine the things the Love-Bot 3000 might do *with* batteries?"

END

SILAS BLISS *lives in the buckle of the bible belt with his wife of over 20 years, Xo. They are active in their deeply religious community while secretly practicing consensual non-monogamy. They use their adventures in the swinging lifestyle to fuel the creation of stories and art to make your naughty bits tingle. He has other things in his life but Xo is all that matters, nothing else need be mentioned.*

790.7
Drj

Erotic Moves

author: **Dr. J.**

category: **Performing Arts**

subjects: 1. Devoted Couple 2. Kinky
3. Seductive Show

Rose Caraway's Library of Erotica

Erotic Moves

Dr. J.

"We don't do this enough."

I pushed the handcuffs under the pillow and slipped my leg between Jessup's, rubbing up and down, careful not to get wound up in the sheets.

"What do you mean?"

He pulled me closer, and I nestled in tighter by his side with my knee against his balls. As his chest rose and fell with his breathing, I played with his chest hair, nuzzling my nose and enjoying the tickle. I basked in the afterglow of our sex as I inhaled the aroma of our intermingled scents.

"Things get so busy with life. We get complacent. I want more time like this. Intimate. Connected. Kinky."

He chuckled. "You are so predictable."

"What?"

"You always revisit this idea when our anniversary rolls around." He pinched my nipple and kissed my nose.

"Don't mock me. Our time together is precious." I touched his face and turned it so he could see me. "I know what I want for my anniversary present."

He pulled back and furrowed his brow. "This is new. You always expect me to surprise you."

I took his hand and kissed the center of his palm. "Are you okay with me asking?"

"I don't know. Depends on what you have in mind."

This is your moment. There is no going back if you say it, Paula. Decide. "I'd like you to give me the gift of time."

He stared at me for a few seconds, and my stomach butterflies took flight. *I've let him down before. Would he go for it?*

"Is this time of your choosing?"

"It is, Jess. Could a gift be more personal than time together?"

He continued staring. I could see his wheels turning, wondering if he would experience disappointment again. Would he take another chance and give me control, free rein to create?

"Jess, it's hard to shop for a man like you, who has everything he wants. When you see something you like, you buy it. I want to surprise you. If you give me the gift of time, I promise a genuine present." Did I sound like I was begging? It did to me.

Jessup rolled and covered me with his hard body. If the erection pressing into my hipbone was a sign, he liked my idea. Maybe, he still had hope.

"Why now, Paula?"

My hands roamed the taut muscles of his arms. I pressed a kiss to his heart, allowing my tongue to absorb the salt on his skin.

"Life's too short. Our culture has been ugly lately with hate and violence. I want to focus on pleasure. I want to take a real risk. And I want it to be with you. For us."

"You have been doing your annual relationship assessment." He rocked his pelvis against mine. "Sweetpea, I'd like to have more connected time with you, too. I have untapped fantasies."

"I know, Jess." My heart rate soared, and the pulse between my legs confirmed I was on track. *Lead. You can do this.* "For now, can you give me this gift?"

"I don't know what you're planning, but I'll go along with it for now. I will gift you my time."

After I spread my legs, Jessup's cock surged into my wetness and brought us home again.

What Jessup didn't know was that my plan was already in action. It had happened so innocently. I had met Aurora for drinks and said, "Do you know how difficult it is to shop for that man?" I gulped my wine. "If he sees something he wants, it's his. How am I supposed to find the perfect anniversary present?"

Aurora had handed me a magazine and pointed to the ad. A workshop. *Under Wraps: Learn Erotic Moves on the Pole.* I contacted them that night and met Michelle, the owner of the studio who would conduct the workshop.

First, I would learn how to dance with a chair, before moving onto the pole. Grounding myself back into my body; that's where I wanted to be. Aging is hard in the physical sense. Your mind knows what it wants, and you hope your body can follow. Learning seductive dance movements, like figure-eights with my hips, body ripples, waves, rolls, bends, and flecks set my body's stage. These moves gave me a tool to get back in touch with myself. Although not as graceful or beautiful as I was in my youth, it was the right path. It was hard work, and by week two, I wanted to give up, but I didn't.

As I danced, I paid attention to clothes that teased my skin, and when it got to be more than I could handle, I ripped them off, piece by piece. It was as if my body had used them up as it came into its own. As I trained, I imagined men watching me as I danced for Jessup. Their want for me would make him burn. I would fuck him in front of them. It was one fantasy he wanted and one I intended to fill.

Two weeks after our discussion, and with months of practice accrued, one of the studio's classes scheduled a performance, and I wanted to take Jessup to see it. I told him one of my friends invited me. I wanted to see how he'd respond, what he liked, and if he squirmed in his chair. He said he'd meet me there, and his tardiness worried me. But he arrived minutes before the start, slipping into the back row.

There were ten performers, and each had selected their favorite style of music. All the dancers' lucky recipients sat in the front row for close viewing. Jessup nodded a lot, keeping time to the music. One of his favorite songs came on, and I stretched my leg over his lap. I had worn a short dress and no panties.

He repositioned himself in the chair, placed his hand on my thigh, and nudged my shoulder. "Do you have plans for the evening, sweetpea?"

I opened my legs. "Maybe a little finger fucking," I whispered back.

A wave of heat rolled off him. "You don't say."

I nodded my head and bit my lip.

I didn't know if it was the music or the thought of my anniversary plan, but I was brimming with lust. Jessup could have thrown me on the floor in front of the audience and done naughty things, and I would have loved it.

My ass was hanging off the chair as his finger began its sultry route of pleasure up and down the seam of my vulva. The music grooved on. The patrons whooped and hollered for the dancers, and I imagined them doing that for me, for us, when it was my time on stage. I held my abdominal muscles tight while I swiveled my hips and added a pelvic push. Jessup's hand met me with every beat.

At the crescendo of the song and dance, Jessup thrust two fingers inside the hot, wet mess between my legs. The cheering crowd covered the chair ruckus caused by my gyrations. As the song ended, the patrons jumped to their feet. That's when Jessup added his thumb to the dancing on my clit. He wrapped his arm around my shoulder and kissed me, a searing maneuver that caused my orgasm to burst through. I shook so violently, I broke the kiss and shouted something incoherent. A guy in front of us turned to look just as Jessup licked his fingers. I felt gooey inside, entirely spent.

Jessup leaned and kissed my ear. "I liked this, sweetpea."

I did, too.

But this was in the back and out of sight. How would it feel to be center stage and have Jessup in a chair as the true recipient while men watched me move for him? Could I dance on stage?

A month later, with my courage bolstered and my training complete, it was time to deliver Jessup's anniversary present. I told him we would visit another performance. He had no clue that tonight would be our debut.

"Wear a skirt again."

"You've been thinking about this, huh?"

"I remember how hot it was."

I had this planned. We would sit in the last row and before my number, I'd tell Jessup I needed to use the restroom as my ruse to get prepared for the routine. Several of us would do a number together, and I would perform the finale solo.

When we arrived at the studio, I held my breath. I had footed the bill for room decorations. I purchased light filters, a shimmery, crystal beaded curtain for the back wall, and a disco ball. The other women knew this was for our anniversary, and I loved how they wanted to partake and make suggestions for my event. Together with our combined ideas, we had created the ambiance of a strip joint with a backdrop that would highlight each performer.

My jitters burst on the scene the moment Jessup and I walked in.

"Let me pick the seats," said Jessup.

"You sure?"

"I told you, I've been thinking about it."

I cocked my head and scrutinized him. "What does that mean?"

"I guess you'll find out." He selected our spot.

"Okay. Be right back. Going to the restroom."

"I'll be sitting here contemplating my fate." He appeared to be ready for anything.

I smiled to myself. Well, maybe not everything.

The music started, and all the dancers were on stage, including the studio owner who held the microphone.

"We have a special event planned tonight. We want to make sure that everyone who wishes to can take part."

At that moment, I walked across the room in between the stage and the front row, like we had rehearsed.

"Excuse me, ma'am. Would you like to join us tonight?"

"Me?"

When I looked back at Jessup and saw excitement etched on his face, I turned and winked at Michelle.

"I'd love too. But only if my partner can sit up front. I wouldn't want him to miss the show."

Michelle nodded and clapped, and I motioned to Jessup to meet me. I pointed to the empty chair at the end of the front row, by my designated stage location.

I saw mischief in his eyes as he spoke. "What are you doing, Paula?"

"Being adventuresome."

He squeezed my hand. "You don't have to do this."

"I know. I need to do this."

"Sweetpea, you don't have to prove anything."

"Maybe, I want to prove something to myself, Jess."

He shrugged. "Okay, pea. I'm here for you."

"That's my hope."

I walked up the steps where Michelle had placed a chair in front of my empty pole.

We had choreographed each song to highlight a dancer.

"She looks like a size seven," Michelle announced to the audience.

"I am."

Michelle handed me my come-fuck-me shoes, and I sat on the chair to put them on. I watched Jessup. He remained clueless. I was sizzling.

"Since we have a new dancer, I'd like to tell her… oh, what's your name?"

"Paula."

"Paula. Stand behind the chair and use both the chair and pole. When the music speaks to you, move, however you want. You can watch the other dancers. Okay?"

"Okay."

I stood up behind my chair and took a deep breath. Now was my moment. Me in charge. Let the seductive show begin.

In succession, each dancer made an individual opening move. I was last.

My heart raced and, on my cue, I put my lefty on the pole and strutted around it, switching hands as I walked. When I touched the cool metal, my inner, naughty self showed up to play. And play she did.

I swayed my hips and alternated bringing one foot to the other, clicking my shoes together as I moved to face the empty chair. Walking my hands down the vertical length, I bent over shaking my ass right and left to the beat of my tapping feet. The crowd roared. I imagined Jessup's mouth hanging open as I dipped my knees in, pivoting on my shoes while sashaying my butt. I pretended he sat in my chair, knowing my ass faced the world. Making him hungry.

When I faced the audience again and gazed at Jessup, I got my gift. He pushed on his crotch and scooted down in his seat to make room for his erection. He'd have to endure the tease until my finale.

As the last group song played, I stepped off stage and changed my outfit. When the song finished, the other dancers left, and I walked back on. I repositioned the chair so Jessup would face the pole with his back to the audience.

Michelle handed me the microphone. My hands shook. I wanted to be succinct. This event was about him and me. My mouth was so dry. I wondered if I could speak.

"Jessup, can you come up here?"

He glanced around the room, stood, and strolled toward me. When whooping and whistling started, it provided the extra fuel he needed for his legs to work.

When he reached me, I smiled and shouted into the microphone. "Happy Anniversary." I switched it off and laid it on the floor.

"What are you doing, sweetpea?"

"I hope to do you, Jess."

His Adam's apple bobbed as he swallowed. "Me? You want to do me, in front of everyone?"

"I want a specific pole between my legs. Yours."

"Now?"

With all these questions, I thought he'd changed his mind. "I thought this was your fantasy."

"Oh, God, it is."

"So, I needn't handcuff you?"

"Hell, no. I'm a willing participant."

I pushed him into the chair, and I swayed my body back and forth. I walked around him, taking off my skimpy top and then dragging my pasties across his face. I had Jessup's full attention as the song I'd selected began playing.

As I faced Jessup, I placed my hands on his shoulders. I repeated the steps from the other song, but instead of clicking my shoes, I kicked his feet wide. I leaned into him, nuzzling his neck and moaning. I stood behind him and repeated the maneuver. I never expected the audience participation to fire me up.

"They are watching my ass, Jess."

"Sounds like they appreciate it like I do."

"Maybe they'll like this."

I circled the chair and placed my back against the pole while I skimmed my hands across my breasts and down my abdomen. His gaze dripped with desire. When I glided down to a squat with open knees, his expression tore at my body, my heart, and my crotch. I pushed myself up the pole, and when I stood, I placed one foot on the chair between Jessup's legs and reached up behind me. I swung my body around in one rotation with my legs open wide enough to land with my feet by his. He rubbed his hands up and down his thighs, blowing out air. His energy was electric. I swiveled my hips and thrust my pelvis in his face while I ran my hands up my neck, and then shimmied my shoulders, shaking my breasts by his mouth.

The music amplified.

"Do me, you sexy slut."

"I love it when you call me names."

I stood beside him and lifted my leg up over his lap like I was mounting a motorcycle. As I straddled him, I twerked my ass and bobbed my body up and down. I felt flush as if the room had grown as hot as my desire. The crowd drowned out the music.

"Take my cock out of my pants. Grind on me, baby. I get all of you, and they don't."

"Rip my thong, Jess."

When I dipped into his lap, his strong fingers hooked the scrap of cloth between my legs and severed it as if it were tissue paper. Following the beat of the music, I lowered myself onto his cock, sucking him in and squeezing him tight, over and over.

To the audience, it looked like I continued my lap dance. For them, it was a fantasy, and for me, it was real. I was there. People whistled. I could feel my climax approaching as the song peaked. With the last beat, I slammed down on Jessup. He grabbed my ass and pulled me against him, grinding my clit as he unloaded into me, and I came.

Jessup buried his face in my neck, kissing me while he clasped my shoulders with his big hands.

I wrapped my arms around him. I'd done it.

Michelle thanked the group for attending and ushered out the other dancers and fans.

"I never expected it to be this good, Paula."

I chuckled. "Wait, what do you mean expected?" I leaned back and saw his sheepish grin.

"I knew you were doing something here."

"How is that possible?"

"After the previous show, Harv sent me a video of you at class."

"How did Harv get a video?"

"He's dating a dancer and came early to pick her up. When he saw you, he took a quick video and sent it."

"Damn him. He ruined my surprise."

"Sweetpea, no one ruined anything. I imagined a scene since we came for the first performance. When I got the video, I created an entire movie in my head."

"You weren't disappointed?"

"Disappointed? I've been a walking erection for two weeks, waiting to see what you'd concocted. Pea, you shined and blew my movie apart. Damn, I'm getting hard again just talking about it."

When I looked up, the entire place was empty, and the music still played.

"Can't waste a good hard-on. What's your fantasy now, Jess?"

"A private show of my remarkable anniversary gift."

END

DR. J. *is a retired sex therapist, who enjoys the island life in Florida. She finds sexy writing inspiration from every corner of her world. When not doing authorly things, you can see her on the pétanque court perfecting her competition moves* *while sipping something cold.*

647.12
Mars

Wet Rewards

author: Sommer Marsden

category: Management of Home Offices

subjects: 1. Talking Dirty 2. Mid-day Fling
3. Four Fingers 4. Little Pussy

Rose Caraway's Library of Erotica

Wet Rewards

Sommer Marsden

Brian was busy on his phone when I set a cup of coffee on the dining room table in front of him. Checking his sales, no doubt. I kissed him on the back of the head, and he hummed happily.

I glanced over his shoulder. "I was about to give you crap and try and tempt you away from work for a while, but what the hell is Wet Rewards?"

He looked up at me, eyebrow cocked. "What?"

"Go back."

He returned to the previous screen and chuckled. "You might need new glasses, babe. Because that says get rewards. And it's just a store loyalty thing."

I shook my head at myself. "I swore it said wet rewards."

He snagged my wrist and pulled me onto his lap. "The only wet rewards I get are from you."

It was my turn to cock my eyebrow at him. "How so?" But I knew what he meant. I just wanted to hear what he'd say.

"Ya know." He waggled his eyebrows and then pantomimed pushing his fingers inside me. When he let out an X-rated movie moan, I elbowed him gently.

"Yes, yes. I understand." I rolled my eyes.

"Are you sure? Because..." He mimicked eating my pussy by flicking his tongue between his fingers, spread in a V shape.

I groaned and tried to stand, but he wrapped a big arm around me and held me firmly. "Where you going, cutie?"

"I get it. I misread the wet rewards."

"I also get them when I—" He stopped mid-sentence and thrust up from beneath me.

I let out a sharp cry but then found myself laughing.

"Christ." The laughter died on my lips when I realized he was hard beneath my ass.

"And now you got me all worked up, so we have to talk about me possibly getting some of these wet rewards."

I stared into his big, blue eyes. He wasn't kidding. "I—"

He jostled me in his lap, and I felt it again, rubbing against me.

My laughter returned, and I clapped my hand over my mouth. "I get it. I get it. You're hard," I mumbled.

His hands drifted up to cup my breasts. He pinched my nipples a second later, and that sensation slid down my center to pool between my thighs.

"Well, you did start talking dirty to me out of the blue," he said, his mouth pressed gently to my earlobe, provoking a shiver.

"Actually, I simply displayed my inability to read."

"But now, all I can think of is you being wet, really wet, and me reaping the rewards of that wetness."

He slid his big hand from my tit to my lap, cupping my pussy through my jeans, pressing a finger firmly against the split of my sex. I could feel my heartbeat there, pounding.

"Is this one of those perks of telecommuting you talked about?" I managed, in a whisper.

His finger curled against me once more, and I drew in a shuddery breath.

"It is. How about we go upstairs?" He didn't wait for me to answer. He simply stood and gently put me on my feet.

I faced him, liking the mischievous look on his face. Before I could react, he grabbed my shoulders and tugged me forward. His mouth, warm and wet, came down on my throat, and he sucked. As I struggled, he sucked harder. The pounding of my pulse grew heavier between my thighs.

When he released me, he winked. "Now, everyone will know your middle-of-the-day-sex shame."

I put my hand to my neck. No doubt I'd wear a reddish-purple mark. When he did that, it did something to me; it turned me on to no end, and I had no idea why.

I knew Brian didn't care why. He did it to get me going. And it worked.

He slid a hand into my jeans, breached my panties, skated a finger through my wetness, and stroked my clit.

"I'm being rewarded already."

My breath caught, and my eyes drifted shut as he touched me.

He pinched my clit gently, and my eyes sprang open.

"Come on, love. Up those steps. I'm gonna eat that pussy like it's my job."

I swallowed hard, and then took the steps two at a time.

He snagged me by the back of my jeans the moment we crossed the bedroom threshold, and I squealed. There was a good dose of anxiety in my anticipation. When he fucked me with his fingers, when he stretched me, it was a pleasure that often skirted the edge of pain. But it got me off like nobody's fucking business.

"Where you going, little girl?" He growled it, and the hair on my nape rose and swayed.

He turned me and popped my button, dragged down my zipper, and pushed down my jeans. He did it all with great precision and ease. My panties were wet at the center. I could feel it before he even tugged them down.

"What's this? Someone's already soaked." His thick finger plunged into me, and pleasure lanced through me.

He withdrew it easily and motioned for me to put my arms up. I put them over my head like a child, and he whisked off my sweater. Beneath, I was bare.

He left his clothes on, and I shivered. That meant, at least for the beginning, it was all about me and the things he was going to do to me with his mouth and his fingers.

He pushed me onto the bed, and I bounced. He grabbed my ankles with his big hands and tugged so that I landed flat. My nipples were twin pebbles, raised and hard in the cool air of our drafty bedroom.

"Now, about those wet rewards," he said, leering at me.

When he was like this, part animal and part man, my pulse always raced with the thrill of it.

"Where shall I start? Mouth?" He dropped a wet kiss on my pussy.

I squirmed.

"Fingers?" He trailed them over my drenched opening.

I wriggled like a fish on a hook and said nothing. Whatever I chose, he'd likely switch to the other just to torture me. If I was silent, he'd choose for me.

"No opinion?"

I pressed my lips together and did my best to stifle my noises of frustration.

"Hmm. I guess I'll just have to decide for you."

His finger plunged into me, deep and fast. My breath caught. I did my best to hold still and behave. Writhing only made him go faster. The pleasure, pain line we skated when he stretched me was amazing.

"Look who's being good," he said. He lowered his mouth to me and gave my clit a fast swipe of his tongue.

I sighed. The pleasure was immediate and intense.

He curled a single, thick finger against my walls.

My toes curled. I shut my eyes.

"Eyes open, lovely."

I forced them open and met his gaze. Eye contact was a rule.

He kept me pinned with his gaze as he slid a second finger inside me, filling me up. He continued to look at me as he lowered his mouth and flick-flick-flicked my clitoris with his wet tongue.

My pussy clenched up around him. He moved his fingers, scissoring them and taking me right to the edge of pain before sucking my clit with a wonderful rhythm. The pleasure tamped down the pain, and my pussy flickered around his fingers.

"How many will I get, I wonder?" He curled his fingers and sucked me, and the orgasm slammed down on me fast and hard, stealing the breath from my lungs.

"There's one," he said.

He moved away from me and took off his sweater. His jeans went next, and then the boxer briefs. His socks hit the floor, and he levered himself over me, his cock hard and ready. I knew he wouldn't fuck me, though. He was teasing me some more.

But as always, he surprised me. He knocked my thighs apart and drove into me easily. I shuddered when his cockhead nudged the perfect, juiciest place inside me. I hummed against his neck.

Brian kissed my shoulder, licked it, and dragged his sharp teeth along the same path.

My nipples tingled with the friction of his movements as he took his time, moving in me. He didn't withdraw much, just kept driving into me while keeping his body close. When he started to rock side to side, rubbing my G-spot with each motion, I bit my tongue.

"So, so close," he whispered, against my earlobe. "But we have some more to do."

He was gone then, his absence from my body staggering. The coolness of the room enveloped me, and I shivered.

He was back between my legs, staring up at me as he pushed a thick bundle of three fingers inside me. My body balked, my walls ached, and I clenched my jaw. He moved his fingers, pushing me closer to that pain threshold. But then, he was lapping at me, working his tongue over my clit in a chaotic dance that constantly kept me on edge. I couldn't anticipate what he'd do. There was no definite rhythm, so I was at his mercy, taking what he dished out.

He flared his fingers apart inside of me, and I ached. My pussy thrummed in time with my heart because what he was doing with his tongue was so insanely good, I couldn't even comprehend it.

His mouth latched onto me as he worked his fingers. A constant dancing motion of wet flesh across my clit. I tried to stay still, but I failed. My body did a dance of its own.

"Look at me, May."

I looked down at him, and he grinned. Leered. Presented his teeth like the

Big Bad Wolf as he pushed a fourth finger into me.

I felt it squeaking in. I bit down on the urge to tell him to stop. I watched his pink tongue dart out and waggle wolfishly against my clit. And then, it was in. A thick bunch of four fingers stretched my little pussy.

I inhaled deeply. He kept them still, letting me adjust. And the instant I did, the instant my body told him I was okay, he flexed them. Working his fingers inside me, he sucked my clit and lapped at me.

I felt the pressure and the pleasure building. Growing. I skated that razor edge between pleasure and pain. He began a perfect rhythm of whorls with his tongue, and I lost it, coming with a cry so loud it hurt my ears.

My pussy was still spasming as he pulled his fingers free, and I whimpered. But then, he plunged his cock into me. Trapping my arms above my head, he worked his hips, and his cock pushed against my still-contracting walls.

He slammed my G-spot, and the breath rushed out of my lungs as I moaned.

"Are you still coming, love? Because I think I can make it happen again."

I tossed my head, overwhelmed by the intensity of my pleasure. He drove into me quickly. My wetness was audible over my desperate sounds.

His cockhead hit the perfect place again, and my orgasm swept upward when it should have dipped, unfurling deep inside me as the pleasure found a second wave, and I rode it.

"There's my girl."

I fought, unintentionally, against the flesh manacles that were his hands, but he held me easily.

When my body began to calm, he stared down at me and thrust deep and hard. He came with barely a sound. That was his way. His pleasure arrived in silence whereas mine showed up like a parade.

I watched his face as he came, and then his eyes cleared. The big bad wolf was gone. My husband remained.

He lowered onto me and kissed my forehead. "You okay?"

"I'm good."

"I didn't hurt you?"

I smiled and touched his face. "Just enough."

He grinned again, showing me a flash of the wolf. "Good."

"All that from a misread." I laughed.

"Wet rewards is way more interesting than get rewards," he whispered against my neck.

I shivered. "Agreed. One hundred percent."

END

Professional dirty word writer, **SOMMER MARSDEN** *is a gluten free baker, a sock addict, a wiener dog walker, an expert procrastinator, and that about sums it up.*

```
306.7
Davi
            His Property
       author:  Eliza David
     category:  BDSM
   subjects:   1. Fetish   2. Pro Domme Career
               3. Kitty Korner   4. Dungeon


Rose Caraway's Library of Erotica
```

His Property

Eliza David

"Again, Mistress…"

I looked down at Walt Channing, who was donning a leather vest he'd kept hidden under his business suit all morning in anticipation of our visit. When the alderman wasn't shutting down rec centers in underprivileged neighborhoods, he was begging me to spank him with exactly eighty-six lashes every Thursday morning.

A part of me loved punishing him, naturally. What kind of person is so miserable they'd close Fremont City's basketball courts to kids? The kind of man who paid a black chick named Roxy Jenkins three hundred dollars an hour to lash his pasty-white ass exactly eighty-six times.

See, Walt had a fetish for black women, which made him my most steady regular. I'd spent the first four years of my pro domme career being cast aside for the traditional raven-haired, red-lipped white girls at the Kitty Korner Dungeon, my place of part-time employment. Then good ol' Walty came in, laid eyes on me in all my bronzed glory, and picked me without hesitation.

"I've given you your lashes, you peasant," I said, legs crossed as Walt panted at my heels. I gave him another smack with my crop. "Now, rise and get back to the office, you racist scumbag."

I watched as Walt scrambled to his feet, so eager to please me. I placed the tip of the crop underneath his chin. "Now, off with you!"

He ran to his white button-down shirt and grey suit. Both lay wrinkled on the floor. He never took the time to undress in the dressing rooms provided to our clients; he preferred to yank his top off and expose his vest to me every week like some kind of sub superhero. It was endearing, but that was my job—to make my client's kink seem completely normal.

Aimee charged in seconds after Walt left my play space, bent over in cackles. "What the hell went on in here?"

I giggled. "Oh, you know Walty," I said, hopping off the red, leather bondage table. "I always have to give him a hard time about his politics. Why? What happened?"

Aimee pointed a thumb behind her. "I was in the lobby with Reggie—"

"Latino Reggie, the diaper wearer?"

"Nah. Black Reggie with the muzzle."

"Got it. Continue."

"So, I'm standing there, checking him out after our appointment, and Walt comes right up to him, pumps a fist in the air, and screams, 'I'm black, and I'm proud.' I about fucking died!"

The cackles flowed out of us again as we walked out of the play space and into the locker room. Being a pro domme may not have been the life my parents imagined for me after I graduated from college, but I couldn't think of a better way to put my psych degree to use. Besides, Kitty Korner paid the bills and never failed to give me a few laughs, especially when my girl Aimee worked the early morning shift with me.

After getting dressed, I stepped out into the lobby to more chuckles from my work buddy. "You go from leather and chains to starched khakis like it's nothing, girl."

I caught a glimpse of myself in my bland Cupz uniform—a dirt-brown polo with a coffee-mug-shaped nametag that said 'Nicole' in peeling, black letters. Again, not what Joan and Darius Foster had imagined for their little girl, but bills. "Don't even."

Aimee tightened the belt on her robe. "Just kidding, chica. I may be needing a gig from you soon." She took her cell phone out of her robe pocket and glanced at it. "My regulars keep canceling on me."

I watched her eyes shadow over with worry. While I only had myself to support, Aimee was a single mother with two redheaded toddlers who waited for her at her mom's house while she made money. If her next trick didn't show up, it would be her third cancellation that week.

I reached for her shoulder, giving it a squeeze. "He'll show, sweetie." I kissed her cheek and headed for the door. "Gotta jet or I'll miss my bus. Call me later?"

Aimee nodded, her eyes back on her phone, though not more than a minute had passed.

I walked to my stop, counting my blessings for what I had in Walt. He was a heartless politician, but he was steady work. I had dozens of clients literally come and go, but Walt was my Thursday guarantee.

But as I stepped into Cupz an hour later, pushing through the crowd to get behind the counter, I saw my guarantee being hauled off to jail on live television.

"Holy shit," I whispered, unable to tear my eyes away from the elevated screen.

"You got that right," a grey-haired lady said. "Feds scooped him up coming into work just about an hour ago."

Right after he left our appointment...our weekly appointment.

"Are they really taking him to jail? Like, jail jail?" I said, to no one in particular.

A preppy-looking Indian guy in front of me nodded, his eyes never leaving the screen to look at me. "Oh, hell yes. Securities fraud will get you up to twenty-five in the slammer."

My eyes bugged. "Twenty-five years?"

"Yeah, but he won't do that much time," the old lady said, shaking her head. "Probably half of that."

The crowd dispersed as an image of Walt being helped into the back of a police car illuminated the screen. I stood there, motionless. Less than a half hour ago, I had been on the bus lamenting about Aimee's bad luck with her clients. Now, I was watching Walt—almost half of my monthly income—get hauled to Sing-Sing. A rush of overwhelm hit me just as my boss yelled for me from the counter. I took a deep breath and walked behind the counter to start the one gig I still had.

I crunched the numbers on my iPhone's calculator app when I got home that night, a vain effort to see if I could make it without Walt's dividends. But between rent, utilities, food, and basic upkeep, I was looking at a loss of twelve hundred a month. Sure, I could pass on mall trips with Aimee and live off of Ramen until I snagged a new Walt, but who was I kidding?

There'd never be another trick as loaded as Walt and without one, making my rent would be impossible.

A knock rapped on my door, and I hopped off my bed. My breath caught in my throat when I opened the door and saw Darryl Winston. You would think that in my line of work I'd get sick of seeing men. But Darryl was a different story altogether. He towered a full foot over my five-five frame with a muscular build that seemed to be all shoulders and pecs. He had a sexy smile framed by full lips I wouldn't mind sitting on if ever given a chance. In short, Darryl was like a big, cuddly brown bear. A big cuddly brown bear to whom I owed rent.

"Darryl, I was just thinking about you," I cooed, hugging myself in the door frame.

He cocked an eyebrow, already over my shtick. "Where's my money?"

"I promise I'll have it for you soon."

"You told me that two weeks ago and again last week," Darryl said, shaking his head. "I can't play this game anymore. Hate to say it but—"

"Then don't say it." I closed the space between us. I swallowed before I attempted the one thing I promised myself I'd never do. But desperate times...

"Maybe we can work something out, Darryl." I kept my eyes glued to his luscious lips.

Then, those lips of his exploded into laughter. "Girl, are you serious? I'm not one of your little clients you spank for a living."

I sighed, forgetting I'd let Darryl in on my profession the last time I begged for a rent extension. "Well, it was worth a try. Can I at least give you a drink?"

"Sure." Darryl paused before moving past me and into my apartment. "I can't believe you just tried that."

"I'm sorry. Besides, I know you have a girlfriend." Yet another fact I kept conveniently forgetting about my hunk of a landlord. Darryl was in love with Gia, a pediatrician who was every bit as gorgeous as he was.

Darryl turned to face me as I walked past him into the kitchen. "Actually, Gia and I broke up."

My eyes bugged as I grabbed a bottle of vodka out of my freezer. "Seriously?" I said, grabbing two red cups out of a plastic sleeve on the counter. "Well, that means you deserve a double, sir." I poured into his cup. "What happened?"

Darryl sat at my kitchen island and took the double shot down in one gulp. "Gia wanted more than I could give. She was fed up and dumped me."

I sat across from him and let my red cup dangle in my hand. "Why are men like this?"

"Like what?"

"You have this intelligent and gorgeous woman in your life, yet you still won't commit." I shook my head before taking a sip, the cold vodka stinging my tongue.

Darryl shrugged. "Men are weird. Besides, I'm holding out for something else."

"You mean, someone else," I said, rolling my eyes, more pissed than I cared to be. I couldn't imagine another woman in our general vicinity that would compare to Gia. She was all legs and long, curly hair. Her boobs and ass were so perky, you could serve a five-course meal on them. In short, Gia was your basic nightmare.

I tipped the frosty bottle into his cup for another shot. "Well, this someone else must be a helluva woman for you to let Gia go."

"Yeah." Darryl's gaze caught mine. "Actually, she is."

I set the bottle down, feeling the temperature in the room rise. *What's with the eyes?*, I thought as I cleared my throat. "So, the rent. Look, you know my line of work. My clientele ain't steady, and one of my richest clients literally just got sent to the slammer today. Walt Channing."

Darryl stopped mid-sip, the cup tipped against his full, brown lips. "The politician?"

"Alderman of Fremont City's Second Ward, to be exact."

"You were..." Darryl pumped a fist, one of those annoying physical colloquialisms men do to describe fucking instead of just saying the word.

"No. I'm a dominatrix. I don't have sex with my clients. Didn't we discuss this when I spilled the beans on my gig?"

Darryl took another sip. "So, men just pay you to spank them? They don't want sex?"

"Sure, some of them want sex, but most of my clients see me for something deeper. Some like to be held. Some just want someone to bitch to about their wife and kids. And yes, some want to be spanked. Or all three. Every trick is different, and every domme has her specialty. Mine is humiliation."

Darryl considered this before rising from his chair and walking around the island to me. "And you?" He set his cup next to mine as he closed the space between us. "What do you want?"

The smell of his woodsy cologne wafted from his skin. This man, this bear, towering over me coursed a strange sensation through me. It wasn't fear. It was want and a need to express a desire I knew Darryl could bring out of me. The heat of his body intermingling with mine was something I'd only dreamed of experiencing. I'd lay awake in bed some nights, touching myself to the fantasy of his muscular body enrapturing mine. I tried to swallow the truth down, but it escaped my lips before I could stop it.

"I want to experience what my clients experience with me," I said, my voice heavy with lust. "And I want that with you."

I took a chance and slid my hands underneath his shirt, feeling the hardness of his burly chest against my nervous palms. "I want you to control me."

"Is this because you're late on the rent, Mistress Roxy?" he asked, in a gruff whisper.

I looked up at him and noticed his slip of a smile framed by his full beard. "No. But tonight..." I stood from the seat and lifted the shirt from his body. "I'm not Mistress Roxy. You're in charge...Master."

His hands cupped my ass. "I don't know. Never done anything like that."

"Sure you have." I dropped my arms from his chest. "Just use your skills as a property manager and tell me what to do. Pretend I'm your property." I raised on my tiptoes to brush my lips against his. "Manage me."

"What do you want me to say?"

"It's not about me." I trailed a finger across the hardened length that was begging to bust out of his pants. "It's all about you. Treat me like you hate me."

Darryl's gaze cast down to my wet lips and back to my eyes. "Get on your knees, you dirty slut."

My pussy ached when he said the word slut. I knelt before him, reaching for the drawstring on his warmups before he slapped my hand away. I looked up at him. "Yes, Master?"

Darryl pulled the drawstring out of his sweats and bent over, taking my wrists behind my back. He fastened the string around my wrists and stood upright, his dick pulsing through his pants. "No hands. Use your mouth."

My wrists twisted in the tight restraint as I bit down on his waistband to pull down his pants. It was a struggle that both frustrated me and made me incredibly wet.

His dick sprang free. It was larger than I had imagined in my fantasies. I took the bobbing head into my mouth and could only get it halfway in.

"Take it," he groaned, his hands in my hair as he pushed himself further in.

My body electrified as my mouth struggled with his thickness. The pain of forcing himself in excited me more than I could have ever imagined. I'd never had sex of any variety with my clients, but if my control over them excited them half as much as Darryl excited me, I understood now why they always came back.

My throat softened, and my need to swallow him whole won out over physical inability. I worked my neck, the salty taste of his hardness making the pulse of my clit quicken. I let out a moan right before I felt another tug of my hair.

"Shut the fuck up," he said, in the same tone one would tell someone the time.

His calm demeanor made me ache even more, speeding up my bobbing head.

He guided me along his length, his sack bouncing against my chin as he groaned above me. He pulled himself from my mouth. "That's enough for you."

"Wait," I panted. My wrists strained in the tight string as I tried to steady my knees on the kitchen tile. "I want you to come in my mouth, Master."

"You don't deserve to swallow me, you whore."

My pussy clenched as Darryl pulled up his sweats. *So, this is how my clients feel when I degrade them.* I wanted more. "What *do* I deserve, Master?"

Darryl stepped behind me and untied the string from around my wrists. My arms tingled with pain at their release.

"A spanking," he said. Behind me, he looped the drawstring over my head.

I gagged for a beat as he tightened it around my neck.

He walked to my front, holding the string and giving my neck a tug. "Crawl."

My hard nipples dragged against the inside of my tank top as I placed my palms on the cold linoleum. I stared up at him, wanting nothing more than his dick back in my mouth. "Please, Master, I..."

"Shut the fuck up." Darryl sat on the couch and patted his lap. "Bend over, you worthless cunt."

I licked my lips, anticipating the feel of his big, bear hands on my tiny ass. I rose to my knees and slid my body over his lap. He tugged down my yoga pants, and I felt the air hit my bare bottom just before the first slap. The second slap made me moan, and the string tightened around my neck.

"What did I tell you? I want silence."

"M-May I come? I'm so close, Master. Please?" And I was. Between the unexpected dominance from Darryl, who had been nothing but a gentleman, and the fantasies I'd had about him coming true, I was ready to cream right then and there.

The third slap reverberated straight to my clit as I squirmed. "Oh, Master! I'm—"

The fourth slap did it, sending an orgasm shooting from my clit to my lower belly as I clawed the hardwood floor. I shivered in his lap as he smoothed his palm over my tender, bruised ass.

He moved his hand to my hair, pushing it behind my ear before he lowered his mouth. "Here's the deal," Darryl said, his voice firm and rough. "You can take your time with the rent. I know you work hard." He slid a finger down my ass crack and into my pulsing pussy, still in aftershock from the climax.

"But when you come home, I'll come knocking and do to you what you do to them. Control you. Degrade you. Give you the spanking you need for being a bad girl all day. You hear me?"

I weakly nodded against his knee, arching my ass into his hand. "Yes, Master."

I was his property.

END

ELIZA DAVID *is an erotic romance author living in Iowa City by way of Chicago. She enjoys reading Jackie Collins, bingeing on Sex & the City marathons, and indulging in the occasional order of cheese fries. You can often find her on Twitter talking all things men and manuscripts.*

```
618.25
 Verd
        In the Practice of
           Her Calling
         author: Alegra Verde
       category: Medical Specialties
     subjects:  1. Hospital Room  2. Vertebra Slippage
                3. Saturated Sex

 Rose Caraway's Library of Erotica
```

In The Practice Of Her Calling

ALEGRA VERDE

"Shh," she said, lifting a finger to her lips as she came into the hospital room, closing the door behind her.

Silently, he watched as she neared the bed. A little, questioning wrinkle appeared between his brows as she slipped off her thick, white running shoes, and then bent down to pull off her socks.

She noted that he was resting comfortably and seemed alert, his eyes following her every move. The bed had been raised to a thirty-degree angle so he could sit up. There was no evidence of pain, and he hadn't requested any meds in more than three hours—all proof that he was improving, even though he'd been having trouble sleeping.

Catching his gaze with hers, she slowly loosened the knot of her cotton drawstring pants and let them slide down over her hips before kicking them away. Her serviceable white cotton panties followed. They caught mid-thigh, so she did a little shimmy to help them slither down her lean legs, and then she stood and waited.

His gaze, which had been unwavering and a little tense, was temporarily interrupted by a grin that closed his eyes briefly.

He stared at her neatly trimmed bush, the narrow rectangle of down barely concealing her slit. His eyes took in the length of her, he swallowed, and then nodded, his eyes almost pleading.

She smiled and wet her lips, her tongue touching the corner of her mouth, and then the center of her top lip before she pulled her bottom lip in to glaze it with a bit of moisture, an unconscious gesture. Her fingers found the bottom of her cotton scrub shirt and pulled it over her head to reveal a pair of full breasts gently cradled in a thin, lacy, black bra. Her nipples, already hard, pressed meaningfully against the wispy lace.

Tugging the coverlet, he shifted as though to spread his legs, his eyes never leaving her. Even though his thick head of dark hair was messy and he'd lost some weight in the weeks he'd been confined here, he still looked hearty. He was a big guy, just over six feet. Before the accident, he'd been a very athletic and competitive soccer player and something to do with horses—training jumpers—she'd heard. The accident had been a fluke; grass had obscured a deep rut in his path. He'd apparently taken a fall that caused some vertebra slippage, but he'd kept pushing through the pain. Had he continued without treatment, he could have done permanent damage, but the pain won out.

He was really quite attractive, she mused as she cupped her breasts and used her forefingers to pinch her nipples.

His tongue darted out as though it wanted to replace her teasing fingers. The action sent a jolt of pleasure straight to her center, and wetness pooled between her legs. She had planned to remove her bra too, but she liked the way the lace cradled and lifted her breasts as though making a present of them, so she left it on. Placing a vertical finger over her lips in the universal sign for silence, she nodded and waited for him to acknowledge the command.

He nodded.

Bending over the narrow bed, she pulled back the coverlet, and then the sheet.

He was still and nearly breathless as though the sound of his breathing might break the spell, and she would be gone in a poof.

She unbuttoned his pajama top. The pale-blue cloth parted to reveal even paler skin. Leaning in, she pressed her lips to the center of his chest, trailing the length of his sternum. Then, her lips and the tip of her tongue played over his taut and quivering abdominal muscles.

His fingers found her nape and stroked the short hairs there.

Relinquishing the smoothness of his skin, she rose to slide his pajama bottoms down, slipping them gently under his backside, down his legs, and off. She dropped them to the floor to join the growing pile of clothing.

His legs were long and strong-looking, and there were wisps of hair on his pale calves. He stirred, his leg moving, a knee bent in an aborted attempt to place a foot flat on the bed. He winced.

She waited, surveying him. There was nothing wrong with his legs; they were strong and well-formed as one would expect of an active man not yet thirty. It was his slowly mending back that had kept him here.

There was certainly nothing wrong with his libido; his cock stood up strong, hard, and eager. His eyes searched hers.

She smiled and leaned forward, taking the tip of his penis into her mouth. His hand found her back, and then her naked hip as she took in more of his hard cock, sucking, and then sliding her tongue up and down its length.

He groaned appreciatively, and her jaws hollowed, sucking harder until he was squirming and breathing heavily. She ran her tongue up his ever-hardening cock once more, then she climbed onto the bed to straddle him.

Balanced on her knees, she let him touch her, his fingers cupping and stroking her sex as though he were fondling a compliant pet. His thumb ruffled her furred triangle, and his fingers dipped into her moist slit and wet depths. They teased her sensitive tissue, stroking and sliding, causing her to moan and sway before remembering the narrow limits of the bed.

If she'd had her eyes open, she would have seen he watched her closely, taking in the way her lips pressed together and her body moved. His mouth was slightly open, and his lower lip trembled as he touched the silky, slippery layers of her wet pussy.

She purred and moaned and continued to let him touch her, enjoying the tingles and jolts his fingers elicited. But when she heard the rustling of the sheets at his feet as he tried to bend, perhaps so he could kiss or suck the trembling lips of her pussy, she opened her eyes and pressed his shoulders back to steady him. Then, she scooted down, her knees carefully skirting his hips until her sopping sex hovered over his straining cock.

He looked up at her, eyes bright with anticipation, and she smiled as she slid down, slow and easy, each inch eliciting a groan from his nearly closed lips. Finally, when her hot, wet pussy had claimed the entire length of him, his large hands gently squeezed her lace-covered breasts and tugged at their soft buoyancy, his thumbs pressing and smearing her protruding nipples.

The scent of hot sex permeated the room. She closed her eyes to better inhale their combined scent. The sweet muskiness lingered in the air, a savory mouth-watering spice.

"I want to taste you," he said, softly.

"You'll always remember my perfume," she whispered.

He filled her, his cock expanding, pressing against her nearly inflexible walls. She slid up and down, and every time her tight pussy slid down, engulfing his cock in its wet fire, it ignited a new series of sparks.

His hands were on her thighs, grabbing and spreading her. It was like he wanted to get up, up all the way past the tight layers of plush wetness. Like he wanted to hold her still as he burrowed and then pounded into her slick flesh. But she had him encased in her heat, her pussy sucking at him. His fingers sank into her waist and her ass.

She moaned and bit her lip to keep from crying out. At this time of the night, most of the patients were sleeping, and the floor was quiet except for the hushed whir of ventilators and beeps from heart monitors. The near silence seemed to amplify every noise, and she knew the other two nurses on duty would come running if they heard cries coming from a patient's room.

She tasted the salty tang of blood as something deep inside her trembled. The pleasure built, on the edge of exploding and breaking free.

He must have felt her trembling joy and impending implosion too because his movements quickened. She rode him faster and harder. He gritted his teeth and held on as his cock grew more rigid. He made another vain attempt to rise as if he needed to get closer and deeper. The slap of her ass against his thighs punctuated the rise and fall of her sleek pussy. She took him again and again, making crazy, ecstatic music.

"Yes, don't stop."

She barely heard him and understood he didn't want anyone passing by in the hallway to hear but also didn't want her to stop.

Her pussy trembled around him, squeezing his cock like hot fingers milking a cow's teat. The thought made him want to laugh, but it felt so good he wanted to cry. It had been a long while since he'd been with a woman.

For months, he'd despaired, wondering whether he'd ever be able to rise to the occasion again. But she'd always been there, holding his hand and offering encouragement through the traction and the meds. When the pain subsided, he'd noticed the rise of her ass in those scrubs and the way soft curls escaped her bun and trailed down her neck as she leaned over him to adjust his brace. He had imagined, wished, and hoped but never believed she'd come to him.

He'd been so helpless at first, and he was still bedridden. Now, his eyes closed tight, he gripped her thighs, and although he could feel her muscles tense beneath his fingers, she did not stop. Her hot, wet sex tugged and sucked at his cock. His balls tightened, and his cock grew longer as though her sex was pulling and stretching it. It felt good; he felt as though he could die of pleasure.

He tightened inside her as she slid down his length. A thin layer of sweat covered her body, and his hot, slippery fingers gripped her thighs. His grip tightened, trying to pull her closer, to control her descent, but she wouldn't let him. She seemed focused solely on the way his rigid cock made her writhe as it slid along her walls, forcing them wider.

His finger teased and pressed her swollen clit until he felt her spasm. He flooded her then, crying out, his fingers making marks on her thighs.

Quickly, and before the haze began to clear, she leaned forward and covered his lips with hers. Tensing, she looked toward the hall as if listening for footsteps, but there were none. Relaxing against him, she flexed her muscles around his half-hard member.

He smiled, his lips curving against hers.

She rested her head in the crook of his neck.

After a while, she rose and cleaned them both, tucking her patient in and lowering his bed. Then, she pulled her scrubs back on and laced her shoes, slipping out of the room.

END

ALEGRA VERDE *is a native of Detroit by way of Rio Grande, Puerto Rico. Instead of playing Candy Crush or Angry Birds, she writes erotic short stories because writing sexy stories is just as stimulating and cathartic as playing games on her cell, but the afterglow lasts longer.*

652.0
DeLo

Such a Small Thing, Really

author: Kiki DeLovely

category: Processes of Written Communication

subjects: 1. Sexual Yearnings   2. Debilitating Shyness
3. Directional Fornication

Rose Caraway's Library of Erotica

Such A Small Thing, Really

Kiki DeLovely

Such a small thing, really. Just a simple task, an assignment. Almost a dare. But for Xiomara, it was so much more. They had engaged in significant edgeplay and had taken kink to places unknown, yet this child's play felt more like playing with fire.

"I want you to tell me what to do. Aloud. In the bedroom," Malik said.

Give her a pad of paper and pen, a laptop, or even a cell phone, and she would gladly outline her sexual yearnings with the written word. But to speak them out loud?

"I…I…I…" She couldn't do it.

"Just breathe." Malik's firm hands on her shoulders were a comfort. "It doesn't have to be today or even tomorrow. Take the next several days and think on it. Consider what you might need to make you comfortable enough for words to flow. I don't care if you stutter and neither should you. You're always sexy to me."

She had undergone speech therapy, starting at a young age after being teased mercilessly. Her father had seen the effect bullying had on Xiomara's well-being and signed her up with the first speech pathologist he could afford. She was grateful for the lessons, though less so for the fact that they'd all but erased her lyrical, Mexican accent. That had been decades ago, and her speech disorder was only a distant memory, except under very specific

Such A Small Thing, Really

circumstances. Her debilitating shyness, coupled with the fear of sounding stupid in an intimate moment, created the perfect cocktail for Xiomara's stutter to reemerge.

Throughout her twenties and thirties, she had made a series of bad choices in lovers, many of whom helped to contribute to her anxiety by telling her that she sounded sexier if she just stuck to moans or, worse, advised her to just keep quiet altogether. Therapy in her forties finally had Xiomara selecting healthier lovers, but she still hadn't been able to quite get past her aversion to speaking during sex other than the occasional "Yes!" or "Fuck!" Sticking to monosyllabic phrases was her pushing at the edges of her comfort zone. And yet, there he was, asking her to audibly form full sentences, paragraphs even! As her dominant, Malik had explored those edges thoroughly, stretching her in ways she enjoyed. Through it all, they'd grown together. But he had never requested something of her that left her feeling so unhinged and sick to her stomach with nerves, floating somewhere just outside of her body. Her one saving grace that she clung to like a tether was that she could always safeword out of it.

But Xiomara didn't want out of it. She wondered if Malik saw her determination, gradually mounting. She wanted to be free of this burden, no matter how painfully challenging it would be to confront. It could open so many doors.

A smug grin crept across Malik's face. "If you want something badly enough, you'll say it." The top of his head brushed against the chandelier as he turned, apparently leaving her to sort it out.

Xiomara felt as if the stiff, mid-century, modern sofa suddenly grew a soft spot and was about to swallow her whole. Somehow, Malik always knew when she needed to be alone.

"Eventually," he called out over his shoulder, his deep voice resonating down the hallway. "Eventually you'll say it."

The dangly bits from the chandelier above Xiomara's head quieted their clanging as if to further punctuate her predicament.

So, she took several days. And then she took several more. Each day, as Xiomara added to two separate lists, the knot in her stomach loosened ever so slightly. The first, her "creating comfort" list, detailed precisely what she needed from him in order to feel at ease. The second, her "reassurance and reward" list, was private.

At the end of each day, she texted him the latest addition to her creating comfort list, and he followed up with a question specifically designed to make her think harder about her needs and to be as specific as possible. "What will you be wearing, if anything? Should there be music playing or complete silence? How will you be positioned? Lights on or off?"

As she ruminated on each question, she reread her reassurance and reward list aloud privately, of course, giving herself the opportunity to practice. This helped forge new grooves in her brain, firing new pathways, and stoking a stimulating courage inside herself.

I don't have to fear the sound of my voice. And he will get off on it.
I am not defined by my fears. Maybe, this will be my new favorite kink.
I can confidently speak my desires aloud. And I will get off on it.

Such a small thing, really, but it made all the difference as she prepared for her most daunting task to date. In all their time together, they had never gone this long without having sex, so twenty days had been torturous for them both. Although Malik's sadistic taunting had motivated Xiomara to wait it out, she'd fully embraced the challenge. The amplified tension only served Xiomara all the better by working up her nerve.

Malik told her he'd memorized her list of comforts and sent her his final question. "Am I allowed to look at you while you tell me, or would you prefer I not?"

She answered within minutes. "You are, of course, allowed to look at me because…well…we both know you can't help yourself."

Her text was followed immediately by a buzz. "Come into the bedroom."

Xiomara heard his warm chuckle from the living room, and she smiled, blushing hard at the thought of him seeing her displayed on the bed like this. She was, after all, wrapped up quite prettily just for him. And he always had a hard time not staring when it came to pretty things. Whereas she had to keep her eyes squeezed shut so that her courage didn't abandon her. Because when he looked at her the way he sometimes did, all thought would cease. Keeping her eyes closed (in addition to laying on her belly so that she was less tempted to take a peek at him) definitely helped keep her from losing her nerve.

Malik didn't have to say anything. She felt his gaze, her skin goosebumping from the entitled invasion of his gaze. He took his time, tracing the back seams of her stockings with his finger, lingering where they met her garters. Patience wasn't his strong suit, but she knew he was aware of how excruciating this was for her and that he would do anything in his power to support her overcoming this hurdle.

"You can begin anytime you're ready. I'm enjoying my view quite thoroughly so no need to rush."

The sound of his voice and the feel of his energy cascading over her coaxed her to let go, liberating her from her internal editor and motivating her to do this for him, to do it for herself.

It wasn't the first time she had found herself facing incredible vulnerability in his presence. But there was a level of comfort between them that takes time to ease into, and she recognized this sensation in her body. Notably aroused, she was on edge, yet somehow also slightly relaxed. It was because of this level of comfort that Xiomara was able to start talking him through her fantasy.

Exhaling, with determination, she began. "I want…" *Deep breaths.* "…you to admire me." Her heart beat, pounding as steadily in her clit as it was in her chest. "I want…to feel…how much you need me." Battling the tension in her throat, Xiomara felt the perspiration beading up on the back of her neck.

"I want…to taste…your restraint."

As he listened to this fantasy coming to light, slowly dripping off her tongue, something began to stir in the air. "I'd intended to only take you with my eyes while you shared your story, but my hands are formulating plans of their own. After all, you didn't say touching was against the rules. But you want restraint, so I'll fight my nature and let you run the scene. May I touch you?"

"Yes…yes, please!" She couldn't get the words out fast enough.

He adjusted her lacy hemline, giving him full access to her ass. Then, he stopped suddenly. "One of your garters…" Malik sucked in a breath through his teeth. "…is slightly askew. Such a small thing, really…but it makes me want to hurt you."

Xiomara felt her entire body constrict. Her breathing slowed.

"I'll suppress this desire for now." Malik didn't rush into it. "No need to tear these stockings off of you like I did the last pair."

These stockings were special—brought back from their recent trip to Paris. They were silk, designer stockings, and she treasured their perfection, which made his urge to ruin them worse.

"No! I mean, yes! Please, please don't destroy them!" Xiomara scrambled for the right words. "You promised!"

Malik ran his fingers below the ribbonlike strap of her garter, pulling it away from her flesh, shifting it into place. He released it quickly, and it snapped against her thigh with a satisfying pop.

A little noise escaped her lips—Xiomara had been holding her breath and hadn't realized it.

"Stop being dramatic. We both know that didn't hurt. Furthermore, I never told you that you could stop with the storytelling."

"I'm sorry, Sir." Xiomara wasted no time—the apology flowed off her lips with ease—and continued where she'd left off, but her words trailed off quickly when Malik's hand began to travel down her leg, taking in the softness of the back of her fleshy thigh, the dip behind her knee, and the curve of her calf. Her skin felt as if it levitated to meet his touch, craving more. He knew her well and must easily have sensed her need, but that wasn't part of the game.

"You have to say it." He encouraged her gently.

Xiomara didn't want her shyness to take hold, so she flashed back to her reassurance and reward list. The confidence it gave her allowed her heavy tongue to form words. "I want more…more…your hands, I want them… heavy…going higher…ohh…more…"

He gave her more. Applying greater pressure, Malik gradually made his way back up as her storytelling became peppered uncontrollably with sighs and moans. When his movements slowed as he neared her inner thigh, her words synched with his pace. Words barely managed to trickle out between her sound effects.

Grabbing a considerable handful of flesh, he gripped tightly, claiming that section of Xiomara's inner thigh for himself. He seemed so lost in the revelry that he didn't appear to mind that her words had become a jumbled mess of vocalizations.

The surrender of his grasp reminded her of the task at hand, and she quickly corrected herself, so he didn't have to. "Tease me…" Each syllable was shaky on her tongue. Beads of sweat collected along her collarbone and dripped onto the mattress below. "Make me…need it." Xiomara spat her desires after each exhale. "Even more than you do…"

He snaked farther up, his fingers stopping just shy of her pussy, and pressed his knuckles adamantly into the spot where her inner thigh met her ass. Her hips rose involuntarily, meeting his resistance, giving back as good as she was getting.

Malik took the opportunity to finger the intricate design of her panties. Delicate bits of ribbon woven together in a way that left little to the imagination. His attention to detail afforded them both even more build-up time.

"I want you…naked…stroking your cock as you touch me…"

He was up, rustling out of his clothes, and then right back to teasing her before Xiomara could even miss him.

"I demanded this, and now you're calling the shots? What a dramatic switch in our dynamic!" She heard the excitement in his voice, tinged with a hint of dismay.

She felt the shift in the air and emboldened with a charge of energy, the lingering bits of hesitation in her voice fell away.

"Wrap your palm around your shaft and squeeze tightly while rubbing your thumb across the tip." Xiomara spread her legs wide, sticking her ass out for his enjoyment.

"Ohh…" It was Malik's turn to go nonverbal.

"Now…push my panties to the side…and use your other thumb to tease my pussy…and play with my juices. Mmm…just like that." Xiomara buried her groans into the pillow. Her movements became frantic. Soon, she could no longer help herself, slicking up the length of his thick thumb. Facing this fear of vocalizing her needs head-on, indulging in this particular vulnerability like never before had left her wetter than she'd ever been, even during some of their most intense scenes.

"More…give me more…I want you to fuck me with three fingers."

Malik obliged, adding his fingers to her greedy cunt. She was so open and sopping wet that they slid in, up to his knuckles, with ease.

Xiomara calmed her writhing long enough to give one final instruction. "Now, press yourself up against my inner thigh, hard. Ohh, fuck, yes…and drag the tip of your cock along my lips, get as close to my hole as you can."

He dipped into her wetness momentarily before starting anew with his fingers. Malik fucked her hard with his hand while jerking himself off with the other. She felt him behind her, spastic and clumsy, as they moved against each other at a furious pace.

There was no controlling their orgasms at that point and no telling who came first. Xiomara clenched down on his fingers. They both wailed incoherently, her desire seeming to drive him over the edge too, her own edge slipping into an abyss of moans and shudders and forgotten fears.

And in the grand scheme of things? Such a small thing, really.

END

KIKI DELOVELY *is a kinky, queer, witchy femme who moonlights as an erotica writer when she's not helping others through energetic healing or spiritual coaching. She strives toward erotica that reads as fine literature, makes you think, assists in folks connecting with their highest selves, and makes the world a more open-minded and sex-positive place.*

200.00
Chat

Confession

author: Emma Chaton
category: Religon

subjects: 1. Forbidden 2. Intense Shame
3. Demand Penance

Rose Caraway's Library of Erotica

*C*onfession

Emma Chaton

Raised in the Church, you've always had some kind of religion in the background, from catechism to Sunday mass to the high holidays. The ritual, the music, the chants, they've always been there in some form. It's a more complicated relationship now, as an adult, between you and the Church. The normal everyday trappings of life, work, and more…it just all gets in the way. Like most other professors of the faith, you're not exactly very good at being Catholic. But you try, despite whatever mortal failings you might have.

One of those mortal failings, of course, is your sexuality. In many ways, being a woman creates no shortage of attention—the look that lingers a little too long in your direction, the momentary dart of eyes from your breasts to your face, the distracted silence in a conversation when you walk by. Sometimes, it's an annoyance. Other times, attraction works its charms and you give into temptation.

The dance can be anything from a nice dinner with expensive red wine, leading to somebody's bed and a quick, dirty fuck in a bathroom stall because you just need to be filled. Men are predictable, and it's not difficult to read their intentions from the moment they introduce themselves.

Men of the cloth, on the other hand, are also predictable, just in a different way. They tend to be asexual, a bit out of reach in terms of age and social position. Like a quiet, funny uncle who remains the eternal bachelor, ready to crack an awful joke on cue. No one thinks of a priest as a matter of physical compulsion, not without some feeling of guilt. And you certainly never had a reason to think of any in that fashion. Not from the time of your youthful indiscretions to your current ones, in your bedroom, with or without a man. But times change.

You don't remember exactly when you started coming back to confession, but you do know why. Father Martin strikes an imposing form in black with the white Roman collar. His broad shoulders fill out his clerical wear and complement his farmer-tanned skin. At the end of the day, a shadow of facial hair fills in along his cheeks and chin, framing his mouth, which is somehow kind and authoritative at the same time. His eyebrows and hair are a soft black, tousled, and perhaps a bit unkempt, which is not surprising given a priest's lack of vanity. And when he looks at you with his deep, dark-brown eyes, you can't help but feel undone like he's looking past you.

You would describe his gaze as intense, but there's more to it. The way he walks with deliberateness, the certainty with which he carries himself. Even the casual banter you overhear between him and parishioners. If Father Martin were any other man, you would have acted on your instinct by now. Brushing his hand, you'd have given him your phone number. But you can't do that.

He is forbidden. And maybe that's what drives you toward him. Lying in bed, after the first time you rubbed your clit as you fantasized about him inside you, you felt a combination of incredible release and intense shame. *I shouldn't be doing this*, you thought. But the feeling was so powerful that it was hard to let go, and you wanted to feel it again. And so you reached for your vibe. And the more you thought about him, the more you realized the idea of him wasn't going to be enough.

Complicated relationships lead to complicated feelings.

The only way to guarantee being in his presence alone was in confession, a small quiet closeted room. You couldn't have him physically, but perhaps you could find a way to inspire your own arousal. Besides, in your experience, there's nothing hotter than making a man uncomfortable, especially when he can't do anything about it. So, a sexual tease it was.

At your first confession, getting on your knees in front of him was hard to do. You came to be forgiven, not to look eager. Telling him of a recent affair, while thinking of him in your bed, was intoxicating. You certainly enjoyed it, but Father Martin seemed…bored? With a blessing and a demand for penance, he waived you on.

Your next confession was just as perfunctory. And the third came with a tired warning that perhaps you should become more serious about finding someone.

Father Martin was unmoved.

This made you angry and challenged. Fingering yourself to another orgasm with him on your mind, you resolved to make it more difficult for him to dismiss you. You wanted him to think of you in the way you thought of him. Uncontrolled, aching, wanting to get fucked senseless. Not stoic, silently judging.

What made it all the more difficult was that you simply couldn't walk in there and lie. As ridiculous as it sounded, you needed to confess, and lying about it was committing a sin, to a priest no less. You couldn't go through with it. This whole fantasy struck you on more than one occasion as insane. But you were determined to experience every sexually deviant act and seducing a priest topped your list. A man here. Two there. A woman. Swallowing a stranger's cock here. Taking your boss's cock in your ass. You needed to fuck, to come. To sin. And you needed to confess to attract your Father Martin.

Complicated relationships lead to complicated feelings.

So the lips got a bit moister with gloss. Your bra got a size too small, showing more than a hint of bosom. The skirts of your dresses got a little higher. And each confession got wilder. And like with every other man, you began to wear him down.

A man trying to hide his attraction still gives up subtle hints. A deep breath as you describe the taste of semen hitting your tongue. Shifting of the legs over another when you disclose having one man fuck you deep from behind while face deep in your ex-boyfriend's ex-girlfriend. Fingers fidgeting on the chair as you reveal that despite your efforts, you couldn't resist the temptation of getting sodomized while having your hair pulled, especially when someone was watching. And the bulge you're certain you saw grow against his thin black pants.

You almost began to feel sorry for Father Martin as you confessed about the hot splash of cum on your stomach last Thursday night. The more details you provide of your latest cock, and how it felt inside you, the quieter the room gets, and the more imposing his silence, and his penance offered. Watching his discomfort, you're dripping before you get off your knees, and by the time you get to your car, you have to rub yourself to orgasm before you can drive off.

Soft sweater, pink wet lip gloss, a blouse with one button accidentally left undone, and a skirt completely inappropriate for doing anything but getting on your knees. On a whim, you decide not to wear panties, and the thought of that alone—having your slit uncovered nearby a man you can't have—makes you wet before you even enter the confessional room.

Locking the door in usual fashion, you walk in front of him, dipping your hips side to side, ready to perch on your knees, when you suddenly hear him with great force say, "Stop."

The single word jerks you out of your joyful routine, shocked by the power of his voice.

Father Martin is clearly angry, a storm in black judging you from a few feet away. As he narrows his eyes on you, you start to tremble. Whatever you've done, you've stirred something dark in him.

He leaps to his feet and stands in front of you, inches away. You can't meet his eyes, because every time you do, you see the accusation in them. Slowly, he steps around you, and for the first time in this confessional, you feel truly powerless. Your tease is over. Walking in here to regale Father Martin with your latest sexual escapades is never going to happen again. And the ache you felt is no longer anywhere near your still soaked pussy but has moved to your chest, to your heart. Whatever lust you had is overcome by guilt.

He's slowly circling you as the lions did the Christians in the Colosseum, ready to pounce and devour. Minutes pass before he speaks. His voice is a low growl in your ear from behind. His hot breath whispers authoritatively, "I will hear your confession now." In his words, you hear his lust, his torment.

You suddenly and sincerely regret what you've been doing, and desperately hope for his forgiveness. You're about to begin your mea culpa to Father Martin, but before you can say anything, he instructs, "Face the wall, and put your hands against it."

You swallow, looking away, unable to meet his eyes before you half-heartedly comply. Eyes downward, you stare at the wall and you obey your priest.

As you place your hands against the wall, that great force returns. "Higher."

In fear, you raise your hands a little more.

Angrily, Father Martin kicks your feet apart and forcefully lifts your arms above your head, pinning them against the wall. "Did you hear me," he whispers once more, rasping, "I said, 'higher.'"

And there you are, standing prostrate and vulnerable in front of an angry man of God, helpless, hoping beyond hope that your skirt covers your bare, goose-pimpled ass. Your entire body starts to quake against the wall as you try to still yourself.

"Tell me why you are here," Father Martin's angry growl inquires.

You pause, breathing in. "I wanted to confess."

Father Martin comes behind you, his arm sliding in front of your belly. His hot breath is on your neck, and *my God* his hardened cock presses against your ass. He whispers, "Confession requires true remorse for what you have done. True remorse is required for forgiveness. Are you truly remorseful for the sins you committed?"

Without hesitation, you lie for the first time in confession. "Yes, I'm truly remorseful."

He lifts your skirt, and you gasp in shame, start to turn around. Father Martin grabs you by the arms and prevents you from turning, pushing you hard against the wall again, pins your hands above your head once more. "I didn't say you could move." The growl returns. "You have the nerve to walk in here, demand forgiveness from me, and yet you don't have the decency to cover yourself?"

Shame echoes with his words, and your eyes search upward for salvation, but none comes. His grip tightens around your wrists, his firm, olive-skinned hand holding you. Your body shakes with embarrassment, and you tear up from the hot guilt, not sure how to extricate yourself from a justifiably angry priest.

And then you feel it. Jerked back into reality, your eyes fix on the wall and you try to catch your breath. It's unmistakable. His cock is positioned between your ass cheeks. Comfortably. Unbearably warm. Hardened without weakness.

And then, you realize the uncomfortable truths of this room. You were never in control here. The cock you've been teasing, it's hungry for you. But it is forbidden, you can't have it. Yet, you crave it. More than any other dick you've ever had, or wanted, or imagined. You want this man, this man of the cloth. You're ashamed, wanting what you can't have. You'll do anything for it, to feel it inside you all the way in. For the first time, in quite some time, you feel humble.

Closer, meaner, Father Martin growls, "I will hear your confession now. Tell me why you are here."

There's only one truth here to acknowledge, one confession to be said. You lift your eyes upward once more, and whisper, "I want you to fuck me."

"I'm sorry, why are you here?" Father Martin demands once more. "Say it."

And you confess, louder, "I want you to fuck me."

The hardened dick pulls away from your ass cheeks and slides toward your cunt lips. You cry out softly as his cock pushes inside you. You squirm, eyes wide open as you feel his balls press against you. His hands grip your shoulders.

"Again, why are you here?" Father Martin commands.

This time, more forcefully, you have no choice but to confess as you feel him slide in and out of you, your hands still raised against the wall, bracing for the hardest fuck you've ever received.

"I want you to fuck me, Father Martin."

Whether it was the constant teasing over the last several months or the pressure of celibacy as a man in the prime of his life, Father Martin pounds into you in a way no man ever has before. With every thrust, powerful and fast, your body shakes. He holds your hips, thrashing into your pussy again and again, while you scrape your fingernails against the walls. It doesn't take you long to come. As your breasts are forced loose from your bra, you stifle your cries and bite your lower lip. Your cheek pressed hard against the wall as you come.

Your priest fills you, deeper and deeper, again and again. And when it's time, he pulls out, turns you around, pushes you down, onto your knees. You take him into your mouth, swallow everything that pours out of him.

You look upward and briefly catch his stern eyes watching his dick at it disappears into your mouth, again and again as he finishes.

Father Martin dresses and returns to his chair. He watches you as you

Confession

straighten your clothes and smooth out your hair, then he waives his hand for you to kneel in front of him.

Father Martin formally asks, "Are you truly remorseful for what you have done?"

You slowly nod, truthfully, meeting his eyes for the first time since you swallowed his cum.

"Good. In the Name of the Father, the Son, and the Holy Spirit," he says, blessing you. "Go forth from this place and sin no more." And with that, you are dismissed.

You stand and turn toward the door. From behind, you hear, "I expect to see you in confession weekly." You can tell this isn't an expectation; it's an order. Closing the door behind you, and making your way out of the Church, you lick the taste of Father Martin from your lips, realizing, there's a whole lot more you can't wait to confess.

END

EMMA CHATON *is pure and innocent, and a role model for those around her. When not reading, writing, or teaching, she is a terrible oil painter and an even worse baker. She greatly enjoys entertaining thoughts that she's not supposed to have or allowed to have.*

613.2
Clif

My Tantric Surprise

author: M.P. Clifton

category: Promotion of Sexual Health

subjects: 1. Massage Parlor   2. Full-Service
3. Sexual Curiosity

Rose Caraway's Library of Erotica

My Tantric Surprise

M.P. Clifton

When you've been married for nearly three decades, intimate surprises are rare. But when one does come along, it can be wickedly satisfying.

All the preparation, presentation, and cleanup after a week of holiday entertaining of family and friends were behind us. The only thing left to do this quiet Saturday afternoon, in the now empty house, was to relax in bed.

Though we shared an unspoken expectation of intimacy, my husband, Alex, could not have guessed in a million years what was coming his way. As we had done increasingly of late, I asked him to read erotica to me to set the mood. While we enjoy adult videos, this mellow day called for something subtle to complement the tranquil pace we sought.

Alex grabbed his tablet and scoured one of several online sites offering erotica submitted by writers from around the globe. The first story was too short. The second didn't quite set the right tone, but the third showed real promise. It chronicled an adventurous couple's first visit to a massage parlor where they had booked two female masseuses for a full-service session. The writer described the scene vividly, painting tantalizing visuals of those involved. Then, they heightened the anticipation before successfully depicting the orgasmic conclusion.

I could easily see the story's effect on Alex who hardened as he read the descriptions of the nude women. He throbbed when the wife climaxed with the help of both masseuses.

Since his hands had not touched me, Alex was unaware of my reaction until I flashed an impish grin and said, "I'd consider something like that."

"You would?" he stammered.

The stunned look on Alex's face was priceless. It seemed he was trying to determine what to say in response to my admission of allure about something he'd probably never imagined would actually happen.

"Well, it did make me wet," I purred.

"Really?" Alex asked. He slipped his hand inside my underpants as if to confirm what I'd told him. A sly smile brightened his face, and he looked ready to come right then.

Truth be told, over the years, our lovemaking had expanded to include honest expressions of fantasy. With my encouragement, Alex would talk about another woman in bed with us. At first, the women he mentioned were purely fictitious or were one of the adult-film actresses we had watched perform.

But more recently, he'd described someone known to us—one of my coworkers, a neighbor, or a mutual acquaintance. Alex told me repeatedly that his fantasies were not about wanting sex with another woman. Rather, they were about him watching another woman ravish me. Alex described the scenarios in great detail as he caressed, kissed, and pleasured me with his body, his hands, and, most deliciously, his tongue. His visualizations were intensely stimulating, especially when they involved someone we both found very attractive.

Sometimes, Alex ran his glistening, wet fingers across our joined lips as we kissed and asked, "Would you rather have a woman go down on you, or would you want to go down on her?"

Although there are instances when the idea of tasting another woman intrigues me, I usually told him I wanted to receive.

After bringing me to orgasm with his tongue, Alex often explored my mouth and whispered, "Taste good?"

I'd just smile, though I became increasingly enthusiastic about Alex's sapphic suggestions.

When we watched porn in bed, our hands roamed beneath the covers. I usually got aroused faster if the scene involved two women or a threesome in which the women pleasure each other as well as a man. My confession of this often drove us to ecstasy of the most wonderful kind.

Today, not wanting to waste the arousal of the moment, I asked, "Think you could find any videos of a Tantric massage?"

He quickly navigated to a video-streaming website and located a video of a woman giving another woman an erotic massage. Unlike other porn, this clip had minimal dialogue, soft music, and high-quality production values. The masseuse wore a loose-fitting, armless t-shirt that offered glimpses of her swaying breasts as she delivered multiple orgasms to her naked customer during the thirty-minute scene.

After listening to the story Alex had read and watching the video, I needed immediate satisfaction. My hand rode atop his as he cupped my mound and stroked me slowly and teasingly.

When the video ended, Alex showed me the website of a voluptuous brunette in British Columbia who provides Tantric body massages to couples.

I laughed. "Guess we're going to Vancouver for our next holiday."

Alex countered, "We could look for someone closer."

"Okay."

Obviously, having expected a swift dismissal, Alex looked astonished at my casual agreement. He found the website of a place in the city that offered couples two masseuses who would work in tandem. While not inexpensive, the rates seemed reasonable. Since this facility was one of several located in major cities across the country, I felt reassured it was not just some shady storefront. Together, we viewed photographs of the rooms and staff. The goddesses, as they were called, looked pleasing.

More than once, Alex asked if I was really serious or just leading him on.

I admitted to nervousness. "But as long as the place isn't sleazy, it could be an interesting new experience." I no longer felt it necessary to hide my growing desire to explore my sexuality with another woman.

Alex correctly took my arousal as an invitation. Obviously excited by the prospect of our fantasy coming true, he rested the tablet on the nightstand as we made love with renewed passion. Our bodies intertwined while visions of multiple hands and tongues inflamed my imagination. We both came easily.

In the warm afterglow, I reaffirmed my sexual curiosity to Alex, and we agreed to pursue the possibility.

He called the place we'd found the following Monday and spoke to a representative. She assured him the facility was clean and safe and said the goddesses were reputable. All potential clients had to meet certain criteria before acceptance. The person also said while release was sometimes the natural result of a Tantric massage, they were not providing sexual services. In fact, the posted rates were considered donations and were all handled by someone other than the masseuses.

After Alex shared the details with me, I suggested we incorporate a ninety-minute session with two goddesses into a weekend stay in the city.

Alex could hardly contain his excitement. While I appeared to go about my life with my usual composure, more than a few times, I secretly fantasized about what awaited us and sometimes satisfied those urges in the shower.

Three weeks later, we checked in at the hotel, went for a leisurely lunch at a café near the park, and shopped at chic boutiques as we strolled the tree-lined boulevard. That evening, we enjoyed a delicious dinner in an exclusive, nouvelle cuisine restaurant on the east side, then stopped for a nightcap at a jazz club not far from the hotel. Even though we were horny and handsy when we returned to our room, we agreed that to heighten the experience of the session booked for the following morning, we would not have sex that night. Nervous anticipation made falling asleep a challenge for me. My dreams were vivid and stimulating.

After a light breakfast in the hotel café, we returned to our room and showered before taking a cab across town to the Golden Temple Spa. The unremarkable entrance was located in a non-descript, commercial building. The elevator to the fourth floor was spotless as was the temple lobby. A personable young woman welcomed us, confirmed our appointment, reviewed basic policies, and directed Alex to present the donation to the manager who joined us from an office behind the reception desk.

Though non-threatening, the man's chiseled physique and imposing presence made it clear he could easily handle any problem that might arise.

The subtle chime of a teak rod striking a small, brass bowl summoned the masseuses we had selected. Both looked like their photographs but wore less makeup. The robed women greeted us before leading us down a dimly lit hallway thick with the scents of jasmine and sandalwood. Asian flute music echoed overhead as we sat in a small anteroom where the masseuses discussed the services they were about to provide.

"Have you ever enjoyed a Tantric couple's massage?" Goddess Serenity, a tall woman with auburn hair, asked.

"No," I replied, my eyes dipping to the plunging neckline of her robe.

"Well," Goddess Serenity said, "it can be an intense experience. Our role is to guide you to a higher level of consciousness about your body and that of your partner. We will demonstrate sensual techniques that you can employ in the quiet of your home." She outlined what we should expect.

"Please follow us to a shower where you can refresh, and then we will begin," the young blonde goddess, Mitra, added in a soothing whisper.

We undressed, stepped into the sandals we found near a rack of thick towels, rinsed quickly in the shower, and wrapped ourselves in terrycloth robes before walking through a curtained doorway into the massage room. The modest space was a serene study in earth tones and gold and saffron, all softly illuminated, all very Zen.

The goddesses eased the robes from our bodies and helped us onto the tables that stood side by side, separated by barely enough space for the women to move between.

Alex and I smiled nervously at one another as we lay face down on the tables.

The seductive scent of sandalwood infused the room as Mitra draped a thin, batik-print cloth over me from shoulder to thigh. With her hair woven tight in a French twist, Goddess Serenity did the same to Alex.

My stomach fluttered as I realized that my erotic fantasy was about to become a reality.

The first twenty minutes were like other couple's massages Alex and I had enjoyed at the local day spa. Our leg muscles were oiled and soothed, our feet caressed, arms worked over, and necks relaxed. I was surprised and, yes, even a little disappointed that Mitra's hands did not venture anywhere near my ass.

More than once, sleep threatened to take me in its embrace. I silently told myself, *Gwen, there's no way in Hell you're going to sleep through this.*

"May we move to the next phase of your massage?" Mitra asked, almost inaudibly.

"Please," I replied, whispering.

The goddesses unfastened the cords coiled around their waists and stepped from their diaphanous gowns. Their naked bodies were fit and womanly, but not intimidating. I studied them. Mitra's long, blond hair cascaded over her pale shoulders. Serenity's hair remained up. Her body was tanned and toned. Their self-confidence was impressive.

"This phase," Serenity said, "will focus on the entire body. To do this, our contact will be more than just our hands. Is that acceptable?"

As instructed before the session, we answered every question they posed. Only then did the masseuses lift the sheer cloths from our bodies so we could turn onto our backs. Though Alex and I were lying there, fully exposed, I didn't feel vulnerable, just incredibly aroused. It was obvious Alex was beginning to feel the same way.

Switching positions with Mitra, Serenity started working my neck and shoulders. As she moved down my torso, she leaned close. Her breath warmed my skin. At times, her body brushed mine. Her naked breast was the first woman's body to touch my own. It was exhilarating.

I watched and welcomed her every move—every light stroke and every gentle caress. My nipples stiffened when Serenity's mocha-tipped ones grazed mine. More than once, she bowed low, her nipples only inches from my lips. I wanted them in my mouth. Instead, Serenity cupped my breasts gently and massaged them, spending time on my sensitive rosebuds.

I turned toward Alex and smiled as Mitra mirrored Serenity's every move on him. Oddly, I felt no jealousy, which both surprised and pleased me. I was free to concentrate on my own pleasure, knowing Alex was doing the same.

Serenity pampered my upper torso before moving toward my hips. Her freshly-oiled hands glided over my stomach and circled my navel several times. With each revolution, her fingers inched closer to my vulva. The sensation was maddening. Were I alone, I would have satisfied the urge myself.

"May I now begin your yoni massage?" Serenity asked.

"Yes," I said anxiously. Though no woman had ever touched me so intimately, I craved her caress.

Serenity stroked slowly and deliberately like she knew my body and its needs. My loins burned as her fingers slipped between my labia. Warm oil mixed with my wetness, and I ached with a desire that could be quenched only one way.

After Alex granted permission, Mitra commenced his lingam massage. Her oiled hands slid up and around his shaft, then cupped his testicles. Her pink-tipped breasts swayed and brushed his body. She smiled at Alex, me, and Serenity.

Alex turned to me and mouthed, "I love you."

I replied, "Love you too."

I had never felt closer to Alex than I did in that moment of anticipation, a moment we shared and wanted not only for ourselves but for each other as well.

Serenity inched me toward satisfaction. My oiled body felt weightless as though it could rise from the table to welcome her sensual touch. Although my clitoris throbbed, I felt no urgency for release. My body felt electric, and I wanted this heightened arousal to continue forever.

Serenity nodded to Mitra. In unison, they lowered their mouths onto our nipples. They teased us with their tongues, tracing the rims of our areolas. Having other women stimulate us at the same time was another first. The hot breath of the masseuse, bathing my body, only intensified my lust.

"Gwen," Serenity said, "may I culminate your yoni massage?"

"Yes," I replied breathlessly, desperate for the climax my body demanded.

In seconds, my hips rose to meet Serenity's fingers as they caressed my clitoris. She slid two fingers of her other hand deep into my hot, wet pussy where they found that sacred spot. I thrashed and moaned as an orgasm overtook me. My every cell was alive and pulsating. My body shuddered while I surrendered to the carnal pleasure delivered so magnificently. While the atmosphere in the room was tranquil, the excitement coursing through my body was beyond anything I had ever known. My fantasy of being with another woman had become a reality.

Serenity slowly eased me back to a delightful place of quiet repose. Her hands never left my perspiring, satisfied body. I opened my eyes and looked to Alex. His expression told me he had relished seeing me climax in response to Serenity's experienced touch.

Mitra had continued his lingam massage during my glorious, erotic journey. Her hands gripped and worked his erection, spinning around its swollen head until Alex began to thrust.

"May I complete your lingam massage?" Mitra whispered.

"Please," Alex begged, his body shuddering. His heart pounded visibly.

Mitra brought Alex to satisfaction with several deliberate strokes. Cum erupted from his rock-hard cock, glazing Mitra's fingers and dotting his oiled torso. Like Serenity had done for me, Mitra slowly brought Alex back from the dizzying heights of sexual gratification.

The two goddesses had done the near impossible, giving me and Alex orgasms far more exotic than anything we had enjoyed before. The entire experience had been not only intimate but also free of tension or embarrassment.

Mitra washed her hands at the small sink in the corner, then added new oil to her hands and ran them from the soles of Alex's feet to his scalp. Serenity did the same to me, reaching my head at the precise moment Mitra crested

Alex's.

Each masseuse brought her hands together as though in prayer and bowed. "Our journey is now complete. Please, feel free to shower. When you are ready, we will meet you in the anteroom. Namaste."

I was amazed at the wanton, raw hedonism the goddesses had so wonderfully guided us through. After several minutes of languid bliss, Alex helped me off the table, steadied me as I showered, and, then gently patted my body dry. We kissed deeply before rejoining the goddesses who embraced us warmly as we gave them the extra gratuity they clearly deserved.

After escorting us to the reception area, Serenity took my hand and with a playful glimmer in her smoky eyes said, "We hope you will return."

I smiled and answered immediately, "Oh, we will; and soon."

END

Writing erotica for over two decades, **M.P. CLIFTON** *loves to uncover the dark secrets of neighbors, friends, acquaintances, and coworkers who are often much kinkier than anyone suspects—or willingly admits. If it's taboo, you're likely to find it in one of M.P. Clifton's steamy stories.*

392.5
Byrn

Nights in Red Satin
author: Emily L. Byrne
category: Marital Maintenance

subjects: 1. Shoe Salesman   2. Lingerie Shop
3. Changing Room

Rose Caraway's Library of Erotica

Nights In Red Satin

Emily L. Byrne

Adela held up the teddy and frowned at her reflection in the mirror. This had to be her worst idea yet. Gleaming red satin with lace insets covered her forty-five-year-old body, outlining her every bulge and lump in shiny or see-through fabric. The lace trim concealed a few ills but not enough. What had she been thinking? This was never going to work.

She pivoted slowly, imagining what Joaquin would say when he saw her. Her gaze fell on the reflection of the shoes she'd gotten to go with the teddy. In the store, they'd looked sexy. The man who had sold them to her had said they made her legs look like the legs of a twenty-year-old.

Now, in her bedroom, she realized she'd been seduced by flattery and a handsome face. So seduced, in fact, that it had shocked her at the time. The shoe salesman at the mall had been unbelievably sexy. She had wanted to run her hands over his whole body, then follow her fingers with her mouth. When he'd bent forward to pull her battered, old shoe off and put the new, red one on, Adela had to restrain herself from running her foot up his thigh.

What had come over her today? Her hormones had galloped away with her, and she was in no mood to rein them in, not today. Not on their anniversary, their first with no kids at home. She wanted to be sexy and wanted Joaquin to want her, teddy and all. The shoe salesman at the mall had just been fantasy hors-d'oeuvres.

Despite herself, she had imagined exploring and tasting the man kneeling before her. She could almost feel him pressed against her naked body. The image had sent a hot flash of pure desire running through her, right there at the mall, surrounded by women shopping for bargains, piped in music and holiday decorations and everything.

It couldn't have been more inappropriate than that, could it? But her imagination had turned to an image of the salesman pulling off her stockings and slowly, carefully sucking on each of her toes. Adela pictured the man's warm, moist tongue caressing each toe, sucking and nibbling on it. She imagined all of her toes vanishing into his mouth at once and had caught herself gasping for air and squirming in her seat.

The salesman had given her a knowing glance, but she must have imagined the light stroke of his fingers on her calf that followed. She knew she'd imagined the way he seemed to slow down, his hands lingering on her feet and legs. She had gotten so hot, so hot and wet sitting there in that chair in the mall, her foot in the salesman's hand as those red, red heels were wedged on first one foot, then the other. He'd slowly, oh so slowly, laced them up, and she'd been afraid she might come right there.

In the end, she'd dropped the salesman's card into the trash outside; best to leave temptation behind her. But it was no wonder she'd come home with the shoes. Remembering it all later, she was surprised she hadn't humped them in the bathroom or on the bus on her way home.

And all that had happened before she'd even gone into the lingerie store. Well, she'd almost walked in but walked past it, looking sidelong at the window display. She'd gone to three other stores before finally going back and walking in.

Inside, there were bright, buzzing lights and soft-pop music and jewel-toned fabrics and chirpy, young women shopping. She pretended to be interested in bras and pantyhose, circling and sidling up to the racier lingerie section like she was hunting a timid woodland animal.

A dark-skinned saleswoman appeared—stern, motherly, and near her own age. All the fantasies about having her toes sucked vanished in a wave of shame.

Adela hung her head and mumbled, "Anniversary...sexy lingerie...that red thing on the mannequin."

It was excruciating, and she had been horribly embarrassed. Especially when the display turned out to be the last one in that color and size, and the saleswoman had to undress the mannequin. Adela pictured a giant sinkhole in the mall's floor, opening up and swallowing her before it got more embarrassing.

She'd slunk into the changing room behind the woman, imagining what the saleswoman must think of her. She slipped into the indicated room, nodded mutely at an offer of help, and undressed with hopelessness she'd thought she'd left behind in high school. What did she think she was doing anyway? Joaquin was a quiet guy. What if he didn't go for this kind of thing and just hadn't told her? Maybe this whole surprise thing wasn't a great idea.

She'd pulled the teddy on over her underwear and stared at her reflection in the mirror. If she thought she was depressed before, this was definitely worse. A frumpy, dumpy, and lumpy figure in red satin with lace trim gave her a tired stare back.

A sharp knock at the door made her jump. The saleswoman poked her head in, took one look at her and said, "Oh, honey. Not like that. Let me show you. Take off your bra first."

Adela could feel a blush heat her cheeks. Not that the woman was anything other than professional, but she was so together. So firm about expressing her opinion. Her hands felt nice, too, as she unfastened Adela's bra and pulled it off her shoulders. She pulled up the straps on the teddy, gently positioned Adela's breasts in the cups, then began lacing up the strings in the back.

After a few more tweaks, she'd met Adela's eyes in the mirror. "Better?"

Adela nodded, and there were more tweaks and pulls, each one firm and authoritative. She watched her body transforming in the mirror. The saleswoman reached for the bag with the shoes in it, after a brief glance at her as if asking for permission. She pulled out the red heels, and Adela saw they weren't the same shade of red as the teddy. But the woman had her stepping into them before she could dwell on that.

"My, oh my, don't you look a picture?" The saleswoman murmured in Adela's ear, tugging between her legs to pull the lace down on her thighs.

For one crazy moment, Adela had imagined it going farther. She pictured the woman using her bra to fasten her hands to the coat hook, spreading Adela's legs wide with her thigh. The fingers adjusting the lace around her cleavage could slide down, pinching her nipples into pebbles beneath the satin. Then, they could move down her body to her ass and give it a playful, experimental slap. Maybe something a little harder when she bit back a moan.

Adela had closed her eyes, almost feeling the other woman's fingers between her legs, testing and probing their way into her wet slit. She wondered if she'd have to be gagged to not alarm the other customers. The unexpected idea had excited her, and she imagined the clean handkerchief from the woman's pristine blazer stuffed into her mouth as she sucked her own juices from those long fingers.

The saleswoman's voice had cut through her fantasies like a knife, and she'd opened her eyes and shook her head with a start. The saleswoman had vanished, and the door closed with a click behind her. Adela had taken a deep breath and piled her hair up on her head, trying to decide if it looked sexier that way.

The woman had unlaced the teddy before she'd left, and Adela cupped her breasts through the satin for a moment. The lace covered a mole she was self-conscious about as well as a couple of wrinkles and was soft enough that it was a caress against her bare skin. She liked the symmetry of the lace trim and the lacings up the back and on her shoes, even if it did make her feel self-conscious.

Pulling it all together for Joaquin would require a bit of finesse, and she needed to get home and get dinner made before he arrived.

Despite the ache between her legs, she'd made herself slip off the teddy and unlace the shoes. She hadn't looked in the mirror again until she was back in street clothes and almost ready to leave. A light touch of lipstick and a comb through her hair made her as ready to face the outside world as she could be.

Armed with her charge card, her bag of shoes, and the teddy, she gave the saleswoman a tremulous smile and said, "I'll take it."

Home was the two-bedroom apartment she shared with Joaquin. He wasn't back from work yet, but dinner was nearly done. But now, the mundane walls of their tiny kitchen made the mall seem so far away, the red lace and satin like they belonged to another world, another Adela.

Now that she had time to think about it, she was embarrassed by her fantasies. What kind of hormonal mess was she to be thinking about sex and bondage and toe sucking with complete strangers, one of them another woman? That had been some wild stuff, like nothing she'd ever felt before. Or at least nothing she'd ever admitted to feeling before.

But even as she had that thought, she knew it wasn't completely true. She'd been looking for something new, something different. That was what had sent her to the mall, armed with her newly-paid-off credit card. She'd wanted to surprise, no, startle Joaquin. Wanted him to see the woman he'd spent the last fifteen years with like a wild sex goddess ready to take him by storm.

Adela's pussy throbbed at the thought, and she gave the clock a quick glance. She had just enough time to clean up, get dressed, and get everything prepped before he came home, assuming his asshole manager didn't make him work late again. She imagined going down to the tire shop and demanding that her husband come home with her right now, cowing the manager into cooperation with the power of her new-found sexiness.

She laughed and turned the stove off before she headed for the shower. It was going to be a fast one, no time for fantasies or touching herself. No time at all. Her hand wandered between her legs. Everything ached so desperately. It would just take a minute, and then she could still…but no, she had planned a special evening for the two of them. And she wanted Joaquin, dammit, not a bunch of strangers who happened to touch her at the mall.

She was out of the shower, dried, and in the bedroom in ten minutes. Then, she faced agonizing choices—wear the teddy under her clothes or change into it after dinner? Maybe she should meet him at the door wearing it and the heels. But then, what about dinner?

Adela rolled her eyes at her reflection in the old dresser mirror, pulling herself back into the present. She was too old for this crap and this uncertainty. She pulled her best dress out of their shared closet and dropped it on the bed before she tugged on the teddy. Lacing it up by herself took some doing, but she managed it. Not as well as the saleswoman had, but it would have to do. If all went well, it wouldn't stay laced for long.

She ran her hands over the satin and rearranged the lace. It had a lovely swirled pattern that set off her brown skin nicely. She imagined that she looked like an antique jewel, all dark gold and red, especially once she dimmed the lights. The image made her smile as she finished getting dressed and fixing her hair. She smiled more once her makeup was done.

Nothing to do but sit for a few moments and wait. She perched on the edge of the bed, reveling in the satin and lace beneath her clothes. Her thoughts wandered back in time to the third time she and Joaquin had made love. They'd known more about the rhythm of each other's bodies by then, and the shyness and awkwardness of the first few times had been behind them. His hands, his tongue, and his dick had seemed to be everywhere at once, exploring and tasting and hunting for all her sensitive spots.

Now, her skin tingled, and she lost herself, remembering. She had discovered he liked having his balls cupped while she sucked on him, and he had figured out how to get his thumb positioned just right to get her to very nearly come.

He had pulled her on top of him, so she'd rode him while he rubbed his thumb in slow, then fast, circles. They'd moaned and gripped each other as she worked her pussy muscles to make him come, though he had tried to hold back for her. In the end, she'd come first, shuddering and shivering as she collapsed on him, still riding him, her hips moving like they had a mind of their own.

He'd come a few moments later, his back arching upward, his hands grasping her hard. The bed had smelled like sex, and it was the hottest thing Adela had ever breathed in. They'd rolled on the sheets, finding each other.

The sharp ping of a text yanked her from her thoughts. She grabbed her phone. He was on his way. She stared at the shoes, and the shoes stared back at her. No woman her age should be caught dead in those shoes. She didn't even know if she could walk in them. But that wasn't going to stop her.

With a tremulous breath, Adela stuck her feet in them and stood up, swaying unsteadily. She put one shoe up on the chair and laced it, then she did the other. They were like corsets for her feet, holding her in and holding her up. Her legs looked impossibly long in them, and she drew herself up straight, her hands going to her breasts, then sliding down over her hips. For an instant, she was the woman of her fantasies, open to possibilities and sexy with the weight of experience.

She faced her reflection in the mirror, the light of battle in her eyes. She would be fierce and fabulous. She and her lover deserved nothing less. Adela walked out of the bedroom with a strut, not a wobble, and she was there to greet Joaquin when he came home.

END

EMILY L. BYRNE *is the nom de plume of another lady. She spends her time thinking up extravagant disguises, wearing her sunglasses at night and fantasizing about being a spy. When not doing those things, she likes a really good cup of tea and some chocolate.*

```
813.8
Walk
```

Home for Good

author: Saskia Walker
category: Romance

subjects: 1. Bad-Boy Ways   2. Body First, Mind After
3. Unrelenting Thrusts

Rose Caraway's Library of Erotica

Home For Good

Saskia Walker

Ellie did a double take. For a moment, she thought she'd seen her ex, Jack Malone, sitting across from the cafe. Had she imagined it? It was entirely possible. She thought about Jack often enough, even though months had gone by since he'd last sat there, waiting for her to finish her shift at The Coffee Oasis.

It can't be him. She shook her head, chastising herself for her imagination but craned her neck just to be sure. People moved across her line of vision as they headed for the exit. It was almost closing time.

Inhaling sharply, she gripped the edge of the counter. It really was him.

Grabbing a cloth, she wiped the marble-topped serving area, determined not to give him the satisfaction of acknowledging him. Even so, she couldn't help taking a quick side-eye glance. She caught sight of the familiar stubble shadowing his jaw and his sand-colored hair brushing his collar. The breadth of his shoulders showed through his worn leather jacket. Jack Malone was right there, following her every move with possessive eyes. It made her pulse race.

He rose to his feet.

Ellie went hot and cold all over, panic setting in. If only he'd texted or called in advance to let her know he was back, it would have been okay.

It was the way he was sitting in the same place at the same time of the evening, waiting, as if the intervening months had never happened—as if the announcement he was going to work in Germany for a few months hadn't devastated her.

And now, he was on his way over.

People were filtering out. Pretty soon, she'd have to lock up, and they'd be alone.

"Hi, Ellie. Got a smile for an old buddy?"

"No." She shrugged. "It's been seven fuckin' months, Jack. Not a word, not a call. Not even a text."

"Four months, surely?" His eyes twinkled.

"Six months and ten days." As soon as she said it, she regretted it.

A smile spread across his face, and the sight of it poured heat through her like warm molasses.

He huffed a laugh. "You always were pedantic."

"Organized, maybe. Was it a problem?"

"No. I like it. You always let me know where I'm at."

"Yeah, well, right now you're here and bothering me while I'm trying to wrap up my shift."

"You used to enjoy it when I called by and waited for you."

"That was a long time ago." Rattled, she lifted her hands, trying desperately to look nonchalant. Why? Because he was acting as if she'd just fall on her back for him. "You do this, walk in here like the prodigal son returned, expecting me to greet you with open arms. I told you I wasn't going to keep getting on and off this crazy ride. Why are you even here?"

Without hesitation, he walked to the end of the counter, stepped behind it, and was up against her in three strides. He held her around the wrist, stroking the soft skin on her forearm with his thumb, forcing her to drop the cloth she held. "I know I've been a waster, but I'm back in London because I've changed, and it's because of you, Ellie."

The seductive grasp of his hand made her heart trip. It was a simple action, but it hinted at so much more—his intensity, his masculinity, and his self-control. Electrified by his touch, she stared down at his hand on hers. Tension built, and yet her legs felt weak under her. No way was she going to do this, she told herself, but she ached for him, and the touch of his hand sent her into overdrive, her will to resist vanishing. Desperate to maintain her dignity, she shook her head. "A drive-by shag for old time's sake? No way."

"I want you," he whispered. "I've come home to be with you, Ellie. You and nothing else brought me back here."

Floored by the weight of his remark, her pulse missed a beat. Could it be true?

Secretly thrilled but determined not to flatter him, she flashed her eyes. "How do you know I'm not in a relationship?"

"Because you would've said right away. You wouldn't have let me come around here behind the counter and touch you like this."

Her heart hammered in her chest. Unable to answer, she attempted to pull away. He responded by arresting both wrists, drawing her in against him. It knocked the breath out of her lungs. She'd always loved his demanding nature and his arrogant, bad-boy ways, but she needed to hold her chin up and deny his power. "Don't assume anything."

He ducked his head and brushed his mouth over hers.

It was the briefest, most tantalizing of kisses. But it made her moan for more.

Drawing back, he grinned. "Your body always lets me know how much you want me, even when your sexy mouth denies it."

His voice, deep and husky, was another trigger on her libido, affecting her in dangerous ways. And what he'd said was so true. Why was he always right? *Because I love him, and he knows it.* She wilted against his shoulder, seeking his closeness and the familiarity of his worn leather jacket and his favorite cologne.

How long could she hold back? Not long.

He kissed her properly then, and it was deep, slow, and hungry.

How could she not adore that? She did love him. That would never change, even though he annoyed the hell out of her.

He pulled her inside the storage area, away from the windows and curious looks from passers-by.

"I need to lock up."

"It'll wait. The closed sign is up. We need to talk." He pulled her t-shirt up and over her head.

"This doesn't feel like talking. This feels like sex."

"We always talked this way. Bodies first, minds after. It's our ritual."

When he went for the clasp on her bra, she halted him. "Things aren't what they used to be, Jack. I've got a scar there now."

If anything would scare him off, that would.

"A lot of things aren't what they used to be," he responded, "but the important things are. You and me."

The look in his eyes touched her deeply. He was serious, and he wasn't turning away. Everything that had been good between them leaped to the forefront of her mind. Even while she denied it was happening, heat pooled between her thighs. "Jack…"

He locked her in against the wall, and the nearby shelves rattled. Something dropped to the floor. She swayed unsteadily, but he held her hips, keeping her still, taking charge. He rocked his hips from side to side, and she had to bite her lip when she felt just how hard he was.

Ducking his head, he kissed her under the jaw. The sensation of his mouth there tantalized her, the brush of his lips so brief, yet so suggestive. He breathed along her skin, then slipped his hands under the hem of her uniform skirt.

She moaned aloud. So much for keeping him guessing. She never could hide her reactions from Jack. She caught his smile just as he tugged her skirt up, exposing her panties.

She fought the urge to beg. "I need commitment as well as hot sex," she declared, eyeballing him as fiercely as she could.

He responded by pushing his hand down the front of her panties. "You do." He stroked one finger into her groove. "You're very wet. Seems like my presence here might be fortuitous."

"I hate you," she hissed.

Laughing, he shoved her panties down.

She felt the flimsy barrier drop around her ankles, and she shuffled her high heels to kick the panties out of the way.

"Hate me?" He nudged one knuckle right against her clit, rocking it back and forth. "Surely not?"

Pangs of pleasure shot from the point of contact, suffusing her groin. "Oh, please, stop teasing me!"

"You want this instead?" He shifted direction, plunged one finger deep inside her while his thumb manipulated her clit. "Or maybe like this?" He pulled out and stroked his slick finger over her clit.

Pleasure swept through her groin, the need for more needling at her, keeping her on edge.

"What is it you want most of all?"

"You, inside me." Her hips rocked, her climax closing.

"That's good because that's exactly what's going to happen next."

Her core clenched, anticipation edging her closer still.

His finger moved faster. He was touching her with self-control, with complete knowledge of what she liked, and she was enslaved to it.

She peaked, gasping for breath, her fingers locked on his shoulders. It was fast, and it shocked her. Tears blurred her vision, emotion and desire tying her in knots.

The sound of his zipper reached her. She was gone on her climax, but Jack brought her back to him fast, lifting her, shifting her to the nearby shelves and wedging her there before slipping inside her.

"Oh, God, yes!" The feel of his cock filling her made her emotions soar.

"I've longed for this," he murmured, when he was wedged deep, "longed for you every moment I've been away." Possessive hands outlined her hips, holding her tightly.

"You say that, but do you really mean it?" She blurted her question out.

Cursing, he locked his hands around her bottom, claiming her in deep, unrelenting thrusts.

The shelves rattled and quaked, canisters and stacks of napkins falling to the floor.

"Oh!" She was totally locked onto each thrust. Another climax was already looming, and when he moved faster—lifting her onto him—she panted aloud. Her core spasmed just as his cock arched and jerked over and over. She felt his hand at the base of her spine, and she wilted over his shoulder, her breath rasping.

"Round one?" His eyebrows lifted, and his eyes twinkled. Renewed lust seemed to ooze from his every pore.

Ellie tried to level her head, which was hard because she was dizzy and high. "Is this another crazy fly-by? I need to know."

"No," he insisted.

She shook her head, unable to believe him.

"Let me see you," he whispered, his hand going for her bra again.

"You didn't listen. I have a scar. I had to have a biopsy."

She thought he'd leap away, put off by what the result might have been. He looked her in the eye. "Let me take it off. I'll kiss your scar better."

She unlatched her bra, letting it fall away.

He ran his lips over the spot, giving her the gentlest of kisses.

"It was benign, but I have to keep watch. The situation could change."

Holding her gaze, he nodded. "I can help with that. I'm here to stay."

Was that a promise?

His gaze softened, and he stroked her lower lip with his thumb. "I love you, Ellie."

Her heart tripped.

The outside door chimed. Someone had entered the cafe.

Pulling her clothes back into place, she darted past him. Turning at the door, she looked at him. "I'll be right back, so hold that thought."

"Forever," he promised, nodding. "Like I said, I'm home for good."

END

SASKIA WALKER *mostly lives in her imagination, happily spinning yarns and telling tales. Her home is on the edge of the Yorkshire Moors, and when the wind is in the right direction, she swears she can hear Heathcliff out there at Wuthering Heights calling for his Cathy. Yes, she's a desperate romantic! Luckily fiction keeps her sane. Just about...*

```
708.0
Boek
```

Hard Art

author: Jaap Boekestein
category: Private Collections

subjects: 1. Antiques 2. Negotiation
3. Bids/Counter Bids 4. Lowballed

Rose Caraway's Library of Erotica

Hard Art

Jaap Boekestein

Unlock the front door. Open it. Get the groceries in. Get your bag in. Close the door. Lock the door. Home!
     Esther dropped the groceries in the tiny kitchen. *Later!*
It was only five o'clock, but it was November. The room was dark.
Click, the Art Deco vanity lamp of milk glass. *Click*, the mermaid lamp (a Tiffany) above the piano, and *click,* the bronze reading lamp (an Edgar Brandt, found at a flea market!). Her apartment wasn't a dark, empty place anymore. Now, there was light and beauty. Yes, it was a small apartment, but it was not crowded. Every piece of furniture, every painting, and every book had been selected with the greatest care. This was her own treasure cave, her own little place where she could relax. This was home. Esther took off her shoes and returned to the kitchen to make tea.
     Sorting her groceries, getting her tea ready, Esther thought about her plans for the evening. She had to review a student's paper about German Expressionism and early twentieth-century horror movies. She sighed. That could definitely wait a few days. *A light dinner and maybe some reading?* She didn't feel like reading tonight. *Watch a movie?* She still hadn't seen that one Garbo-movie she bought a few weeks back. *Maybe.*
     Tea, phone. With one swipe she killed the architecture picture (the Sagrada Família). *Any messages?* The usual stuff and a message from Hausmann's

Antiques! Her pulse quickened.

Click.

Hi Esther,
I think I have found something you will love. If not, I still would like your opinion.
If you're interested, I will see you sometime this week? You know where I am.
Regards,
Julius

Now, Esther knew what she would do tonight. She would fuck Hausmann, or maybe, he would fuck her. Anyway, there would be fucking.

Nowadays, Hausmann sold most of his antiques online, but he had a shop in the city center for those with money and time—the bored rich wives and the weekend antique hunters. It took Esther forty-five minutes to get there. The little street was cold, windy, and empty. Her coat was buttoned up all the way, but the cashmere didn't protect her legs. Like a dirty old man, the wind caressed her stockings with ice-cold fingers. She hurried over the uneven street cobbles. *Click-clack, click-clack.* The window of the shop was as dark as all the others, but Haussmann would be there; he practically lived in that shop.

Esther rang the doorbell, and after fifteen steady heartbeats, Hausmann buzzed her in (He had gotten careful after a robbery a few years back). With experienced ease, Esther maneuvered through the overstocked, almost dark shop. The antique dealer would be in the back.

Julius Hausmann was shaking hands with a stunning blonde, very Eva Marie Saint. "I'm sure you will enjoy this, and please come back if you need anything else."

Customer. Esther stepped aside when Hausmann walked his client to the exit. One blond woman, one slightly graying Cary Grant. A short moment of eye contact. "Good evening." The other woman didn't whisper, but her voice was like cigarette smoke in a George Hurrell photograph.

Esther nodded. "Good evening."

The blonde walked on and Esther waited. She didn't look back. She heard Hausmann turn on the light, unlock the door of the shop, say goodbye, then close the shop door.

Haussmann returned and smiled. "A late client. Maybe I'll introduce you?"

Esther didn't take the bait. "Good Evening, Julius. You texted that you have something special?"

"Do I! I think you will like this!"

The figurine was delicate. It was a young girl with a *putto* on her shoulder and another chubby angel at her feet. *The putta and the putti*, Esther thought. Hausmann would get it and would like it, but she was not going to give him the satisfaction. She didn't do dirty jokes. Only in her mind.

"French," she said. "Auguste Moreau. Is it signed?"

"At the base."

Carefully, she checked, but she already could tell it was an Auguste Moreau. Hausmann knew better than to try to unload a fake on her, but she checked anyway. *Always check.* "How much do you want for her?" Carefully, she put the figurine down. *It would be lovely in the corner near the window of the living room.*

"So, you're interested? You can have it for $1,500. And that's giving it away. These bronzes are really popular."

The negotiations had started. He would try to fuck her over, and she would try to fuck him over. Those were the unwritten rules. Esther started unbuttoning her coat. She deliberately waited with her bid until she had undone the very last button, and Hausmann could see what she was wearing under her coat. "$500."

He looked at her as though appraising a piece of art. The original twenties ivory, silk chemise, the laced, satin cami-knickers, the black garters (not red. That was no color for a lady), her stockings, and high heels (nothing authentic about those, but the effect was stunning, Esther knew).

"I like the pearls." It sounded like Hausmann had a dry throat. "$1,490." Of course, that was a ridiculous bid, but so was hers.

The negotiations would be long. That's how they both preferred it.

"Got them on eBay. Japanese." She played with them for a moment. They were smooth and made tiny clicking sounds. "Are we going to stand here all evening?"

"Oh, eh. No! Please!" He took her coat.

His momentary confusion was a sign she had made an impact. Maybe, she could get the Moreau cheaper than she'd thought.

He gestured to the part of the shop where he kept the bigger pieces and the furniture.

She walked in and took inventory. There was the Empire sofa they had used several times. The heavy French farmhouse table had gone. *Too bad. Good memories.* The Regency chair was still there, but it really was too fragile. In the corner, there was something new. *Yes!* "Here." Esther pointed at the large art nouveau mantle mirror. It had a lovely gilded wooden frame with cut out flowers and branches. In the top right corner, a dryad looked down. Not really Esther's style, but a beautiful piece nonetheless.

The mirror stood against the wall, and Esther could see herself from top to toe. Her image admired her. Esther put her hands on the wall, left and right of the mirror, and then spread her legs, leaning a bit forward. "$520."

"Ridiculous!" Hausmann put his hands on her legs, just under the black garters. Slowly, he moved his fingers upwards.

Warm, strong fingers. Garters, stockings, her skin, and thighs. She shivered and closed her eyes when his fingers moved upward again over satin and silk. He felt her up and ended with her breasts which he caressed through the lace and silk. He found her hardening nipples, but he didn't stop there like too many men would. Very gently, his fingers danced over her still-covered breasts, almost tickling them.

His body rested against hers. Subtle eau de cologne filled her nose. *Man.*

"$1,450," he whispered, against her ear. His face was a lot closer than she had realized.

She opened her eyes again and saw him in the mirror. An expression of dreamy concentration was on his face. This was the first time they had ever used a mirror. *Nice. Sexy.*

"Noooo." Esther sighed lazily, rubbing her ass against his groin. "$530."

In the mirror, his nostrils flared. Less gentle hands now. He pulled her knickers down and groped her flesh. He got down, and his lips, tongue, and teeth kissed, licked, and bit her ass. His hands moved upward again under her chemise. A new counter bid. Of course, she refused.

And down again his hands went. On his knees, he tasted her from behind, the tip of his tongue almost penetrating her, moving slowly in circles, stimulating her lips.

"Oh!" she cried

He continued—circling, circling—without mercy.

"$590!"

He stopped for a moment.

"$600! Oh, yes, please!"

His tongue still didn't move.

"Damnit, bastard! $610! Do it!"

He unlocked her with the tip of his tongue. His warm, wet flesh tasted her. Esther moved her feet a little farther apart.

His fingers massaged her thighs with the same slow rhythm of his mouth and tongue.

Bid, counter bid, bid. At this point, she had a disadvantage, and the price was running up fast, but Esther was patient. Her time would come. Oh God, her time would come.

She grunted. Julius Hausmann knew his stuff. His tongue flicked in and out of the hot wet spot between her legs. He nibbled her lips with his. Esther tried to suppress a shiver. It felt so good, but she couldn't let Julius know how good. *Like he doesn't taste how well he is doing.*

She whispered her bids now, trying to stretch the time between them as long as possible but not so long that Julius would actually stop. He countered her bids with higher numbers, diminishing the red-hot pleasure between her legs if her bids were too low.

Bastard, bastard, bastard. Go on!

He stroked her stockings as if he loved them. His hair got ruffled by her ass. Esther was sure he loved that too. *Well, that makes two of us.* There's was a purely physical, purely business arrangement. There was nothing between them except mutual lust. He used her lust against her, but Julius Hausmann didn't control her. Oh no, he did not. She knew what he wanted. She only had to bide her time and ride out his evil administrations.

Once, she had tried to compare his cunnilingus to the brush strokes of a master painter, or the notes written by one of the great composers. But those analogies just didn't work. What he—they—did was just too vulgar, too villainous (from the Latin root *villānus*, meaning a farm servant, a commoner). Sex wasn't art. Not delicate art anyway. It was wet and dirty, nasty and so fucking good. It was take and be taken. Wild brushstrokes, coarse images, pornographic sounds.

Esther ground her pelvis against the antique dealer's face, leaning as far back as she dared on her heels. "Deeper! Deeper!"

It cost her fifty, but he obliged.

His tongue reached that one spot and stayed right there. The tip of his tongue wriggling quickly.

"Oh, fuck yes!"

It cost her another fifty, but he continued, seemingly caught up as much by her lust as his greed.

No more brakes. Full throttle now. "Shhhhhttttt," she hissed, not cursing. Esther's fingers rested on the delicate carvings of the art nouveau mirror, but she didn't dare hold on to it, fearing pulling the antique from the wall. She staggered, only held up by Julius. The hot flood inside her exploded and drenched her, costing her yet another fifty. But it was fucking worth it. *Fucking worth it.*

With a wet grin, Julius Hausmann rose to his feet. He had given her pleasure and driven up her bids considerably. But now he wanted. He wanted.

Esther knew what he wanted. She looked in the mirror, blinking a little sweat from her eyes. Now it was her turn. She watched the antique dealer unzip his pants and take out his dick. He was not very thick, but he was pretty long. Long enough anyway.

Panting, Esther leaned forward, almost horizontal, offering herself. Her breasts dangling in the loose chemise. The flimsy fabric teased her sensitive nipples.

"$1,390," he suggested, entering her carefully from behind.

It was nice, the way she liked it.

He started moving as did she. Flesh against flesh, flesh in flesh, hot blood, hot bodies. A new round of bids and counter bids.

He worked her, she worked him. Sweat and moans. But now, she had the advantage. He wanted her, wanted her so bad. "I'm going to fuck that tight, wet pussy. Fuck you until you beg for mercy," he said.

He wanted to come, but he did not want to lose money. This, she knew.

He kept banging her, groping her, kissing her, and trying to please her until she surrendered.

It was not going to happen. Not with his dick. No matter what. All she had to do was to hold out while the price dropped and dropped. It wasn't easy, though. They had fucked many times before. He knew what she liked, and he used it. But so did she, and in this phase of the negotiations, his need was always bigger than hers.

He pulled her hair, grabbed her throat, and pushed deeper and deeper. There was no love in it. Absolutely none. But neither of them cared. Neither wanted love. This was business.

Julius pounded into her, losing more of his self-control with every thrust.

"I want to finish. I want to finish. I want to finish," his movements seemed to call out, like some old-fashioned steam train.

The sound of wet flesh. Grunts. From Julius. Oh, he wanted her.

Back and forth, rubbing, pushing, and stimulating a million nerve endings.

Esther blew a lost lock of hair from her eyes, her legs and arms shaking. She held on, directing Julius's energy. She'd had her pleasure. Now, it was her turn to subjugate him.

She lowballed him, dropping her bid, which got the reaction from Julius she was counting on. The antique dealer doubled his efforts behind her. Red-faced, squinting eyes, his mouth half open. Esther could see it all in the mirror.

He wanted to conquer her with his dick.

He never would.

He called out a bid, and she countered with a minuscule raise.

Julius cursed, pushing in and out of her.

Esther wriggled her ass, her mirror-self looking her in the eyes. Her hair was sweaty, her mouth open. It was not very stylish, but Esther didn't fucking care. Only two things mattered: getting the price down and keeping control of what was happening between her legs. *Concentrate! Fucking concentrate, bitch! Get. It. Down!*

The bids were coming together. More than a hundred difference, less now.

"$1,050!" Julius cried…almost there.

With all the power she could muster, Esther put her legs together, locking his penis inside her. Of course, he could get free, they were soaked, but he wouldn't come inside of her. Not if she didn't allow him to.

"$1,020," she said, panting.

"Oh, God! Fuck! Yes! It's a deal!"

Esther released the pressure. So did he. He came. She received.

His hot flood filled her. It was not the warm ecstasy of her own pleasure, not true pleasure, but it was satisfying in its own way. Esther's true joy came from her victory. *$1,020!* A whopping deal for an Auguste Moreau original!

Sweating and panting, they leaned against the mirror, his body against hers, his head resting on her shoulder. Their joint breath fogged the glass. For a handful of moments, they were just two people. No deals, nothing to be gained or lost. Two people, gasping for air, feeling each other's heat, moisture, and racing hearts.

"Julius," Esther said, after a while. She had made up her mind. Beauty was there to be enjoyed. "Can you get me in touch with that blonde woman, the one who was here earlier this evening?"

"I'm sure I can arrange something," Hausmann replied. Teasingly, he kissed her neck in an act of tenderness they both knew they would never really share. Tenderness was for lovers. "I will set up a meeting, for free. On the house."

"Thanks."

END

JAAP BOEKESTEIN *(1968) is an award-winning Dutch writer of science fiction, fantasy, horror, thrillers and whatever takes his fancy. He usually writes his stories in trains, coffeehouses and in the 16th century taverns of his native The Hague, the Netherlands. Over the years he has made his living as a bouncer, working for a detective agency and as an editor. Currently he works for the Dutch Ministry of Justice and Security.*

```
398.0
Jaku
```

The Mermaid's Necklace
author: Maxim Jakubowski
category: Folklore

subjects: 1. Shiny Scales 2. Tribute Paid
3. Master of the Fuck

Rose Caraway's Library of Erotica

The Mermaid's Necklace

Maxim Jakubowski

This is the sorry tale of how I lost the woman I loved to a merman and, later, lost my penis to the sea.

April and I were already on the second chapter of our lives, silently dreading the inevitable twilight and eager to enjoy the time we had left together, all too aware of the sundry mistakes we had both made repeatedly and varyingly in previous years. We were all too aware that time had already passed us by too rapidly and seemed now to accelerate perilously. Too many pages in the books of our lives had prematurely been turned, and we knew all too acutely that not many of our remaining moments could be wasted.

Her name was actually April Dawn.

And we had met in the month of April. In a bar, in a club, in a hotel that catered to the lonely. Or the damaged. Drifters coming together. Beggars who could no longer afford to be choosers. I was a widower, and she was a nude model who had turned forty, whose assets were no longer in sufficient demand.

Initially, we lived in a big city in the North, drunk on the lights and the noise, the culture, the food and the infinite choices, even though in the heart of night it was just the two of us, spooning in bed against each other, relishing the warmth, the closeness and, in my case, the delirious softness of her body, her curves, her touch and the caress of her voice in the dark when we invariably played the games of the flesh. Even though I increasingly had to rely on the magic of the small blue pills to waken the reality of my ardor. In my mind; however, I was always hard for her.

During the daytime, we worked, hard, but always arranged to speak on the phone a few times, never allowing the ties that bind to weaken, until we would meet up again in the evening and could swim anew in the tide of our contentment. All too easily, the months swept by, days and hours ticking away uncounted.

We were happy, in our quiet, unspectacular way, content with the banality of love and the sound of our own voices. We had few friends and, even then, we preferred our own company, so even those we made or had accumulated from our earlier lives began to drift away.

One morning in December, two weeks before Christmas, there was a thin layer of snow on the ground, and the car on the drive was peppered with frost.

It was the beginning of a weekend.

"Looks cold, feels cold," April said.

"Yes," I agreed. "Maybe we should take a break somewhere, a holiday. Go somewhere warm."

"Why not?"

We went online. Surfed. Read. Pondered. Places with exotic names, resorts with fancy descriptions, promising the earth on an all-inclusive budget. Some, we had been to separately before we had come together. Others, neither of us knew about or were attracted to for good reasons.

I'd gone to the kitchen, to get myself some lemonade and a cup of strong brew for her, leaving April exploring possibilities at the desktop screen.

I set down her coffee on a corner of the desk.

"What about a cruise?" April asked, looking up at me.

I had never even contemplated the idea. When I had been a teenager, we had lived in Paris, and every half term my parents would pack me off to London to spend time with my aunt. I had always hated the ferry crossing the Channel as I was invariably seasick, in some cases, rather violently and unforgettably. Disgustingly so.

I expressed my reservations.

"I just thought it sounded glamorous," she said.

We examined the various itineraries on offer and gradually succumbed to the idea. After all, there were a lot of stops on dry land along the way, in places that had once sounded like expensive mirages and were now within our financial reach. I could stock up on sea sickness pills. It wouldn't be the end of the world, even though that felt like our actual destination.

The ports were pleasant, the boat surprisingly steady like a city on water, and not a hint of nausea plagued me even as we swept across a choppy Bay of Biscay. My stock of pills would remain untouched for the whole thirty-three days of the journey.

We enjoyed the winter sun on the top observation deck, sitting in our deckchairs, reading from the ship's library, and sipping cold drinks which would have cost us less than half the price on land. As ever, we avoided the company of others. In that respect, we were not typical cruisers, a species I observed from close range with both disdain and a touch of horror. And there was nothing like coordinating my gentle thrusts when we made love to the rhythm of the boat effortlessly cutting across the waves, the minimal sway and movement of its massive bulk surging as if through butter, dividing resistance and almost attaining the majesty of flight. Not that I'd ever achieved a mile-high achievement! No woman had ever told me I might have been a superlative lover. But I was content to be average.

At one stage, we had seven days in a row between ports of call, moving invisibly along the wide, limitless sea.

At twilight on the forward deck, waiting for the call for dinner in the main restaurant, we gazed at the sea unfurling with no end in sight and blending with the horizon as the sun set.

"Isn't it just amazing, isn't it?" she said.

"Yes. So much water. And then you remember what a large proportion of the planet is just that—water. More than land. The mind boggles. And all that secret life underneath, too."

"Makes you think," she said.

"Yes."

"How insignificant we are in the scheme of things."

I nodded. There was both majesty and a quiet form of serenity to the moment.

I turned to April, looking into her grey eyes with their curious, evanescent speckles of green like miniature jewels sparkling in their depths at irregular intervals, depending on her moods.

Miles from civilization, from even the smallest of islands, heading for Polynesia, isolated, with plains of water in all directions, she was pensive, more so than I had ever seen her before.

"Makes you think, eh?"

"Yes," I agreed, again.

After our return from the lengthy cruise, we felt adrift for some time, and then, one day, she suggested we move from the big city and go live on a coast, nearer to the sea she now felt such a strong affinity for.

Already, it was calling out to her.

We argued, calculated, dithered, and finally took the jump.

It was a famous beach, a mile long, renowned for its surfers and spectacular waves, and we found a small apartment in the low hills behind it. April was adamant it should feature a balcony from which she could watch the sea in all its splendor over the roofs of the buildings, hotels, eateries, gift shops, and clubs on the promenade below.

It was there we began drifting apart.

I could work anywhere. Have laptop, can travel, but April was now idle and left to her thoughts. While I typed away, she would spend hours on the balcony gazing out at the changing colors of the ocean or would walk to the beach, sit herself down for hours, eyes fixed on the horizon, deep in contemplation. When I asked what was going through her mind on these lengthy occasions, she could never express herself to any degree of satisfaction, mumbling, stumbling on words, and then falling silent again.

Now, I know that it was the sea calling out to her, wrapping its insidious roots deep down inside her mind.

The tourist season faded away. As did the tourists and the surfers.

The silence between us grew deeper with every passing day. I was on a deadline. April spent increasing hours away from our apartment. Often, when I stepped over to the balcony for a breath of fresh air, I might see her in the distance toward the end of the beach, where the rocks rose, sitting motionless like a matchstick woman on the plain of sand with her back to me, seemingly entranced by the swell of the nearby waves and the ebb and flow of the water by her feet.

One day, as I watched her in the distance, I saw the elongated silhouette of a man emerge from the sea, ambling towards her. I became frozen to the spot. The man reached her, standing tall beside her, and the image froze as they remained fixed like statues. Squinting hard as I was, I was unable to make out his features, let alone what he was wearing. His image shrouded in eerie darkness, just a somber silhouette, his shadow fell on her lanky form, the warm, brown shades of her skin offset by the white of her skimpy bikini.

They were immobile for an eternity. In conversation, probably.

A call of nature stole me from the balcony. By the time I rushed back, the man was no longer at her side, and I saw April slowly walking down the beach on her way home. He was nowhere to be seen. Returned to the sea where he had come from?

"How was it?"

"It was good. The sea is always so beautiful." No mention of the man she had fallen into conversation with. Probably because it meant nothing, just an idle encounter not worth mentioning.

For the next four days, April returned to the same spot on the beach and, invariably, the man emerged from the sea at some point and joined her. He never sat. April never rose. What could they be talking about?

"Saw you chatting with someone. Anything interesting?"

"No." She looked me in the eyes, almost defiant in her response. "Just someone. Nothing of importance."

I bought a pair of binoculars at one of the gift shops on the promenade where they also sold giant, embroidered towels, swimwear, and surfing accessories.

I stood on the corner of the balcony, ashamed, furtively watching her in the distance. Lines of white on a sullen sea echoed the streaks of her bikini against her tanned skin.

A dark blur upon the breaking wall of waves and the man appeared as if from the very depths of the sea. I adjusted the focus. My heart seized. He was naked. My attention was inevitably drawn to his cock—thick, long, straight, dangling proudly between his massive thighs as he cut through the flow of the water lapping its way toward the edge of the beach. I swallowed hard next; the rest of his body was covered in shiny, dark scales. His ebony hair fell to his scaled shoulders, wet and dripping with salt.

He looked like a magnificent beast roused from the deep, both human and inhuman.

He reached April.

She stood.

I watched their lips through the lens of the binoculars, my breath tight and irregular, the cold metal cutting into my cheek. Neither of them spoke.

Do mermen even have a language or the capability of speech?

April unhooked her top which fell to the ground while the stranger tugged at her bottom and pulled it down to the sand.

I wanted to close my eyes, but I just couldn't.

I watched them make love.

I tried to feel detached but couldn't pull my eyes away. He was brutal, unrelenting, a master of the fuck. For a brief moment, I remembered the beach scene in *From Here to Eternity* with Burt Lancaster and Deborah Kerr. It was an incongruous thought, and what I was witnessing was in another dimension of sex altogether. Primal. Elemental. Savage.

How long their sandy union lasted, I have no clue about, but I had to eventually stop watching as every successive thrust was a further stab to my heart and gut. Somewhere inside me, I had always known April and I wouldn't last forever but would have never predicted it would happen this way.

Like a film you can't unremember, abominable images had been carved deep into the back screen of my brain. The porcelain white of her skin scraping relentlessly against the off-green texture of his scales; the massive girth of his erection, his cock a rainbow mix of azure colors, its glistening, darker tip digging into her slit, parting her labia with ferocity until it was swallowed whole.

I wanted to close my eyes but could not find the willpower to do so, entranced by the spectacle of their mating, imagining the noises of the sea, the lapping of the waves surrounding their rutting bodies. Witnessing the O of her mouth as he plowed into her, the V of her hard nipples as he played her body like an instrument. I came watching them.

That night, she did not return. Nor the following day.

I had already reached a resigned sense of acceptance. Then, on the morning of the third day since I had witnessed her in the arms of the merman, the key turned in the front door, and she walked in.

She wore a thin sundress, almost transparent against the rising light cavalcading through the window and the white cotton curtains. She was visibly nude underneath.

I looked at her.

She was flushed. There was a length of thick gauze plastered along the right side of her neck.

"What is that?" I asked.

"Nothing," she said.

"It's not," I replied. "Show me."

She did.

There was a raw, deep scarlet scar running along the ridge of her long neck. Between it, a new mouth, a dark maw that gaped open.

"What the fuck?"

"It's not what it seems," April stated.

"Did he do it?" I asked.

"No, he sent me to a doctor in the hills who was willing to perform the surgery."

I fell silent.

April then walked past me and made a beeline for the bedroom.

"You're leaving, aren't you?"

"Yes."

"Why come back at all?"

"I wanted my jewelry. That's all. You can give all my other stuff to charity. Any charity. It doesn't matter."

We didn't discuss what I had observed on the beach. As if she knew I had seen it all.

Later, once again on the balcony, holding the heavy military binoculars. Following from afar her deliberate path along the promenade, then down the stone steps to the beach and her steady progress toward the rocks, where the beach turned into the sea.

He emerged from the water. April shed her sundress and, wonderfully naked and free, took a step toward him. He opened his arms, took her by one hand and pulled her toward the harbor of the sea. Soon, the water was up to their knees, their waists, their necks until they were fully submerged. I caught a brief glimpse of their legs scissoring the waves, fluttering as they both swam under to reach his world. Where she could now live, now that her body had been surgically adjusted, and she could survive under the sea, the gills in her neck like a beautiful new cunt.

I began to cry.

I had no wish to return to the big city in the North, even though the beach resort now held painful memories. I met my deadlines, lived from day to day with a profound pain in my heart and sharp pangs of memory piercing the night sky as I tried unsuccessfully to reach the peace of sleep and dreams.

I now made a daily pilgrimage to the area close to the rocks where April had first met the merman and left with him. I hoped she was happy. But I missed her so much. Damn it I did! And wondered what life must now be like for her, how things functioned under the sea or on the exotic faraway islands where she and her merman and others of his kind maybe lived, took refuge.

Weeks passed, several months, maybe even more than a year, in a state of misery, half alive, submerged by sadness. I often got drunk at a shady tavern to the left of the rocks in the unfashionable part of town where you could be morose with no one making any objection and ignore the slumming crowds and remain seated in splendid isolation.

It was dawn. The sun just a speck rising in the east. The wind mild and caressing. I nursed a mild hangover. Sitting cross-legged in the humid sand. Watching the sea, eternal, steadfast, imperial.

I blinked. A shadow darted across a dying wave that crashed against the nearby shore.

Opened my eyes wide.

The apparition gained focus.

I blinked again. My throat tightened.

It was a woman. She was naked. Her heavy, dark-nippled breasts swaying gently in the muddy water. She had brown hair, falling wet to her shoulders. A strand of seaweed snaked between the valley of her breasts. Her eyes were emerald. Not April. She stopped. Looked across at me with a hint of a smile.

I waved at her, hoping I wasn't scaring her. An early morning swimmer who hadn't expected to find anyone around at such a premature time of day? She looked foreign, different.

She began to move forward in my direction, gliding with uncommon elegance through the incoming tide until the sea swayed sideways as her midriff appeared. She had no legs. A scaled mass of flesh. A mermaid.

She wriggled onto the shore and settled by my side.

She could speak.

I was entranced by her beauty. Her name was Liv Lisa.

It was love at first sight. At least for me.

For several weeks in a row, we would meet at the same spot on the deserted winter beach and talk endlessly. I would tell her about my life, the cities I had seen, the places I had been, the things I had done. She would, her voice imbued with all the dizzying softness of a musical instrument played by a virtuoso, talk to me of the islands, her folk, her legends, allowing my hands to stray across her body, the silk of her skin, the damp firmness of her regal breasts, the hypnotic texture of the scales covering the lower half of her body, her tail. I never even bothered to ask her about April or mermen. That was the past, and this was the present. And Liv Lisa was at its center.

Never had a woman, let alone a mermaid, taken my cock inside her mouth with such talent and devotion, the wetness of her tongue and its salty surroundings like a balm; the movements of her deft tongue like a snake of lust enveloping me in her grasp, her dance, her hunger. Never had my anus been fingered like a piano, the movements of her supple fingers in harmony with the travails of her busy mouth, orchestrating the rise of my engorged fluids through my balls and helpless cock like an experienced conductor who'd entranced every concertgoer in the world.

But, most of all, it was the picture of her face when she looked at me, sucked me, and played with me, that became unforgettable—a thing of beauty, both naive and wanton, childish and as old as the world at the same time, her deep blue eyes reflecting every shade of the sea and the eternal tides of lust.

The sheer perfection of her breasts.

The magic touch of her hands. Her wandering fingers.

The curve of her ass where it merged imperceptibly with scales and her tail.

The phosphorescence of her body, its light bathing us in a force field of time as we merged, made love, fucked, fought, and enjoyed each other as much as we could.

Every day, when the sun had risen properly over the far horizon, she would retreat to the sea, always promising to return the following day. Which she invariably did.

"The seasons are turning, the weather will soon change a lot, and it will be too hot for me to swim these waters," Liv Lisa said, one day.

I knew what this meant—that I wouldn't see her again or, at any rate, for around a whole year. A prospect I couldn't face.

"I can travel to the islands," I pointed out. "I'd be happy to. Not to lose you."

"It's too much to ask," Liv Lisa said.

"Nothing would be too much," I replied.

"But you can't live under the sea. You're human," she stated.

"I'm aware there is a doctor who can operate on me, change me appropriately," I declared.

"I know." Liv Lisa sighed. "But for any man to join us, he must also pay a tribute. It's our law."

I nodded.

We agreed we would meet on the night of the spring solstice by the Bay of Sharks in Nuku Hiva. I knew there was a regular boat service to the French Polynesian island.

That night, at the tavern, I began asking around. Toward the end of a long evening, passed from post to post, person to person, I finally came across a local sailor who knew a man who knew another who knew of a rather particular doctor.

I tracked him down.

Explained.

"I wouldn't if I were you," he said. "Mermaids are extremely unreliable. That's a well-known fact. They lure you to unholy places until there is no turning back."

I was firm. Told him I was ready for the consequences.

I had the operation that would allow me to breathe underwater, the cut along my neck that would match April's. This he did with just a local anesthetic.

Then, he put me under for the other surgical intervention.

When I woke, he had expunged my genitals.

It felt sore, but I knew physical pain always passes.

I looked down at my body. It shone clean, hygienic, almost natural in its absence. Not that I'd had that much use for my cock for some time, I consoled myself.

The doctor's payment, as we had agreed, was in kind. For the fruit of his labors, he would retain my penis. For his specimen collection, he pretended. Little did I know then that he would pass the small flask in which it floated—shriveled, small, pitiful—to Liv Lisa. That they had a deal, and it wasn't the first time she had cleverly pointed a man his way. At least he had been right and speaking from experience when he had informed me that mermaids were not to be trusted.

I arrived in Nuku Hiva a few weeks later and made my way quickly to the Bay of Sharks. There was no sign of mermaids or Liv Lisa.

I returned every single day for several weeks, but she never appeared.

I returned to the long beach, an emptiness in my soul and inside my trousers. By now, the area had fully healed, and the inconvenience of my penis's absence was no more than the wind of a fleeting memory.

A year went by, and I returned every day before dawn to the beach, but no one came to join me. Ever. Apart from stray dogs detached from their leashes, their owners, and material debris, washing up from the sea.

One night at the tavern, I met Volker, an elderly German ship's mate hailing from Hamburg. We became friendly and had been drinking together in a smoky corner of the joint when, out of nowhere, the subject of fantastic sea creatures came up.

"I believe in them," he said, with a deep sigh.

"So do I." I nodded.

He looked me in the eyes as if weighing me.

Tentatively encouraged by our respective reaction to the way the conversation was going, we both hinted at personal experience with such creatures.

And I learned about the legend of Liv Lisa, the beautiful, seductive mermaid who stole men's cocks and, reputedly, had them hanging from her necklace. It was said she now had two handfuls of penises strung along her coral necklace. No other mermaid in the hemisphere had harvested as many—a testimony to her incomparable beauty and powers of seduction.

I visited an occult library in the upper town where I was told rare books about legends and the sea were kept. I had to bribe the librarian to be given access to the rare book section where forbidden texts and images were kept. There, I found in the second edition of a Zafón classic, a collection of sea lore, engravings depicting Liv Lisa and her kind and the necklaces they harvested in their dangerous journeys. There was an image of a cock necklace, and the image captivated me. They came in all sizes, some small, others large. Some veiny, some smooth, all conserved by some dubious miracle of science at the pinnacle of their erect size, it appeared. Both a morbid and fascinating sight.

And I knew all too well that, now, one of them was mine, not so much a stellar but probably an undistinguished addition to Liv Lisa's collection.

And was Volker's there too? He'd been evasive when I probed him.

But there had certainly been a cloud of sorrow floating behind his eyes as we concluded our conversation.

He never returned to the tavern the following days.

I traveled.

I lounged on the beaches of Spain, Thailand, Bali, some of the Maldives islands. Crossed the Panama and the Kiel Canal, navigated the Florida Keys, lingered on Bora Bora, and tramped down the Yucatan Peninsula. Never found out where mermaids and mermen lurked.

But I will keep on searching as I follow the trail of my lost April, the treacherous Liv Lisa, and my severed penis.

And if you buy me another glass of that exquisite bourbon, I might even tell you what happened to me in the dunes of that Caribbean island I am not allowed to mention by name or about the delirious way a mermaid's breasts feel under your wandering fingertips. Just another sea story.

END

MAXIM JAKUBOWSKI *edited the Mammoth Book of Erotica series for almost 20 years. His novels include Kiss Me Sadly, The State of Montana, Skin in Darkness, On Tenderness Express, I Was Waiting for You, Confessions of a Romantic Pornographer, Ekaterina and the Night and, most recently, The Louisiana Republic. He lives in London.*

382.11
Ford

King's Mercy

author: Alexa B. Forde
category: Foreign Trade

subjects: 1. Bedchamber 2. Vendetta
3. Royal Exotic Fantasies

Rose Caraway's Library of Erotica

King's Mercy

Alexa B. Forde

I stand in the line of girls, waiting to be led out. It is cold in the chill morning air, and I only have a thin dress on. I am filthy, my hands sting with cold, and I am trying not to shiver. I do not want my shivers to be mistaken for fear. I need to look strong and arrogant, or I'll never be chosen. Cold mud squishes between my bare feet.

When I had discovered I was going to Movina, I had thought it would be warmer than my last mission. The seaside capital is known for its clear skies and crystal-blue waters. Bordered by mountains and rivers, Movina's geographical location makes it impossible to take by force.

The wooden gate of the cage opens in front of me.

The slave trader pulls on our chains, and we stumble forward. His oily, greying hair flops limply. His too-long arms end in stumpy, white hands tinged brownish-red.

I touch the bruise on my eye, imagining it is the shape of that filthy hand.

The trader played his part well, the fool.

I want to look difficult. I know that's what His Royal Highness likes. King Samuel the Seventh has a reputation for enjoying wilful women, ones who don't comply no matter how much they are conditioned. He'll keep them for a while, then dispose of them.

I don't plan on getting to the disposal part. I know it's a risk, but there are important reasons why I agreed to this; the only people who get to see the king are his most trusted advisers—all men—and the women he enjoys. For a female spy, this is the only way in.

We walk forward into the trading grounds and are led into a pen. The royal slave buyers are in the far corner, making their way around, examining those of us on offer. I know they are in the market for something for the king.

Lord Darian, the king's chief slave buyer, walks through the crowd. He's taller than I'd expected, and his face is cold and calculating. His dark hair and piercing, brown eyes are as reported.

The sun is just starting to rise, and street lamps are being snuffed out. The air is warming up, even at this early hour. Soon, I will be sweating, but at least the shivering has stopped.

A young woman in front of me is pushed forward by the trader. She stumbles, and I catch her. I help her up, but one of the guards still manages to kick her. She whimpers behind a curtain of long, blond hair that sweeps down over her full breasts. Her thin nose and fair skin tell me she's from the southern provinces, lands of ice, where the king's slaves dig day and night for the mysterious minerals that power his cities. Her people have been hurt almost as much as mine by King Samuel the Splendid. I just love the Movinian fondness for alliteration. They might as well call him Samuel the Psychopath or Samuel the Secretive. Either would be a more accurate description.

The slave trader walks along the line, and we stand, waiting. He primps and fusses over us like a fruit merchant with his display of apples. When he reaches the blonde, he rips the front of her dress, revealing more of her bust. She steps back, and he grabs her chains, pulling them hard. Tears spring to her eyes.

"Leave her alone," I say, just as the king's buyers approach. I know that my little act of rebellion will interest them.

"Or what?" the trader hisses.

"Or, I'll break your neck."

He punches me in the stomach, and I buckle forward, his rotten breath at my ear. "If you don't sell today, you can expect to be dead by morning but not before I'm through with you, girl." He grabs my chin and presses his fingers into the bruise over my eye.

Pain sears through my body, but I hold his stare. My defiance is a calculated risk. This mission relies on me being installed in the royal palace before our army starts riding north. When the Elite Guard takes this city, sometime in mid-autumn, his shiny, little face won't look half as smug, and we will finally put an end to his kind of business. I smile at the trader, knowing his pathetic life is ticking away.

Lord Darian and his posse approach from behind the trader. The front of his ceremonial robes open as he moves, hinting at the athletic body beneath. In this attire, he looks almost harmless, but I know better. He is a trained killer like me, just not quite as good. His jaw is square, making him look as though he is carved of stone, matching his stone heart, no doubt.

"Good day, m'lord." The trader turns and greets Lord Darian cheerily.

"We are looking for something special today, sir," Darian says, appraising our flesh as though we are mere trinkets.

"I'm sure you are. Something for the kitchens or something for the king?"

"All you need to know is that I need something…" he pauses briefly. "…with a bit of spark."

"Well m'lord. This young thing is a fine specimen." The trader pulls the bedraggled blonde forward. "She is quite buxom as you can see." He grabs her breast and squeezes. The woman lets out a cry.

"Mmm, a bit too innocent, I'm afraid. I need something…" Lord Darian leads him aside. They talk in hushed whispers. I catch a few words—wilful, pain, fight.

Surely, I'll be recommended, but the trader will want a good price.

Lord Darian looks at me, and I roll my eyes. When his lips draw upward, I know I'm in.

"What about this one?" He walks toward me.

"Yes, that one. I'm afraid she might have a bit too much fight in her, m'lord, even for your tastes. I wouldn't feel right selling her to the palace. She's violent, sir, and dangerous."

"And damaged, Sir Trader." Darian places a hand under my chin. It's surprisingly gentle, considering his occupation. He turns my head from side to side, seeming to appraise the swollen bruise above my eye.

"Yes, well—"

"I certainly hope you're not using brutality with your stock."

This is rich, coming from the man responsible for breaking-in the king's playthings. The king is well known for his twisted tastes.

"Brutality, m'lord? No, no. This one tried to escape, and we merely had to contain her. Sir, she's much too dangerous. Besides, I already have another interested buyer. A chap who runs a fighting pit down at West Wharf. He's already offered me double what she's worth, sir. So, you see—"

The lying little weasel, I think.

"Sir Trader, we'll take her. My man will arrange payment. Unchain her now."

"Yes, m'lord, of course."

One of Darian's fellows withdraws a large chain attached to a metal collar and deftly places the device around my neck, ensuring it is secure. Darian is already moving on while another of his assistants busily counts out silver pieces.

The trader steps back, gesturing to his man to unlock my wrists. He whispers in my ear, "A shame. I was looking forward to tonight." He reaches his filthy fingers up under the tear in my tattered shift to my naked ass and grabs me painfully.

"I'll be back for you later," I say, my voice a low rumble as I stare into his eyes. "You might want to lock your doors, Trader Simon."

His eyes flicker when I use his name. He squeezes me harder, causing considerable pain, but I hold his gaze until he releases me. He laughs, slapping me sharply on the rear, calling out to Lord Darian. "Best of luck m'lord. She's a tricky one. Just remember, we don't offer exchanges or refunds."

Lord Darian's assistant leads me away while Darian negotiates another acquisition. His voice is commanding as he discusses the finer details of the sale. His next choice is tall and red-haired. She looks angry. I can see I will have to prove I am the best choice for His Majesty.

Once we arrive back at the palace, our restraints are undone, offering me the perfect opportunity for a little display for Lord Darian. As the bulky chain around my neck slides free, I run for the gates. The guards are slow to react. I fake a stumble so they can catch up. I hear Lord Darian yell in the background, and I smile.

Two enormous guards stand in my way at the front gate, and I skid to a halt. The larger guard takes two steps and grabs my hair, tossing me to the ground. His dark, tanned skin shines as I stare up at him. He grabs my neck and hauls me back to my feet just as two more guards arrive. They each grab one of my arms and drag me back toward Darian who looks pleased. "A fighter, indeed. Good. Take her to my chambers," he orders.

The guard nods and drags me away.

I am deposited, unceremoniously, in Darian's bedchamber. They attach me to an iron ring fixed into the wall opposite Darian's bed. There are a number of similar rings attached at various locations around the room. I realize that Lord Darian's role in vetting the king's exotic fantasies might be more hands-on than I had thought. Or perhaps, it's just that I have caught his eye.

I wait for what feels like hours until he finally appears.

Bursting into the room, he doesn't waste any time getting acquainted. "That was quite a display today." His anger is obvious. "Another attempt like that, and I'll have you beaten to a pulp."

"Fuck you."

"If that's what you want." He strides over, grabs the front of my dress, and rips it straight down the front, exposing my breasts. He considers them, and the line of his jaw sends a sudden thrill through me.

I stare at him, expecting him to take me then and there, but he doesn't.

Lord Darian surprises me, walking over to a long box on the other side of the room. He takes down a heavy key, making no attempt to conceal its location. I know the kinds of things that are inside a box such as that. I'm well versed in these sorts of fantasies. My mission in San Terra had taught me that pleasure comes in many forms. It was during that particular mission I'd learned that working as a spy didn't have to be boring. A woman may have a bit of fun along the way. If it meant taking the assignments that no one else wanted, while earning some extra royal favor along the way, well, I was happy to do so. But there is more than pleasure involved with this particular mission; I have a personal vendetta to settle with the king.

I realize I'm losing focus and return my gaze to the box. Darian searches through it, seemingly undecided. He removes a long, black robe and lays it carefully on his bed.

Surprising me again, Darian pulls out a long feather. I had expected brutality, his reputation as the king's bulldog is well-known. Perhaps all the rumors are lies. I shift, my chains clinking against the stone wall.

Darian looks at me, feather in hand. As if making an important decision, he pulls a small, leather strap out of the box too. "There are two ways that this may go for you." He says, walking toward me.

Lord Darian is an attractive man. His strong arms are evident through his white shirt.

"If you are a good girl, this might be enjoyable for both of us." With the feather in one hand and the strap in the other, he grabs what is left of my dress and rips it off.

I stand naked before him, still chained, my arms raised above my head.

Gently, he runs the feather down my neck, over my breasts and stomach, around to my buttocks, and across the backs of my thighs.

It tickles, sending waves of warm desire through me. Then, the feather flutters to the ground.

"Or this can be painful. The choice is yours." Grabbing my arm, he turns me, bends me forward, and plants three sharp strokes against my buttocks with the leather strap.

My blood rushes, and desire extends throughout my body. The long chains attached to my wrists clink loudly as I rest my palms on the rough wall. I want to face him, but he's spun me around and holds me in place, facing the wall.

He takes his time examining my body, then finally spins me around to face him again.

My gaze falls level with his chiseled jaw. I spit, hoping to anger him, but he doesn't react. I move to hit him, but he grabs my hand, and the chains rattle loudly.

He walks back toward his box of tricks and places the feather and strap back inside, then he leaves, walking into the next room. I hear shuffling. When he returns, his face looks freshly washed, and he's carrying a wooden chair, another key, and a long, leather belt. It looks ceremonial with a simple, iron loop at one end. He's no amateur.

"I can see that you want to make this difficult." He places the chair next to me, undoes my chains, and slowly winds the belt around his hand.

I try to maintain my focus, but the mission is fast slipping to the back of my mind.

Lord Darian takes a practice stroke at his own leg, then grabs my waist and sits me on his knee. The heat of his body matches mine. He runs his hands down the front of my body, grabbing so roughly at my breasts and thighs that I can already feel bruises will form. Then, he runs the tip of his

King's Mercy

belt up and down my back.

He breathes into my ear. "You belong to the King of Movina now, slave. The king is a man without mercy. As his faithful servant, it my duty to show you exactly how to behave for him."

Lord Darian lifts me and bends me over his knee, his strong arm pinning me into place.

I shift to get comfortable, hoping he will mistake my movement for shame, though nothing could be farther from the truth. The belt brushes my skin, and thoughts of my mission disappear as I submit to the pleasure. Vendettas can wait. I brace myself for the first blow. I know it will come at any moment, and the ache of lust and longing fills me. I close my eyes, curious to know how hard he will strike.

The first stroke bites into my bare ass. It is painful and relieving at the same time. I realize now how much I want this. I want him inside me. I stifle another moan and grit my teeth. Curse Lord Darian. He is not part of the plan.

He strikes again and again in quick succession, then he pauses with his arm in mid-air.

The unpredictability and building anticipation is almost unbearable. With the next stroke, I let out a cry that seems to spur him on. He hits me harder and I cry out as the sensations move to a new level of pleasure-pain. I know my backside will be shiny and red with welts, yet all I can think about is this man's cock, rising beneath me, hot and hard.

Without warning, Lord Darian stands me up and pushes me against the stone wall. He licks my neck and bites my breasts and shoulders. He presses his body against me and the stone wall's hard, uneven surface bites into my back. He presses his cock against my hip.

I pretend to be disgusted and try to stifle a moan, but his hands feel as though they are everywhere, rubbing my breasts and my ass, circling ever closer to my quim. I tilt my pelvis, and he slips his fingers inside of me, making me gasp at the fullness. He withdraws and shows me his fingers, the creamy evidence of my desire on undeniable display.

"If I'm not mistaken, girl, I'd say you're enjoying this."

I try to look embarrassed, innocent, and even horrified.

Lord Darian smirks. "Yes," he says. "You will do nicely. I'm going to enjoy you a great deal."

A wave of heat rushes through me, his words echoing in my mind.

He strokes my hair and leans down, whispering, "There's just one problem with your intelligence, Alanah." His eyes have gone wolfish and something dark stirs in me. I bite my bottom lip.

"They never got you a proper description of the king, did they?" he says.

"I…" I stumble on my words.

"The king prefers to find his own playthings. He always has. He doesn't need a servant to do it for him. You wanted an audience with the king, Alanah, to air your grievances. Well, you've got your audience, slave."

My mind races and realization dawns as the words fall from his lips. As he turns me around and presses me against the stone wall once again.

"I am the king, and lucky for you, I'm feeling merciful today." I can feel the rustle of his pants against my bottom. The press of his hard, warm cock against my sensitized skin. "I should have you executed for treason, but..." He slides his shaft through my slick channel, searching for my eager entrance. "I have a far more thrilling option waiting for you. You want to know all my dirty secrets, Alanah? Where my army's going, what my plans are? You want every graphic detail of how I will crush any army that tries to take what's mine?"

For the first time, I realize, I want the King's cock inside of me more than fulfilling my mission. In one swift thrust he is inside of me, pumping. His sharp, heavy strokes come in a steady rhythm and just as his final thrust hits home, I find my own release. We collapse onto the floor of his chamber; his body deliciously heavy on top of mine.

Revenge can wait a few days. When I finally have it, it will be all the sweeter. If only all my missions were so much fun.

END

ALEXA B. FORDE *is a sometimes TV extra and nude life model who enjoys writing with a glass of wine and her pet rat. She'd prefer to forgo food than settle down and get a real job. ALEXA'S favorite pastimes are walking her dog, reading epic fantasy novels, and listening to eastern European folk music.*

398.2
cumm

The Wicked Witch of the Wet

author: t s cummings
category: Fairy Tales

subjects: 1. Central Park 2. Old Crone
3. Bobbed My Apple

Rose Caraway's Library of Erotica

The Wicked Witch Of The Wet

t s cummings

One eye open.
      Two eyes open.
   That, my friends, was half the battle. Now came the other half.
   My feet found the cold floor and carried me to the window. I threw open the curtains, daring the day to come in.
   Despite every bleary neuron screaming no, no, no, the pre-dawn glow of amber somehow compelled me to finally break in the new running shoes I'd just spent way too much money on. Though traditionally not a morning person—unless one was referring to my preferred time to find my bed—I'd made a New Year's resolution to exercise more. And since Halloween lurked just around the corner, I thought it best to get started.
   Free of the screaming brats and ranting winos that curse it by day, at this hour, Central Park felt like even more of an oasis. As the morning mists glided across the path, curling around my calves before dispersing in the wake of my steady footfalls, my mind retreated into the peace born by the cadence of my gait.
   Not yet through with my first wind, I challenged myself to traverse the

Park's length, all the way to the North Woods. I veered off West Drive to avoid the Children's Glade, lest I encounter any Type-A moms logging quality time with their still-snoozing offspring. Besides, the solitude of the road less jogged beckoned.

The unnamed trail welcomed me with a mid-autumnal pastiche of burnt colors. Completely enveloped in the flameless fire, I misplaced all track of time. Eventually, my brain barged in, breaking the silence. *Haven't we been at this for quite some time? And where are we?* Yes, and I have no clue, were my replies, respectively.

Above my head, a little, snow-white bird sang, its melody both alluring and foreboding. It stretched its wings and flew in front of me, compelling me to follow. The feathered siren led me to a little house in a clearing carved from the dense forest. Logic would have suggested I find it odd that someone could claim a quarter acre within the confines of Central Park and build a house. Of course, had I packed even a nutribar's worth of logic for this run, I likewise would have questioned the owner's choice of materials, as walls of bread, a roof of cake, and windows of clear sugar likely would not pass muster with the city's building department.

Should I, or shouldn't I?

My stomach, denied breakfast in the interest of getting my ass out the door in a timely fashion, immediately and emphatically weighed in on the pro side.

So be it. Wall, roof, or window?

Still holding the gavel, the representative from Hungryville argued that if I was going to carb-load, it might as well be on cake.

A rickety rocking chair next to the stoop offered me a step up. I snatched an ort of the eave. But before the morsel could meet my mouth, a gentle voice called out.

"Nibble, nibble, little mouse. Who is nibbling at my house?"

Now chewing on a gummi gutter, I ignored what I assumed to be my conscience.

The door opened and a woman, as old as the hills and leaning on a crutch, came creeping out, eyeing me curiously. In hindsight, I suppose literally eating a stranger out of house and home would fail the Miss Manner's Test.

"Ma'am, I am so sorry. I realize this is your house, but I was jogging and I was hungry, and..."

A wry grin crept across her face. In one deft motion, she flipped the cane end-over-end, hooked one of my legs, and yanked. My body met the ground in a most inglorious fashion.

I awoke in the dark. After verifying the relative relation between up and down, I stood tentatively and chanced a step. Owing to its success, I tried another, and another, before walking nose-first into a bar. The wrong kind.

The bitch had caged me.

"Hello? Hello-o. Look, I don't know who you are or what you're doing, but I'm calling the cops." *With the cell phone you stole from my pocket.*

A bare bulb several feet away glowed into existence.

"Well, well, my pretty."

"Yeah, yeah. You got me. But you'll never get my dog, too."

She nodded at a filthy mug atop a small table in the corner. "I've left you dinner. A yummy protein shake," she said, sing-song, though I suppose sing-wrong would be more apropos.

"That's very kind of you. But you know what would be even kinder? Letting me out."

"I'm afraid I can't do that."

"You can't?"

"No. I need you."

"Need me? For what?"

"I'm going to fatten you up. And once you're fat, I am going to eat you."

"Lady, that's just gross."

"Fine. Would you prefer to stick out your cock, so I can feel if you are fat?"

Okay. Admittedly, it had been a while since I'd read a Brothers Grimm tale. But I would wager the old witch never said that to Hansel.

"And if I don't?"

"Then no treats, you naughty, little boy."

"You call that slop a treat?"

She snapped her fingers. A Big Mac and a bottle of Jack Daniels materialized at her feet. "Is this more in line with your tastes?"

What did that troglodyte Texan politico say a few years back? If it's inevitable, lie back and enjoy it.

"Give me the booze first. And give me five minutes."

She passed the bottle between the bars. I mainlined a few healthy swigs, sending my head and my inhibitions into a tailspin.

"Five minutes. Are you ready?"

"Sure," I slurred. "What the fuck?"

Her bony finger beckoned me to come closer. With half the fifth under my belt, or cascading happily toward it, the old crone started to look pretty good. Her sister wasn't bad either.

"How you doin'?" I said, in my best New York Italio-gigolo voice.

"I'm fine," she giggled, tugging her dress like a nervous school girl.

"What's a nice girl like you doing in a place like this?"

Oh my god. I'm actually flirting with a real live witch.

"It's my first time here. Do you come here often?"

"I haven't, yet. Perhaps you could do something about that."

She covered her mouth and gasped with what looked like faux-modesty. "I don't know," she said. "We just met."

"Okay. There's other fish in the—"

"Ready!" she said, getting down on creaking knees. She slowly pulled the drawstring and yanked down my sweats and underpants in one motion. She sniffed lightly, then buried her face in my crotch.

"Mmm. You smell like a man."

Yeah, a five-mile jog and captivity in a dungeon will do that.

"My, what a big cock you have."

I was pretty sure she'd mixed fairy tales. But her house, her rules.

"All the better to mouth–fuck you with," I said, grabbing a handful of her greasy gray hair, and thrusting my cock past her lips, into the soft warmth of her mouth.

She responded by reaching through the bars and digging her fingernails—really long fingernails—into my ass, no doubt leaving battle scars that would mandate an explanation to the future Mrs. Me.

She drew me into the deepest recesses of her mouth and her soul. I closed my eyes and visualized Angelina Jolie from *Maleficent*. Actually, that would have been pretty hot; I could have grabbed her horns. Surprisingly, the old crone's technique wasn't half bad. I hazarded a glance down. With tender ferocity, she bobbed my apple, her lips extending to lead the charge down my shaft, then retreating gracefully. Hag-ness be damned. I could get used to this.

Pressure began building in my brain and in points to the south.

She must have felt it. "My, what big balls you have."

"All the better to paint your face with."

"Not a chance, buster. It's cocktail hour." She grabbed my prick with two hands and stroked furiously.

In all honesty, she didn't really need both hands. But she also stroked my ego. The precipice loomed.

"Fill me!" She gasped. "Fill me with your essence! Give me your life!"

I released. And released. And released.

She sampled her taste buds a moment, then frowned a little. "Hmm," she said, smacking her lips, "I'm not all that fond of the taste of whiskey. I think next time it will be Malbec."

"Next time?" I said.

"*Somnus statim*," she said, waving a hand.

I splashed back onto the waterbed.

When consciousness finally feather-kissed me, a chipper "Good morning!" more or less shattered any illusion I'd held that yesterday had been a bad wet dream.

"Rise and shine. And rise," she chirped, smiling less-than-repulsively. "How you doin'?" she said, far more "New Yawk" than I ever could, brushing away a few strands of ginger hair that had infiltrated the gray.

"How long have I been out?"

"Five hours. But you're back," she said giddily. "I thought you might be hungry." She nodded at the little table, now laden with shrimp, steak, a baked potato, and an absurd slice of Boston cream pie. And a bottle of Malbec. "For your entertainment." She clicked a remote. The large-screen television now adorning the wall lit up, the Nets-Knicks game in full swish.

"Sweet!" I said.

"Uh-uh. First, you have to eat. Then, I have to eat. Then, you can have TV."

"If I must," I sighed.

It's now been three weeks, give or take a succulent meal and a mind-bending blow job or two. Getting out of bed has been a chore lately. Little aches and pains invade unimaginable corners of my body. And the bars seem miles away from my bed.

But she sure is looking hot.

END

t s cummings *is a ne'er-do-well who loves wine, women, chocolate, and himself, not necessarily in that order. When not too busy living it, he writes erotic fiction and poetry.*

613.1
Amor

Boy Toy

author: Jaycee Amore
category: Science and Technology

subjects: 1. Loving Companion 2. Customizable
3. Fully Functional 4. Orgy

Rose Caraway's Library of Erotica

Boy Toy

Jaycee Amore

Sometime in 2025....
"Oh my God! Yes! Right there!" The sensation was so intense, she found it hard to instruct him. "Shit! More tongue...further in... Aaaahhhhfuuuuckkkk..!" Leslie's ability to speak intelligently left her as she came on her new boyfriend's tongue, her spasms keeping rhythm with his gentle thrusts.

He continued to tongue-fuck her until the wave subsided, then slowly worked his way up to mount her, kneading her breasts with his mouth, and kissing her neck as he'd been taught. She felt his swollen member press against her slit and gasped in expectation of its entry.

"Size preference?" His husky voice exhaled the words against her neck like a warm wind bringing a storm over the mountains.

"Start with a six." She felt him pushing her folds apart. "More. Go to seven." She felt the difference immediately. "Mmmmmm, up another size. Mmmm...oh yeah, that's a good stretch." She was amazed at the options; clearly, this was the greatest birthday present her husband had ever gotten her. She was on the verge of coming again in minutes, legs splayed wide and trembling as her new lover drove her to deeper depths of ecstasy.

She was surprised when he added his moans to hers. She pushed gently against him, and he dismounted, rolling over onto his back. Curiosity piqued, she went down on him, working his cock with her hands and mouth until she felt the beginnings of his orgasm in his balls.

He moaned again, and his load filled her mouth with an unexpected treat—as sweet as salted caramel. She savored it for a moment before swallowing, then crawled back up to collapse next to him. He was warm to the touch, with a light sheen of sweat on his skin (she wasn't sure if it was hers or his). He made a surprisingly soft pillow when she lay her head on his chest. She dozed lightly, drinking in the scents of lavender and sex. For the first time in years, she was satisfied.

"Well, was it worth the price?" Her husband, Donovan, barely looked up from the paper when Leslie came downstairs. He was in his work chair, the overstuffed leather recliner with power everything, his nose buried in the financial section of the *National Times*.

When they had dated, she recalled, his nose was often found buried between her thighs, but once he started working for his father and started making the big money, all that changed. Honestly, she was surprised he even bothered asking her opinion. Was he just wondering about his investment?

"Reminds me of you, Don, when we first got together." She tried flattery. "Bet you could teach him a thing or two." She winked at him when she said this, letting her robe fall open.

Leslie was proud of her body and loved displaying it for admiring audiences…she just wished her husband fit into that category. She spent a considerable amount of her sweat, and Donovan's money, to sculpt herself into a walking fantasy—tan, lean, firm, with a swagger that told every man she met that they would never know true pleasure until they had her.

Donovan didn't seem to notice.

She dropped the robe completely and stood naked before him, a light sheen of sweat and massage oil making her skin glow like the goddess Aphrodite.

No reaction.

Leslie filled her glass with Riesling and retreated upstairs.

Troy, her thirty-six-thousand-dollar birthday present, was plugged in and charging in his pod when she got back to her room. The pod, a special cabinet that allowed him to re-charge out-of-sight, was built to look like an antique wardrobe and stood in the corner on her side of the room. Leslie stared at it with a mixture of desire and contempt. She drained her glass, cursing herself for not bringing the bottle; now she'd just have to go back downstairs where she'd see Donovan sitting there in his goddamn chair doing his goddamn currency analysis instead of being upstairs in his goddamn bed doing his goddamn wife!

Tears welled up, and she threw the empty glass at the wardrobe. The explosion of glass was therapeutic. She deflated onto the bed, wishing her mind felt as satisfied as her body. She hoped the anticipation wouldn't come tonight.

The anticipation. Leslie hated it, that feeling of going to bed wondering if her lover would choose that night to make love, lying next to him, so close in proximity yet so far away emotionally. Don had a once-a-week policy. Every Friday night he would indulge in pleasures of the flesh (but only certain ones), occasionally slipping in a quickie in the middle of the week just for her. That meant Leslie felt the anticipation three or four nights of the week and often fell asleep wondering why she didn't deserve to feel the complete satisfaction of a lover's embrace.

She and Don had been around and around on this topic. They even tried counseling a year ago, but there seemed to be no resolution. No matter how incredible Leslie looked or how much she tried explaining how she felt, Don wouldn't budge. She knew he'd bought her the toy to avoid doing the job himself. A nice gesture?

"Well, fuck it!" Leslie decided. "I'm gonna wear the damn thing out!" She grabbed the vacuum and cleaned up most of the shards from her wine glass (the maid would get the rest) and headed downstairs for the bottle and her cell phone.

"Ohmagawd Kelly, you will not believe what Don got me for my birthday!" Leslie had to tell someone and, of course, Kelly would be the first. Kelly was her oldest, dearest, friend. They had been besties in high school, went to the same college, and now, lived two houses apart.

Leslie had Donovan while Kelly had, well, a string of guys she'd dated for a few months. They would call now and then, usually when horny. Kelly didn't seem to mind. Hell, Leslie thought, she got laid semi-regularly and didn't have all of the drama of a full-time relationship. Sometimes, Leslie thought she saw a wistful look in Kelly's eyes, though, whenever they discussed relationships, Kelly always denied it. She was free and content to be so!

"Must be something really special for you to be calling me when *Sport of Kings* is on; you never miss that show." Leslie noted the sarcasm; poorly written medieval drama wasn't Kelly's thing.

"I have the Tivo set. No sweat." Plus Leslie liked to re-watch the good parts with a glass of wine and B.O.B., her battery-operated boyfriend. "I am calling a brunch tomorrow. You, Annabelle, Dahlia, and me. You'll have to wait until then, no hints! Shit, you'd never guess anyway. Be here at ten?" They usually got together on Sunday mornings, but today, Don had wanted to take her out for her birthday, so the group had been cancelled.

"Sure, it's another two weeks until tax season, so I can play hooky." Kelly ran a corporate accounting firm, handling several big clients in the state, but she gave her employees as much flex time as possible, so she could justify a few hours for herself.

"It's a date!" Leslie hung up, chuckling at the thought of leaving Kelly's curious mind to think of the most outrageous ideas. Tomorrow would be fun!

Ladies, this is Troy, my birthday present!"

There was a chorus of gasps and "oh my gawds" as the robot, or "loving companion" (as the company stressed), entered the room carrying two trays of hors-d'oeuvres and wearing a French maid's apron and nothing else.

"Les, seriously, did Donovan get you a live-in stripper?" Annabelle's bright-blue eyes were the size of cue balls as she surveyed the muscular form of the server. As a frequent visitor of male reviews, and co-president of the Chippendale's Fan-Club, San Clemente chapter, Belle calling a man a stripper was considered a high compliment.

"Thank you, Belle, but no, he is not a professional, although he appears to be modeled after one!" Leslie decided to let the secret out early in the conversation. "He is an LCX deluxe-model loving companion, fresh out of the box. No pun intended," she added, with a wink. Troy had provided her with two exquisite orgasms during her morning shower.

"Holy shit. No way!" Kelly almost dropped her mimosa, "He's a robot?"

"Basically, yeah." Leslie pulled the brochure out and passed it to Kelly. "Programmable and customizable in the most glorious ways! Troy, honey, put the trays down and lose that apron, will ya?"

Troy placed the trays on the table and shed the apron revealing his manhood, which Leslie had instructed him to set on maximum. It achieved the desired effect. Kelly did drop her mimosa this time.

"Shit! Sorry, Les!" Kelly reached for the napkins on the coffee table, but Troy was already there.

"Allow me," the robot said, picking up the napkins and beginning to clean up the spill while maintaining eye-contact with Kelly.

His husky voice and hint of an Italian accent reminded Leslie of a famous actor, although she couldn't place the name. The temperature seemed to rise about ten degrees. Warmth radiated from just below her bellybutton, building like a rising tide. She was glad she'd worn a panty-liner.

Troy seemed to know exactly what effect he was having on the women. He inhaled deeply through his nose as his gaze slowly worked its way down Kelly's body, stopping between her crossed legs. His eyes met hers, and he winked as if to say, "Oh yeah, you're ready!"

Kelly seemed unable to tear her eyes away from him.

"What does he do?" Dahlia asked. "I mean, you know...is he like fully functional and all?"

Leslie was surprised Dahlia hadn't passed out yet, being the most prudish of the group. Dahlia wouldn't even go down on a guy which explained why she was perpetually single.

"Dee, Troy here will do anything I ask him to and will remember anything I teach him with no hesitation or obligation! Absolutely the perfect man!" Leslie felt guilty for the lie. Troy wasn't perfect. He was programmed to please; he didn't want to please. There was a difference.

The Q and A that followed was pretty much what Leslie had expected.

"Does it feel real?" Kelly asked.

Leslie let them have a turn holding Troy's package, soft and hard.

"What is the size range?" Dee wanted to know.

The looks on their faces during that demonstration were priceless!

After Kelly asked about customizing the model, eye color, body hair, voice and accent, Leslie referred them to the website where there were dozens of videos (definitely not intended for young audiences) and a full list of options. Donovan had ordered this model and apparently known Leslie's tastes pretty well.

When the questions were answered and the mimosas consumed, the conversation turned to Annabelle's pending wedding. "Ohmahgawd," Leslie proclaimed. "I am throwing you one helluva bachelorette party!"

As if on cue, Troy emerged from the kitchen, still sans apron, with donuts displayed up the length of his manly appendage.

"Who wants a cruller? Ya have to get it with your hands behind your back, though," Leslie said. She winked.

Annabelle practically launched herself across the coffee table.

That evening was the typical disappointment for Leslie. Donovan had spent the afternoon golfing with two of his partners and was exhausted, so Leslie decided to have some toy-time. The brochure said Troy was submersible to fifty feet, and he obviously didn't need to breathe, so Leslie took him to their hot tub on the deck to really enjoy the sunset. She had just peaked the first time when she heard the sliding door open.

Don emerged, wearing a towel. "Good idea, babe, great way to unwind from...oh..." He paused when he spotted Troy, completely submerged, still servicing Leslie.

"C'mon in, hun, the...ooohhhh...water is..., ohmagawd, sooo fuckin great!"

Donovan watching was a turn-on she hadn't expected, and her intensity skyrocketed. She tapped Troy to the surface to give herself a breather. An image broke through the fog in her mind, but would Don go for it? "Don, I want you and Troy to share me!"

"Not really up for much right now, Les. Long day today, meeting tomorrow morning."

"Troy can do all the heavy lifting. I just want to share this with you." She couldn't believe she had to beg like this.

"Maybe next Friday. You know I like my routine. That's why I got him for you, something to keep you going in between." He turned and went back inside.

"Shit!" She sighed. It had been worth a try, even if it had been a longshot.

The next two brunches featured the obvious topic of discussion—Troy.

Donovan typically scheduled his golf time for Sunday mornings, so Leslie held her brunches while he was out. The arrangement was perfect, in her view, as it allowed Troy to walk around in various stages of undress without fear of making Don uncomfortable. She had seen Don peeking over his paper at Troy a few times in the past week. If he'd been a chick, she'd swear he was checking him out, but Donovan Pritchard had never displayed the slightest hint of bi or gay curiosity. Leslie chuckled at herself and let it go.

Troy was in the middle of bringing the third round of mimosas when Annabelle posed the question. "Leslie, you keep raving about his abilities. When are you going to let us sample the goods?"

Leslie had thought about it, of course, but felt a little protective of Troy as if he could develop feelings for another and leave her. The idea was so incredible; she laughed out loud.

"You want a personal demo, 'Belle? Let's do it!" She winked at Annabelle and set her mimosa on the coffee table. "Troy, honey, will you show Annabelle a good time, please?"

Once she said the key phrase, Troy's demeanor changed; he walked over to Annabelle and held out his hand. She let him help her to her feet, and he pulled her in as she stood, one hand sliding up her back to her neck as the other traveled down to cup her ass. He kissed her deeply, pressing her close to him as his most important accessory began to throb and grow. His mouth left hers and found her jawline, then her neck, and suddenly, her blouse was completely unbuttoned and bra unclasped (Annabelle always wore a front-release, for just such an emergency). She moaned and arched her back as his mouth gently enjoyed her breasts, moving from left to right and alternating hand and mouth.

"Damn, Kelly, you look like you want a turn too!" Leslie said.

Kelly was pleasuring herself, skirt up to her waist, panties pulled aside, gently circling her clitoris with her middle two fingers.

Before she could react, Troy looked down and smiled at her, holding out his hand. She stood, and he kissed her too, his left hand sliding between her thighs to continue what she had begun and his right unbuttoning and removing Annabelle's shorts while she began stroking his shaft.

"Looks like a party!" Leslie announced, "Dahlia, you in?"

Dahlia had been staring, practically unblinking during the proceedings. She blinked rapidly as if waking from a trance, downed her mimosa, then Kelly's, and stood. In one quick motion, she was topless and moving to join the threesome, undoing her pants en-route. Dahlia embraced Troy from behind, her hands sliding up and down his chiseled chest and abs as she pressed her body against his back. The other two ladies were completely naked by this time, each being alternately kissed and simultaneously fingered, so Dahlia slid between Troy's legs to pop up in the middle. She pulled at his waist, signaling for him to move forward, then she pushed gently back on Annabelle and Kelly, having them sit on the couch. She sat between them, and all three raised and spread their legs as Troy knelt in front of them, two fingers in Kelly and three in Annabelle. Dahlia put her hands on the back of Troy's head and pulled his face into her slit, reveling in the feeling of his hot breath and his probing tongue.

Leslie watched her three best friends orgasm within seconds of each other, each seemingly oblivious to the world beyond their personal ecstasy. Annabelle and Kelly gave Troy the stop sign as Dahlia climaxed and Troy expertly consumed her lust.

"I think we need to get more comfortable. Follow me, y'all." Leslie made her way toward the bedroom.

The rest of the day was a blur of ecstasy.

That night, Donovan reviewed the security footage from the day's orgy. He typically recorded Leslie's brunches, listening to them trade secrets and dark fantasies, reveling in his forbidden knowledge. This time; however, was different. Every inch of their bodies had been revealed to him. The sounds of their orgasms reverberated in his head like a delicious symphony, and as he watched his cock pulsated. He seized it, and it exploded in his hand, like a beast awakened from hibernation; it was hungry. He spit on his hand and stroked himself as he watched his wife kissing Dahlia, pleasured by Annabelle's mouth. Kelly's fingers probed Annabelle's cunt, her own occupied by Troy, who administered long, deep strokes. Donovan mimicked Troy stroke for stroke until his lust exploded twice more. He hadn't jerked off since middle school when his mom caught him and told him about self-control and moderation.

"Once a week," she'd said.

His shame trailed slowly from his eyes and down his cheeks as he reached for a towel.

END

JAYCEE AMORE *could be best described as the offspring of Eros and Asimov: Science Fiction, Horror, and Erotic Romance blended into a steaming, foaming latte...the kind that leaves you with a burn on the tip of your tongue, but a warmth that emanates from your soul. Jaycee enjoys thought-provoking music, historical fiction and biographies, and pugs, the "court-jester" of dogs.*

331.71
Jame

A Star is Born
author: **Janie James**
category: **Sexual Career Planning**

subjects: 1. Shameless   2. Amateur
3. Milky-White Ropes   4. Money Shot

Rose Caraway's Library of Erotica

A Star Is Born

Janie James

Daniel lay atop the bed, nude. Erect. Phone in hand, he recorded my every movement and smiled as I dropped my bra to the floor and approached the bed.

Stripping for the camera made it doubly exciting for me. I get off on being filmed, and Daniel knows it.

I climbed onto the bed and crawled forward, pausing just long enough to run my tongue up and down his shaft. Continuing up, I let my tits brush over his cock, and then his smooth chest. When I reached his face, he paused the video and kissed me, his tongue exploring my mouth like he'd never met me before. I returned the favor until it got too hard to hold my position. Then, I slid back down and took him in my mouth. I heard the tiny beep of the video starting up, and I instantly grew even wetter.

"That's it, you slut. Suck my dick for the camera."

My heart revved. "Mmm," I responded, savoring the taste of him—a little salty with just a hint of soap. I knew my role well. Tonight, I wasn't Daniel's wife. I was a porn star, doing this for my fans.

He grabbed my hair with his free hand and guided my motions. At one point, I released him and spat on his dick. A classic, porn star move.

"Oh, yeah, baby. Spit on my cock."

I did it again, marveling at how something that looked so stupid on video could make me wetter than a drunken teenager. I let my hands massage his balls until I felt them begin to tighten, then I backed off. *Not yet.*

I leaned upward, arched my back, and pointed my tits right at the camera. "You like these?" I asked, kneading my breasts and squeezing them together. God, was I so fucking hot for him! Warm liquid trickled down my thighs.

"Lemme suck those tits," he said.

I shook my head. He was still too worked up. But I needed release. I reached down and spread my pussy lips, exposing myself to the camera. I stroked my clit, and then shoved two fingers into my hole. I closed my eyes and concentrated on fingering myself. In and out, up and down. Pussy-clit-pussy-clit. It only took a minute for the familiar sensation to start. A million electric shocks spread from my clit.

"That's it," Daniel whispered. "Come for your fans, baby. You like putting on a show, don't you?"

His words kicked my imagination into gear. I wasn't finger-fucking for my husband anymore. This video would become part of our online portfolio, viewed by hundreds of strangers, all of them jacking off while they watched me.

That did it. My orgasm exploded, and I cried out. "Fuck!" I came in waves, my pussy the epicenter of an earthquake that rocked me to my core. Colored lights flashed inside my still-closed eyes.

"The show's not over, Neela. Get ready for act two."

He pushed me onto my back and entered me in one swift motion, my hole so lubed and ready it offered no resistance. The fire inside me roared to life again, stoked by his motions. No subtlety, just hard and fast fucking, exactly the way I craved it.

"Fuck, yeah!" I shouted. "Fuck me hard. Fuck me like the slut I am!"

His fingers dug into my thighs as he lifted my legs and shoved in deeper.

A few more strokes and I screamed as another orgasm rocked me, this one different but just as good. No electric explosions, just red-hot fire erupting from my center. Warmth filled me until my skin prickled, and the hairs on my arms stood up.

I was still riding the waves of my orgasm when Daniel pulled out and crouched over me. He was going all out for this vid, and I was more than happy to oblige. I grabbed his well-greased cock and stroked it. "That's it, baby. Come all over my tits!"

He did, his hips jerking as he spurted milky-white ropes across my chest. He let out a series of grunts and collapsed on top of me, his skin sliding across mine on a sheen of sweat and body fluids. He rolled off and lay next to me. Our chests heaved.

"Damn," I said, once I could finally talk.

He echoed me, and then leaned over and turned the camera off. He'd edit it later and upload it to one of the amateur porn sites. We'd watch it together tomorrow night. That got my motor revving again, imagining all the lonely men and women doing the same thing. In the meantime, I needed a shower. A very cold one.

Neela, you ready?" Daniel's voice floated up from downstairs.

"Two seconds," I replied. I quickly brushed my hair and turned the light off. The weekend getaway had been his idea. I'd been a little disappointed when he said we were going upstate instead of to Manhattan or Atlantic City. Those places had sex clubs. What did upstate New York have to offer?

But then he'd said we were staying at one of the new casinos, and that made things more interesting. No wild sexcapades, maybe, but shopping, gambling, and nightclubs would still make for a fun weekend.

And we'd have his phone. Maybe we could make a little movie while we were at it.

Now that would be a weekend to remember.

Really?" I said, holding up a see-through teddy. I knew I shouldn't have let Daniel pack for me. I rarely wore stuff like that unless we were filming because it always ended up coming off so quickly.

He winked at me, his blue eyes twinkling. "I've got a little surprise planned for tomorrow."

"Oh, yeah? What?"

"You'll have to wait," he said. He flashed a sly grin.

All day, Daniel refused to give me any hints, although he did a good job of getting me worked up. We went shopping in the lobby mall, and he insisted I wear a miniskirt and no panties and had a salesman help me try on shoes. He dressed me for dinner too, in a sheer red blouse that made it perfectly clear I wore no bra. It also exposed plenty of cleavage. The way the waiter stared at me all throughout the meal got my juices flowing in more ways than one.

I figured we'd go back to the room after dinner and bang all night because judging from the bulge in Daniel's pants he was ready to fuck me three ways to Sunday.

Instead, he told me to go to the piano lounge. "Sit at the bar, not a table or booth," he said. "Flirt all you want but no inviting anyone back to the room."

I frowned at that. It was a weird thing for him to say because we'd never picked anyone up in a bar. Well, except that couple in Vegas. But Vegas doesn't count. Everyone does stuff there they wouldn't do anywhere else.

It didn't take long for a man to approach me. Mid-fifties, balding, wearing a sports coat over a black t-shirt. I guessed he was a salesman of some kind, based on his cocky attitude and his flashy rings. He tried to chat me up, his gaze alternating between my eyes and my tits. The attention was nice, but he wasn't my type. I brushed him off nicely. He shrugged and wandered off. Two minutes later, I felt a warm presence at my side. When I looked up, Adonis was smiling at me. *Wow*.

He was tall, muscular, with blond hair that almost touched his shoulders, and blue eyes that glittered like precious stones, bluer maybe than even Daniel's. He smiled, and I thought I might come right there. "Buy you a drink?" He took the seat next to me. "I'm Lars," he said. He asked my name and where I was from.

Our small talk quickly turned into flirting. Before I knew it, we had another round of drinks in front of us, and my hand was on Lars's arm, my dark skin contrasting nicely with his pale complexion. He responded by placing his hand on my back, just above my ass. Like most men in bars, he didn't seem at all bothered by my wedding ring, and he certainly didn't complain when I leaned forward, giving him a full view of my tits, right down to the nipples.

"You like what you see?" I asked, the combination of wine at dinner, three martinis at the bar, and my growing lust making me brazen. I felt no guilt; this is what Daniel had told me to do. And while I hadn't seen him enter the bar, I was sure he had his eyes on me from somewhere.

"I do. I'd like to see more." He winked at me and smiled. "But I have to leave. Business. Maybe we'll meet again." He leaned down and kissed me, sending a thrill up my back. Then he was gone.

Disappointment cooled my ardor. I ordered another drink, and I'd just about finished it when Daniel showed up.

"Ready to go?" he asked.

I nodded. After the missed opportunity with Lars, vanilla sex didn't hold much interest for me.

When we got to the room, Daniel paused and held up his wrist so I could see his watch. "It's after midnight. You know what that means?"

I shook my head.

"It's tomorrow. Time for your surprise." He keyed the lock and pushed open the door. I stepped inside. And froze.

A half-dozen people were in the room. Two spotlights shined on the bed.

"Surprise," Daniel said, pushing me forward.

A man came up to us. The middle-aged salesman from the bar.

Behind him stood Lars.

"What the hell?" I looked from the salesman to Daniel.

"Congratulations, baby. You're gonna be a movie star."

"What?"

"Neela Cosini, allow me to formally introduce myself." The salesman held out his hand. "Nicky Boyle, owner and senior producer, Naughty Nice Productions."

I shook his hand and looked past him at Lars who was smiling and waving at me.

"You've already met your co-star, Lars Nilsson."

"Nicky makes movies, hon," Daniel said, putting his arm around me. "He specializes in amateur housewife films. This one is going to include you. If you want."

I should have been mad. You didn't just spring something like this on someone. Sure, we'd talked about how sexy it would be to fuck in front of real cameras, to be a porn star for a day. But that had just been a fantasy.

"You did this for me?"

"Your big chance. A real movie. Millions of people will see it."

Millions of people. My lust came back in a rush.

On the other side of the room, Lars stepped out of his jeans and into a satin robe. His cock swung like a third arm, larger than anything I'd seen outside of real porn.

"Are you sure about this?" I asked.

Daniel grabbed me and kissed me, long and hard. "My wife, the porn star. How could I not love it?"

I looked at Nicky. "Where do I sign?"

Fifteen minutes later, I lay on the bed, dressed in a see-through nightie. Lust and anxiety warred inside me. Behind Nicky, Daniel gave me a double thumbs up.

The setup was simple. Lars was a bellhop, and I was seducing him while my husband watched through the phone I'd left on the bed.

"Come get your tip," I said, making sure to look at Lars and not the bright-red light atop the camera. Off to one side, a second cameraman filmed the action that would later be dubbed in as the phone recording.

Lars peeled off the pants he'd changed into for the film, exposing the magnificence of his cock. It stood at half-attention.

My desire to see it fully erect made me sit up and grab it as he stepped to the edge of the bed. I wasted no time getting my mouth on the head of it. I slid forward, slowly engulfing him. When it hit the back of my throat, I still wasn't anywhere near the bottom, so I grabbed it with both hands, the way I'd seen the girls do in the movies. I let my saliva flow all over it, getting it good and slimy. At the same time, I stroked him and played with his balls. It must have been the right thing to do because he moaned, grabbed my head, and began fucking my mouth. I fought to breathe, gasping and choking around his enormous dick while it grew larger.

Without warning, he pulled out and pushed me onto my back.

"Look at the phone, and say your line," Nicky said.

My line. I turned my head. "Sorry, baby, it's too good to resist. You can punish me when I get home."

Lars spread my legs. I wanted his dick, but instead, I got his tongue, which he expertly used to massage my clit while he shoved two fingers inside me. I was wetter than ever before in my life. Watching Daniel watch me while a stranger ate me out on film had me practically gushing.

"That's it!" I shouted. "Fuck me with that tongue. Oh, shit, I'm coming, I'm coming!" I hadn't expected it, not so soon. Lars pressed his mouth on my cunt and did something with his tongue that made me twitch like I was having seizures.

"Yes!" someone yelled. I opened my eyes and saw Nicky pumping his fist in the air.

"Keep rolling. Position one," he said.

Lars lifted my hips. His cock probed the entrance to my pussy. Somehow, he'd put a condom on while I was lost in my orgasm. He pushed against me, and, for a moment, I didn't think it would fit.

Then, it slipped in, and the most amazing sensations burst through me. Daniel is big. I've always had a thing for big men, big vibrators, even a big zucchini one time back in high school. But Lars was bigger than big. He was giant. Mammoth. His immense dick stretched the limits of my cunt in every direction.

I couldn't get enough of it. "Fuck me! Fuck me with that monster cock!"

He did. In and out, fast and hard.

I screamed. Clawed at his back. "Fuck that pussy! Fuck it hard!"

I lost track of time. It might have been three minutes or ten. I know I came at least once, a small but powerful orgasm.

Then Nicky yelled again. "Position two!"

Lars withdrew, and I fell onto the bed, my chest heaving

"Get on top of me," he said.

I did as I was told, climbing onto him and lowering myself onto his pulsing member. We moaned in unison.

"Jesus, you're hot," Lars gasped. He bucked his hips, bouncing me on his huge, flagpole dick.

I caught his rhythm and matched it, swinging my ass up and down to meet his movements. My nails dug into his chest, and he countered by gripping my thighs so hard I knew there'd be bruises the next day.

I rode him like that for a while. Shouted his name, shouted for God. I came again, my body bucking so hard I feared I might break his prick.

"Keep going!" Nicky shouted. "Position three!"

"Doggy," Lars whispered.

"Aim toward the phone," Nicky called out.

I tried to remember where it was as I got onto all fours.

Lars turned me.

And there was Daniel. Right past where the phone sat on the bed. The bulge in his pants was unmistakable.

I caught on to Nicky's idea.

"You like that?" I called out. "You like watching your wife fuck a stranger? You—oooooh, fuck!"

Lars entered me like he was drilling for oil. It seemed like his cock went all the way into my stomach. He was like an enraged beast, and I responded in kind, never taking my gaze off my husband.

"That's it, fuck me. Fuck me, you animal. Show my husband what he's missing. Fill that pussy! Fill it!"

I tried to see myself through Daniel's eyes, covered in sweat, hair plastered around my face, tits swinging wildly each time Lars plunged deep into my cunt. I clenched the sheets as the beginning of another orgasm burst to life deep in my core.

"Yes, that's it. Make me come. Make me—" It exploded, a violent orgasm that made me throw back my head and howl like a wolf. My limbs shook, and my cunt squeezed around Lars's dick.

"Money shot," cried Nicky.

Strong hands pushed me onto my back. Lars's cock loomed over me, a fleshy missile. He stripped the condom off and I wrapped my hands around his dick. Three strokes was all it took. Thick, hot sperm sprayed across my face, streams of it like sticky rain falling on me.

"Aaargh!" Lars bellowed. His cock was like a firehose, dousing my tits and neck this time. I didn't think he'd ever stop.

When he finally did, I scooped up some cum with two fingers, looked right at Daniel, and did what I'd seen so many porn actresses do. I slowly licked it off and let it drip down over my lips.

"Cut!"

Lars climbed off the bed, bent down, and kissed my cheek. "You were fucking amazing. Your husband is a lucky guy. Any time you want to make a sequel, I'm your man." He walked away, calling for some wipes.

Angie, the assistant producer, came up to me. "Outstanding. You're a natural. Let's get you cleaned up." She helped me off the bed. As I passed Daniel, I couldn't help feeling embarrassed and guilty. Had I gone too far? Was he mad? Jealous?

He put his arms around my waist and looked into my eyes. "I think maybe we've found your new career."

My heart soared. Lars was wrong. Daniel wasn't the lucky one.

I was.

END

JANIE JAMES *is a former scientist with a lust for love and life. After years of toiling in laboratories and photographing crime scenes, she gave up the 9 to 5 routine to write erotic fiction. When she's not writing, she enjoys sleeping late, overdosing on coffee, and watching online porn.*

About The Editor

"A short story is a different thing all together – a short story is like a kiss in the dark from a stranger." — Stephen King

Rose Caraway is a native Northern California writer, editor, audiobook narrator, and podcaster for the #1 Erotica show in iTunes, The Kiss Me Quick's Erotica Podcast. She freely celebrates all things erotica with her wonderful husband and Lurid Listeners, and is fondly known as *The Sexy Librarian*.

You might also find Rose Caraway over at, The Sexy Librarian's Blog-cast where she not only discusses her own journey in writing and her latest book and audiobook projects. She also interviews some of her favorite erotica authors, fellow narrators, and anyone else interested in engaging conversation, while along the way, offering helpful tips of the trade to aspiring writers. The Sexy Librarian's Blog-Cast is a new way to get to know Rose Caraway and her husband/producer, Dayv Caraway, and their amazing friends!

Rose's writings have prominently showcased her sex-positive approach to life, as well as shown her commitment to both feminism and masculinism. She believes that people of all genders and orientations should be considered complementary and interdependent and are necessary for a truly healthy and functional society.

In addition to writing, Rose's other passions revolve around her soul mate, Big Daddy—Dayv Caraway, their three children and her two dogs. Rose keeps an active lifestyle and has earned a Black Belt in Kenpo Karate. She loves the gratification of gardening and has become a beekeeper!

THEKISSMEQUICKS.COM
STUPIDFISHPRODUCTIONS.COM
@RoseCaraway

The Kiss Me Quick's Erotica Podcast

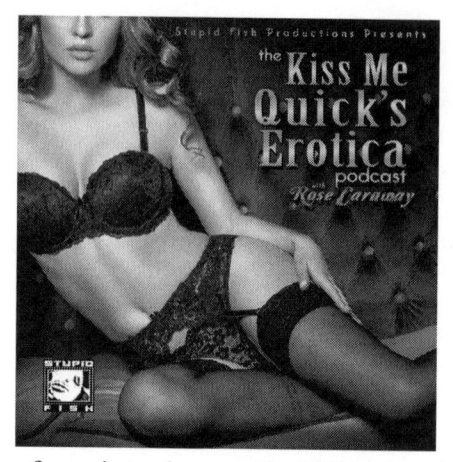

Rose Caraway and her friends will arouse your senses and inflame your imagination with tales of love, lust, loss, romance, suspense, and adventure! Come, experience intense fantasies that are sure to seduce your thoughts and leave you and your partner/s wanting more!

Enjoy the best erotica authors today as they show off their limitless imaginations with smart, provocative stories, with just the right amount of moxie and sensuality! There's a lot of 'em so pace yourself. The Kiss Me Quick's Erotica podcast is bold erotic fiction that will beautifully but explicitly delight, and thrill you, so please enjoy carefully and judiciously.

This show is for mature adult audiences only.

TheKissMeQuicks.com
@theKMQ

THE SEXY LIBRARIAN'S DIRTY 30, VOL.1

The Sexy Librarian is at it again! This time, it's after hours. Forget the card catalog just for tonight. Come to the back of the library, peruse *The Sexy Librarian's* private stacks. Smart and edgy, with just the right amount of moxie, these stories illustrate the limitless imagination of some of the best erotica authors today. Allow The Sexy Librarian to introduce you to some of her favorite and most trusted Erotica authors, who understand that sometimes you like it hot, intelligent, and occasionally, very, very…dirty!

THE SEXY LIBRARIAN'S DIRTY 30, VOL.2

The Sexy Librarian returnz with another library of Erotica just for you! Enjoy 30 adventurous, fantasy-filled tales that span this sexy bibliotheca from Fair Tales to Torrid Literature, Bi-Curious Rendezvous to Sex Cult Acolytes, Clandestine Military Adventures to Public Punishment and so much more! This is your very own, hand-held library! So grab your partner, peruse the card catalog and see which sexy stories pique your libido first.

THE SEXY LIBRARIAN'S DIRTY 30, VOL. 3

Lose yourself in these thirty risqué adventures, loaded with fabulous characters in provocative situations. Get ravished by flirty-frills and sassy petticoats in our hot bodice-ripper romance. Keep it strictly confidential as you fall in love with a dangerous undercover spy. Feel your heart quiver as you lust after two brothers on the lone frontier. The choice is yours in this library of sexy-sharp stories! Aphoristic and lively, these tales are perfect for a mid-day quickie or an evening kiss before bed. Do you have twenty minutes for a brazenly sexy jewelry heist? Or maybe take that once in a lifetime cruise vacation and discover that mermaids really do exist! You can savor the heat rising in your cheeks as you confess your deepest desires to the town priest, then finish-off your evening with a run in Central Park and stumble upon a house made of…gingerbread?

More Books By Rose Caraway

TONIGHT, SHE'S YOURS: CUCKOLD FANTASIES VOL. I

Go beyond traditional fantasy, cuckolding is where it's at! Cuckolding is deeply layered. From privately whispered scenes between a Hotwife and her Cuck, to a wide range of humiliation play requiring the adept skills of a big, beautiful Bull…or three. "Tonight, She's Yours" is guaranteed to get you randy. I must warn you though, with this much 'One Handed Reading', you may experience a bit of a hand cramp. I do hope that you have a good time.

TONIGHT, SHE'S YOURS: CUCKOLD FANTASIES, VOL. 2

This collection of 18 steamy stories brings LOTS of heart-pounding erotic action. Featuring 1800's India, paranormal characters, MMA fighters, BDSM experts, made-to-order robots, cuckolding first-timers, well-practiced cucks, humiliation play—cucks of all varieties and persuasions are all found within these pages. Get ready for the ultimate in cuckold fantasy fulfillment.

FOR THE MEN: AND THE WOMEN WHO LOVE THEM

Rose Caraway presents an anthology intended for the fellas and the women who have an appetite for bold, adventurous erotic storytelling. Escape into the fantastic, the outlandish, and the literary. Get ready for; a space pirate, a cowgirl, an anxious odd man out, an undercover agent, lonely ghosts, a taxi driver with an unexpected topsy-turvy fare, a burly biker who just wants to be cuddled, a bride-to-be with one last oat to sow, The Devil offers a golden deal, a mysterious hitchhiker, strangers and a spontaneous three-way, and a reluctant hitman.

LIBIDINOUS ZOMBIE: EROTIC HORROR
An 8 Authors Project

This book is erotic.

This book is horrifying. This book is cunning.

This book is edgy, seductive, violent, fiendish, indecent, and unfair.

Made in the USA
Columbia, SC
22 August 2019